Wall

WIND OF DEATH

To Lucien Nahum, who opened the way

The English-language debut of a prize-winning French thriller

GILBERT GRELLET and HERVE GUILBAUD are Washington-based journalists for the French news agency Agence-France Presse. Their work has taken
them around the world and enabled them to depict international locales with
extraordinary realism.

"An adventure novel to take your breath away."—Le Pariesien

"Compares with the best American thrillers."—Le Monde

"Each of their chapters could appear one day in one of our newspapers."
                                                    —DOMINIQUE LAPIERRE, Figaro

Gilbert Grellet—Hervé Guilbaud

WIND OF DEATH

Translated from the French by
Joanna Biggar

BERGH PUBLISHING, INC.
276 Fifth Avenue, New York, N.Y. 10001

© 1990 by BERGH PUBLISHING, Inc.
Originally published in France by FLAMMARION, Paris.
© by FLAMMARION, 1988.
Paper ISBN 0-930267-28-1
Case ISBN 0-930267-25-7

Manufactured in the United States of America

Sales and distribution: The Talman Company, Inc.
150 Fifth Ave, NY, NY 10011 Tel (212)620-3182
Fax (212)627-4682

CHAPTER 1

Kaokoveld, northwest Namibia, November.

The heat. . . . Yves Arnold should have been used to it, but the cockpit of the Jet Ranger helicopter was almost unbearable. How hot was it? 105, 110? Maybe more, Arnold thought as sweat rolled in fat drops from his face onto the controls. Luckily he wouldn't stop much from now on.

About fifty yards below, the ground ran past him at full speed. With the cape to his west, the helicopter skirted the fertile fringe of the Cunene River which marked the border between Namibia and Angola. On the left he caught sight of the imposing, desolate spurs of the Zebra Mountains in that part of Namibia which the Germans, the first colonists, had baptised Kaokoveld.

Arnold had just dropped two South African engineers at the pumping station of the Ruacana dam. Two or three kilometers north of the Namibian border in Angolan territory, it was controlled and used by South Africa. The pair hadn't really been such bad company, but they just kept asking the same old questions. What future did Namibia have? How big was the risk of terrorist attack?

Arnold had been stationed in Namibia since 1963 and was fed up with these endless discussions about the country. He'd learned about that kind of situation twenty years ago living in Algeria. The territory was all eerily familiar. Algeria had been such a painful period of his life, he only wanted to forget. Yet in unguarded moments, memories rose up from the horizon and carried him back to the heart of that tortured, beloved country.

To shake himself from such memories, he decided to make a

little detour over the Zebra Mountains to see his old friends the Ovahissas before returning to Windhoek, his "home port." He had come to appreciate the hospitality of this tribe of gentle pastoralists. Their proud, noble features were said to resemble those of the Masai of Kenya—a mystery anthropologists hadn't succeeded in unraveling.

Out of the corner of his eye, Arnold saw the familiar loop of the Cunene. A glance at the map on the seat next to him confirmed that was it; he was approaching the *kraal*, the Ovahissa village. As soon as he spied the first mud huts surrounded by high wooden stockades, he cut back his Allison engine.

He still had his hand on the throttle when he saw the first corpses of cattle sprawled in the sand. At the approach of the chopper, a cloud of vultures took off, beating the air with their heavy wings, and flew out over the river towards Angola. Puzzled, Arnold changed course slightly. Then he saw the carcasses of beasts scattered over the earth, as though mowed down by a powerful blast of wind, their stripped flanks an offering to the voracious appetites of vultures.

Passing over the outer stockade of the *kraal*, he saw the first human bodies, lying every which way among the huts.

"Shit! What's this?" he said out loud. This part of northwest Namibia, kept in tow by South African forces, was supposed to be calm despite the mines planted by guerrillas.

Barely lifting over the last gate, he turned sharply to the right and brought himself over the river. Then he picked up a little to make several passes over the village, scouring the bald mountains on both sides of the Cunene for any sign of activity. Finding no movement, he approached the *kraal* again, chose a clear spot and landed the helicopter. When the skids rested on the sandy soil, he opened the door, unstrapped himself and waited for the turbine to stop wheezing. Soon there was silence. Total silence.

Arnold waited a good five minutes listening for the slightest sound, his hand gripping the Colt 45 that never left his side when he flew. Throat tight, he climbed down slowly from the Jet Ranger and inched toward the entrance of the *kraal* about fifteen yards away. Creeping like a cat, his eyes strained their sockets as he turned every few seconds to look in all directions. He had almost reached the opening of a hut between tree trunks stuck in the ground when he stumbled across a body.

It was a woman, lying on her stomach, one arm on the ground and the other bent under her, her head thrown in the sand. Like all the Ovahissas, she was naked to the waist, wearing only a loin-cloth the color of red clay. Immediately he noticed the strange blisters which covered her back.

He knelt beside her and tried to expose her face. Unable to do it with one hand, he carefully set his gun down on a scraggy patch of yellowing grass and turned over the body.

He knew it wouldn't be a pretty sight, but he didn't expect what he saw. Sickened, he let go of the dead woman and half-way stood up, turning his head away in revulsion. The features of the Ovahissa woman, who looked about thirty, were bloated beyond recognition and her mouth twisted in a grotesque grin. Hundreds of ants filed out of the sand which stuck around her glassy eyes, her nostrils, her mouth. In some places the pigmentation of her skin seemed changed. Swallowing painfully, he stooped over to pick his gun, checked to make sure there was a bullet in the chamber, then moved carefully toward the entrance of the *kraal*. He crept lightly, turning around to look back every few seconds, until he got safely outside the stockade.

Before he could even see them, the stink given off from decomposing bodies hit him in the face. Moving in a little closer, he was suddenly overcome by the odious buzzing of flies, amplified by the encircling stockades that turned the enclosed villa into vibrating drum. For a brief moment, he was tempted to run, to get back to the safety of the Jet Ranger—to get out of this nightmare. Instead he kept going.

The ground was covered with bodies—men, women, and children. With each step, Arnold scattered clusters of flies and ants from their macabre banquet. As the bodies began to bloat, the stench became unbearable.

Dazed by the spectacle around him, he stumbled about the *kraal*, poking into the honeycomb of little rooms ingeniously laid out inside the village. Even though their faces were deformed by horrible scars, Arnold could still recognize several members of the tribe, especially Vita, the chief, who over the years had become a real friend.

Like all the others, Vita's body showed no trace of blows or wounds. Clearly the village hadn't been attacked by another tribe—always a possibility—nor by SWAPO commandos, the armed group who were fighting in the bush for Namibia's independence.

But what the hell killed them? He thought about the temperature of the Kaokeveld in November, the heart of summer in the southern hemisphere, and figured that the mysterious phenomenon which had wiped out the little tribe must have struck two or three days before. Maybe a deadly epidemic? But the marks on the bodies didn't resemble anything he'd ever seen.

In turning into the narrow passage leading to the last room in the *kraal*, the one reserved for meetings of the council of elders, he heard a faint groan. He stopped sharp and listened. Hearing nothing more he started to walk away when the moaning started again.

"Hey! Somebody's alive!" Arnold yelled and burst into the room. He had no trouble finding where the sounds were coming from; leaning against the inside wall of the hut, a man sat in the sand. His head thrown back, he stared up with an empty look, mumbling weakly. From time to time his body shook uncontrollably, and wild-eyed, he tossed his head from side to side. Horrible blisters, like the ones Arnold had seen on the others, covered most of his body.

The pilot pulled the safety catch on his gun, slipped it under the belt of his khaki shorts, and knelt next to the man, whom he didn't know. Repulsed at the idea of touching him, Arnold tried to speak in Herrero dialect, the language of the tribe.

As soon as he heard a few words, the man became silent, locked in his delerium. Arnold repeated himself patiently and slowly, carefully articulating each word. Herrero was not the Namibian language he knew best. He got along better in Kwanyama, the main Ovambo dialect. But if he took his time, he could communicate all right with the Ovahissas.

"My friend, my friend, what happened?" he asked over and over. He also repeated the word "peace" three or four times to give the poor man a sense of security. After five minutes of speaking without any response, he was just on the point of giving up when the man stammered something.

"Burning . . . night . . . pain . . ."

Overcoming his disgust, Arnold forced himself closer to the Ovahissa, who wore only simple shorts of gray cloth. The man weakly blurted some jumbled words which Arnold vaguely grasped—words about children, about death.

He asked his questions again in Afrikaans. Whenever there were problems communicating in Herrero with certain tribes, he automatically switched to Afrikaans, knowing that many black Namibians understood it despite their reluctance to use the language of those who occupied their land.

After a short silence, the man again said a few words, interrupting himself often, while his mouth opened grotesquely wide, as though he were suffocating.

"Children, women then men, all dead . . . three days . . ."

"What are you saying my friend?"

"Burns chest, blisters . . . container . . ."

"Container?"

Arnold wasn't sure that he had gotten this word. He didn't see what a container had to do with this story.

"Container . . . plane . . . death . . ."

"Plane? What plane?"

Arnold couldn't make sense of it. He knew that the Ovahissas were used to seeing airplanes fly over for anti-guerrilla operations—he himself, with his helicopter, had helped make them used to "flying machines."

"What plane? A plane with white soldiers?"

"No, not plane green soldiers white. Plane yellow . . . yellow like sun . . . Orlog beside river, see plane come . . . container from plane . . ."

He moaned and a rattle escaped from his chest.

Arnold was dumbfounded. What was the story? Was the Ovahissa simply out of his mind? Yet Arnold had the impression that he was really quite lucid and that it was only pain which prevented him from speaking clearly.

"Orlog, did you say a container from the plane?"

The man didn't respond, and Arnold believed he was dead. He had an urge to put a hand on his shoulder and shake him, but he stopped himself, not daring to touch the swollen skin. At that moment, the Ovahissa's head flopped toward Arnold, the frantic eyes fixing on him for a minute, while the man clawed his chest with his right hand, as if to tear out the pain which ate at him. Then he said a few more words.

"Container fall plane . . . *kraal* die. . . ."

A pinkish foam trickled out of his mouth. He contracted suddenly, convulsed. His head fell forward, and he couldn't move anymore, his face contorted with suffering.

Arnold stood straight again, profoundly shaken. He had seen death before. It had never been far from the commando unit of the French army he'd been with in the Algerian mountains. But that hadn't prepared him for what he'd just seen.

He had loved this tribe, where, after so many visits, he was greeted like a member of the family. He'd known more than half the adults by name. There weren't that many of them, 200 or 300 at most. Semi-nomads, the Ovahissas were very independent and had hardly any contact with other Namibian tribes. For several years now, the war had kept them from making their annual migration towards Angola. They had stayed peacefully in the same spot on the Namibian side of the Cunene.

There seemed no point in hanging around the *kraal* any longer. Arnold decided to get back to Windhoek, the capital of the territory, immediately. First he'd have to alert the authorities. Then he'd come back with the team to bury the dead and open an enquiry. He glanced at his watch. It was 1:30. He could be back in two hours. Jumping over some bodies, he rushed out of the *kraal* to the safety of the Jet Ranger, which appeared to him now like the vision of an oasis.

The plexiglass door had remained open, and Arnold was ready to slip his right leg into the cabin when he suddenly had the acute sensation of being watched. The impression was so strong that he spun around, instinctively taking out his gun.

He checked over the surrounding hills to see if he could make out anything which might have provoked this unexpected feeling. Nervous, his eyes swept in a full circle around the *kraal*, but he saw only rocks hardened by the sun and the Cunene, which flowed slowly toward the Atlantic.

Repressing a shudder, he climbed aboard the chopper, strapped himself in, and without waiting another second, fired up the engine.

CHAPTER 2

Paris, November 27

A lingering grey cloud cover hung over Paris, as usual, but Steve Denton didn't notice. He no longer paid attention to the perpetual sadness of the Parisian sky. The "City of Lights" had other ways of justifying its name.

Besides, he hadn't even been outside and was just as happy to have stayed in. After more than a week of grinding away, the article on Bordeaux and the chateaux of Medoc was finished at last! He closed the folder on his knees and called out toward the kitchen, "Caroline, could you fix me a little whisky?"

"O.k., but wait a second."

Sprawled comfortably on the couch facing the large window of the living room with a Keith Jarret record on the stereo, he relished the end of the afternoon, the peace he had found in his life in Paris. What a contrast to the frenetic pace of living in New York, where a few years ago, he had been scrambling to make a deadline, trying to beat the clock. It was a race he could never win.

He thought again about that hot and stormy evening when he had decided to bail out. It was 5:00 o'clock when the World Desk asked him to do a piece for the next morning's European service about Jimmy Carter's woes. He slowly finished his cigarette in front of his office window. Below, office workers and business-men dashed for their cars or the subway. Jets of steam rose from the damp pavement of 50th St. The city seemed like a giant cauldron ready to explode any time. Like his brain, crammed to its limits with a million facts, most of them useless.

Sitting in front of his terminal, he stared at the green screen for a long time, trying without success to start the piece in a way which was at least slightly original. Then, without typing one letter on the keyboard, he got up and went out, swearing to never again set foot in the offices in Rockefeller Center. It was a decision he had rejoiced in every day since.

Now he worked for *The National Geographic*, a monthly which published only one or two of his stories per year. His articles even carried his byline and were printed on good glossy paper which readers fingered with love before religiously placing the yellow-circled magazine in their libraries. It was a good feeling to do something lasting—something unconnected with the anonymous, impersonal work of the wire service.

One day he would have to go further and write a book, if only to leave a trace of his brief passage on earth. At forty-two, he figured he still had plenty of time. Or did he?

"Here's your whisky, Steve." Caroline, in a simple mid-calf shirt-dress, handed him the glass.

Denton took the glass and gave her his wide, easy American grin, at once natural and spontaneous. The slightly prominent forehead, the small, straight nose and determined chin, the full, wavy brown hair, and dreamy, far-away looking blue eyes, often gave him an irregular sort of good-looks.

"Thanks. You're good to me. What are making?"

"A *tarte aux pommes*."

"Mmmmm. That's what smells so good . . . don't mind if I do say so myself, nobody can cook like a Frenchwoman," he teased her, smiling.

"Oh, I get it. Tonight's cliche night . . . You're just like the oven," she said "full of hot air." She looked at him with mock sarcasm and turned to go back to the kitchen.

For the two years they'd lived together, they had rarely had an argument. He wanted so much to preserve that almost magical harmony, so far from the domestic warfare which had badly marred his last months in New York.

He had taken the opportunity of quitting A.P. as a chance to leave New York—and his wife. The city was exciting, but neurotic. Like his wife. Judith was one of these business-women obsessed by her career and eaten away with fear that she wouldn't make it to the top. He couldn't stand any of it any longer.

They had met soon after his return from Johannesburg, and had married almost right away. He had been taken with her energy, her sexual ardor, her New York elegance, while she had been fascinated with the tall, nicely built reporter who had just dashed through South Africa in pursuit of big game and freedom fighters lurking in the bush. . . .

But trapped by false images of each other, they couldn't hold up long under the stress of daily living in New York.

Judith worked for First National Bank, where she moved up through the ranks quickly, taking advantage of a quota system instigated by a management sensitive to feminist demands. But the further she climbed up the ladder, the more long hours and fatigue took their toll. Evenings when they didn't go out, they sat down to sandwiches or frozen dinners. And as she collapsed into bed, she became increasingly cool to his advances, while he felt more and more awkward in touching her.

He found her frenetic scrambling ridiculous, and their incessant fights—almost caricatures toward the end—drained them of all energy and made their marriage a living hell. It hadn't been difficult, then, to pack his bags and to say good-bye to Judith, to his *Wall Street Journal*, and to their 5th Ave. apartment.

Now he'd been in Paris for eight years. Luckily, he was free from financial worries, because his father, a rich New York lawyer who had died of a heart attack ten years before, had left a fat inheritance which he split with his mother. Along with what he earned at the *National Geographic*, he could live very nicely in Paris.

As for Caroline, she taught English at Jeanson de Sailly, a high school not far from his place. The apartment, on the corner of ave. Henri Martin and rue de la Pompe, was close to the Bois de Boulogne. That's where he'd met her, jogging. He'd taken it up in New York, where he'd begun running around Central Park as much to calm his nerves as to keep in shape. And she too loved to run.

After a few weeks, she moved in with him. He loved her slim, firm body, her slender hips, and her face, serious and soft at the same time beneath short, wavy hair, cropped like a boy's. What Denton appreciated most about her was what made her the polar opposite of Judith: her lack of ambition and the fact that she was able to enjoy life from one day to the next. That was a rare gift in a perpetually dissatisfied world.

Lost in his thoughts, he didn't hear until the phone had rung three times. He hesitated a minute, then decided not to get up to answer it, thinking it was for Caroline.

Her mother called often about this time of day to see if she was all right and to make sure that "the American" was treating her well. Every time she called, Caroline was annoyed to have to repeat that everything was o.k.

But this time it was somebody else. "Steve, it's for you. An overseas call. Somebody called Steve Arnold, if I heard it right."

Denton jumped up. Thin, muscular and slightly taller than average, he was very fit for his age. Jogging helped keep him in shape. With his jeans and Lacoste T-shirt, he could have passed for thirty. He walked toward his desk wondering what the devil Arnold could want. He'd known Yves a long time—since he'd first come to Namibia after leaving newly independent Algeria and his days as a paratrooper behind. Just about a month ago, Arnold had taken him all over Namibia in his helicopter, which gave Denton the chance to do a piece about it for the *Geographic*. In fact, he had to go back in about ten days to finish up the reporting. Maybe Arnold needed something from Paris?

"Hello, Yves, how's it going?," he asked, sitting on the corner of his desk.

"Hi, Steve. I'm glad you're home, because I had trouble getting a line. Tell me, are you still planning to come down here next week?"

"Right. And I hope that you've saved me those dates for the chopper."

"No problem—but would it be possible to move your trip up and come right away?"

"Uh . . . that would be tough, because I've got a lot of little things to take care of here before leaving. But why? What's going on?"

"Look, I discovered the most incredible thing today. A whole tribe exterminated up in the north. . . ."

"What happened?"

"I'm not exactly sure, but it was horrible. Some sort of weird epidemic. Look, this could be terrific stuff for your article. I spoke briefly to the last survivor just before his death. He mentioned a yellow airplane which flew over the village and dropped a container just before the catastrophe. I don't know any more than that. I'm going back there tomorrow with some guy from general administration. The shit is really going to hit the fan with this one."

Arnold spoke so fast that Denton could feel his agitation through the receiver, almost as though he were right next to him.

"Look, take it easy, Yves. You know I've given up that kind of reporting."

"Yes, but nobody else knows a thing about this. This could be the scoop of your life!"

"Oh look, real scoops are rarer than hen's teeth." Denton smiled to himself at the cliche. "Anyway, my article won't even come out for another six months. By that time, this'll be old news."

But he had to admit that his curiosity was piqued and he felt a little prick of excitement. The reflexes of his old profession rose to the surface after being put to bed for eight years.

What day was the weekly South African Airways flight between Frankfurt and Windhoek anyway? Thursday? Then he could be in Namibia in four days.

"O.k., Yves, I'll try to come. I think there's a flight from Frankfurt in three days. I'll see if I can get on it."

"Yeah, there's a flight Thursday, and there ought to be space. It's not the end of the year rush yet. But are you sure you couldn't come a little earlier via Joburg?"

"No, really, I've got some stuff to take care of here. It's already going to be complicated to move the trip up by a week."

"O.k., o.k., never mind. I'll come get you at the airport. So long. See you soon."

"So long."

Denton hung up the phone and began thinking about how he was going to get everything done in order to leave Thursday.

"Who was that? Anything important?" Caroline leaned casually against the doorway startling him. He hadn't heard her come.

"It was Yves Arnold. You know, the helicopter pilot who lugged me all over Namibia last month. He wanted to tell me about an interesting development. I think I'll have to get down there Thursday instead of next week."

"So soon! We haven't seen each other much this time."

Her face wore a familiar expression of love, at once dreamy and provocative. Just seeing her, he felt a sudden, strong desire rise up in him.

"So, are you happy with your article?" she asked a propos of nothing. It was part of the love game they played that she liked to talk of anything else when she was in the mood for love. Her pretended aloofness only made his hunger for her grow.

"Oh, I think it's all right." He got up and moved closer to her. Her body pressed tightly against him. He kissed her and felt her lips and breasts tense with desire that she didn't try to hide any longer. He suddenly wanted to take her there, where they were, against the wall of his office, and began to unbutton her shirt to free her breasts while he pushed a leg between her thighs. Sometimes they made love like that, almost brutally, carried away by the violence of their desire, seeking that wild, disturbing pleasure which left them breathless and a little afraid.

This time Caroline didn't want it that way. She bit his lips before pushing him gently away.

"Let's go in the bedroom, Steve," she said softly, taking his hand and leading him out of the study.

He followed her, and as he left, automatically glanced at the map of the world pinned to the wall near the door. He suddenly wondered why he had said yes to Arnold and agreed to move up his trip. Why rush to the farthest ends of Africa?

He turned and glanced at the telephone on his desk.

No, it was too late. He had promised to go.

CHAPTER 3

New York, November 28

"**G**entlemen, we agree completely. John, you check with First National to see about the financial arrangements."

"And if there are any, shall we say, 'diplomatic' objections?"

"No problem. We'll find the money somewhere else—but I don't think they'll give us any trouble—we're representing a very sound investment and they've been burned badly enough by their loans to Brazil or Argentina. Don't forget, we have solid guarantees to offer in the States."

David Cullum got up slowly from his seat and acknowledged the men across from him with a nod of the head. They were John Baska, his finance director, Richard Mayberry, head of industrial affairs, and George Newton, his legal advisor, an expert in international legislation. They had just completed the finishing touches on a deal for the expansion of a uranium mine worked by the Cullum Company in Namibia. The three men got up in turn and left the room without saying a word. Now that they had the green light from the boss, they knew exactly what to do.

Cullum remained standing a minute and looked toward the large window which faced his desk. Light clouds underlined the clear blue of the New York sky. It was almost noon, the midpoint of a magic autumn day with fresh air and a bright sky washed by the wind. The atmosphere was charged with a feeling of powerful energy—nowhere more noticeable than at the corner of Central Park South and 5th Ave. The flags of the Plaza snapped in the wind and long, silent limousines fought for space with battered yellow cabs, tireless workers in the anthill of New York.

The offices of the Cullum Corporation, a family conglomerate controlled by David Cullum, were there, in the white General Motors Building at 767 5th Ave.

He sank slowly back into the leather armchair. The man who only five minutes before had appeared alert and focused, deciding on investments approaching $50 million, seemed suddenly to have lost his spirit. The square, willful face sagged, as if all the facial muscles were loosened one by one. Holding his head in his hands, he sat motionless, as if trying to distance himself from the luxurious atmosphere of his office.

The sound of the phone made him jump and sit up straight. He forced himself to try to look normal.

"Sir, your wife's on the line."

"Thanks, Kay, put her on."

"Hello, dear. How's everything? Have you noticed the weather? Magnificent, isn't it, for this time of year?"

He tried to make his voice sound cheerful, but his face still reflected a profound sadness.

"Yes, David. It's really a long Indian summer this year, isn't it? I enjoyed it—went out a bit. You haven't forgotten that we're supposed to meet the Davises at 21 at 1:00?"

"So we are. It had slipped my mind. Shall I meet you there, or will you come by my office?"

"I'll meet you there. See you in a bit."

"Right. I'll be there soon, Liz."

Cullum winced, then hung up the receiver. He'd almost forgotten the lunch organized by his wife, a Frenchwoman he'd married in London in the 60's. The Davises were nice enough, but they evoked too many memories he'd just as soon forget. Why did Elisabeth like to see them so much? He seemed to understand her less and less. And to make matters worse, he didn't really like the 21 Club—the restaurant had become too much an institution and too trendy for his taste. Well, there was no point in hurting Elisabeth. Besides, it was too late to back down.

At that moment, the door to his secretary's office opened discreetly and Kay White came in, a file with mail in her hand. "Here are some letters for you to sign. Nothing very urgent. Can I bring you something? You look very tired."

"No, thank you Kay. You are very kind, but I'm going out soon. A bit of fresh air will do me a world of good."

Cullum forced himself to smile at his secretary. Pushing fifty, this woman with the determined but intelligent face was actually more like a collaborator. She'd been with him now for more than ten years, and if for some reason she ever left, he worried he could never replace her.

Kay White looked at him attentively. For months she had watched his physical decline, but was powerless to do anything to help. Although still elegant with his Brooks Brothers tweed jacket and flannel slacks, his silk handkerchief and club tie, he was no longer the fit-looking man of fifty whose athletic build and luxuriant graying hair had only recently attracted the admiring glances of women. Now his face appeared hardened and his hair thinning. The charming smile had disappeared altogether. And the open, direct manner had become fixed and distant.

His secretary decided not to press the issue. She disliked playing mother hen and knew he hated it. He went on signing letters, barely looking at them. The telephone rang again. He picked up the receiver and held it to his ear, continuing to sign the letters. The call came on a direct line which had been installed only six months before. He had given the number to very few people; even his wife did not have it.

"Hello, yes. Marais. Hold on a minute please." He covered the mouthpiece and turned to his secretary who waited patiently next to his vast mahogany desk.

"Thanks, Kay. You can come back in a few minutes and get letters. They'll all be signed."

She hesitated a moment, then turned on her heels and left.

Cullum waited until the door was firmly closed to pick up the receiver again.

"Hello Marais. Go ahead. Everything all right?"

"Good evening, Mr. Cullum. Or rather, good morning. I'm calling you from Windhoek. We're having a little problem I wanted to tell you about."

"What's this all about? Nothing serious I hope."

"No, just a little hitch during one of our operations."

"Which operation?"

"I'll tell you about it later. But the problem is that we had an unexpected visitor. It's a bit troubling."

"Why? Can he cause problems?"

"Yes. We've tried to clean things up, but you never know."

"What are your options?"

"Limited. It's a simple choice, really. And we've already made certain arrangements. Don't worry. Everything will be fine. I only wanted to let you know."

"Good . . . all right. You know you have a *carte blanche*. How's everything else going?"

"Very well. The men are in fine shape."

"All right, Marais. Don't forget that the deadline's approaching."

"I assure you we'll be ready according to plan."

"O.k. We'll talk about it again soon and you can give me all the details. One more thing, Marais, we've reached an agreement about expanding Naukluft. This wouldn't be for several months, of course, when the operation is over. No doubt Mayberry will go to Windhoek next week. I'm going to spend a few days in Palm Beach."

"Yes, sir. I'll call you there. We'll be in touch soon."
"Good-bye, Marais."

Cullum sank back in his chair and gave a little spin to the globe he kept on his left, just next to the desk. It was an old Weber Costello globe; he looked pensive as it turned slowly in his hands. Then the yellowing sphere came to a stop, and he stared for a few moments at a certain spot before nodding his head violently, as if to shake free a thought stuck deep in his mind.

Before getting up to go to the luncheon, he looked again at the picture frame next to the telephone. A moment's glance, and his face tensed with feeling . . .

CHAPTER 4

Kaokoveld, November 29

"**N**o, it can't be. I don't understand. . . ."

Shocked, Arnold turned toward his companion, who barely hid his irritation.

With his pale blue shorts, wool knee socks and cheap black leather shoes, he was the picture of the Afrikaner bureaucrat in the bush. Nothing was missing—not even the comb forever sticking in one of the socks. Built like a linesman for the "Springboks," he was a good head taller than Arnold.

"If this is your idea of a joke, it isn't very funny. I doubt that Mr. Howe appreciates this sort of humor, either," he grumbled.

But Arnold, completely dumbfounded by what he saw in front of him, didn't answer. He took out his handkerchief to wipe the sweat which was trickling down his forehead and closed his eyes a moment to reassure himself that he wasn't dreaming. . . .

He saw himself climbing into his Jet Ranger only two days before, after discovering the disaster. The return to Windhoek had been very fast, one hour and fifty-five minutes exactly. The chopper had flown like a whiz and he'd almost never gotten below 200 kph.

The only problem was the radio which had suddenly gone out. So he couldn't send a message to the bases at Ondangwa and Oshakati further east. And he hadn't wanted to take time to stop there either. He had a good reason to be in a hurry to get back—it worried him that he hadn't been careful enough.

He wanted to make sure as fast as possible that he hadn't caught the mysterious disease that devastated the tribe.

Despite nerves and fatigue, Arnold felt good when he touched down on the tarmac at Eros, the airfield just outside the Namibian capital.

After a quick hello to Mary, the young South African who was his secretary and also worked for several other local bush pilots, he put away his pilot's license and helicopter papers, and jumped into his old, faithful Peugeot without saying another word.

Leaving the airport area, he headed in the direction of Katatura, the section of Windhoek where 50,000 blacks and coloreds lived in misery. Ten minutes later he arrived in front of the ultra-modern hospital of the "township" and rushed into the office of Dr. Piet du Toit, one of his few real friends in the capital.

Fortyish, bright and good-natured, du Toit was one of a rare breed: a liberal Afrikaner. Originally from Capetown, he had left the south right after graduating from medical school and had buried himself in Windhoek. For the last four years, he'd worked in this hospital, putting in ten hour days for barely a living wage.

Arnold had met him at Windhoek's only decent night spot, the Kaiser Krone Bar. After downing several belts of "Namib," the local blond beer, the pilot and the doctor had discovered many things in common and a real friendship sprang up between them.

By chance, du Toit was able to squeeze him in right away between a Damara woman and an old man with Asian-looking features and copper skin. Listening to Arnold's tale, the doctor was troubled. He had certainly never heard of such a phenomenon either, and hearing the symptoms of the strange malady, he drew a blank.

"Could this be something like the story of the volcanic lake in the Cameroons? You remember dozens of people were killed by that leaking gas not too long back?"

"I suppose it could be possible. Except there isn't even the shadow of a volcano in the whole Kaokoveld," Arnold answered.

Du Toit gave him an examination and drew some blood.

"At first glance, you're healthy as a horse. But that's not to say there's nothing wrong with you. Invite me to dinner tomorrow, then I'll bring you the results and have the chance to work my charm on Laura at the same time."

"Roger," Arnold said, playing the pilot. He knew that his friend was quite taken with his beautiful wife, a tall brunette with green eyes, and that in a way, Piet envied him his family life, despite his ringing declarations on the glory of bachelorhood.

"Look, I must caution you against being too optimistic. If the cultures turn out to be positive, it will take me a few days to identify what bug you brought back from up there."

"*Mektoub*, Arnold shrugged his shoulders. "I'll be patient."

He left the hospital quickly. The temperature had become slightly more bearable, and the hilltops around Windhoek were beginning to turn pink. He looked at his watch: 4:30. He had just enough time to run in and see Howe.

He was just starting to turn on the ignition key of the Peugeot, when again he had the strong sensation of being watched. Immediately he turned toward the miserable cardboard hovels with corrugated tin roofs which lined the other side of the street, but saw only the usual crowd of blacks and coloreds coming home after work. In front of him the automobile traffic was thick with motorbikes zooming like Kamikazis between cars and "bakkies," small local trucks with open backs. A glance in the rear view mirror showed nothing. Everything seemed normal.

"Good God, if I'm really fine, what's got ahold of me?" Arnold murmured to himself. "I'm worrying like a little old lady . . ."

Without waiting longer, he started the car and plunged into the stream of rush hour traffic. Darting between "bakkies" and army trucks, he nearly hit a dozen bicycles in the process. But he arrived in only fifteen minutes.

The offices of the South-African "pro-consul" on Goeringstrasse in Windhoek looked like a huge and luxurious vacation villa—except for the soldiers, sombre beneath bush caps and automatic RI rifles over their shoulders, who were posted at the entrance. SWAPO hadn't made any strikes in town for a long time, but the South Africans were still uneasy, and armed soldiers were everywhere in Windhoek.

Arnold gave his name and asked to be seen right away by the administrator, or, if he weren't there, by one of his top assistants. He had no trouble getting in; in this country, like anywhere south of the Orange River, it was enough to be white.

Reginald Howe, the General Administrator, was not there, and Arnold was received by one of his deputies, Johan Van der Mewre. The Frenchman didn't know him at all—he'd only just come to Namibia—but he could tell from the moment he saw Van der Mewre that his job wouldn't be easy.

As calmly as possible, Arnold explained what he had seen, pointing out the village on a map pinned to the office wall. Van der Mewre couldn't have cared less, and made a point of acting as bored as possible. Finally he interrupted.

"If I understand correctly, 150 or 200 Kaffirs are dead in the bush, out in the middle of nowhere . . . but what's that to me? From what I can see on the map, their closest neighbors, other Kaffirs, are a good 150 km. to the east. If this is an epidemic, it will disappear as quickly as it came. This is Africa . . . Besides, how do you know it's an epidemic? With the blacks, you never know. It might turn out that another tribe wiped them out to steal their women. It wouldn't be the first time, you know!"

Arnold was prepared for this kind of reaction. He knew Van der Mewre's type only too well—the bureaucratic bigot who had come to Namibia to earn a few extra *rands* per month, and who basically hated the country and its people. And this one had no doubt never set foot in the north."

Still, Arnold managed to contain himself.

"It's true I don't know for a fact what happened," he said. "But there's the story of the yellow airplane flying over the village . . . that seems a bit strange. And the one thing I'm sure of is that this wasn't some sort of tribal squabble. Not one of the bodies I saw had any trace of a wound. In any case, you're in charge of the administration of this territory, and you can't just leave these bodies unburied. You've got to begin an investigation right away to find out what went on up there. What if the same thing shows up at the bases in Ondangwa or Oshakati?"

"Look, Arnold, I know what I have to do, and it's not up to you to tell me. The General Administrator is in Pretoria for a week and I'm practically alone here to take care of all the red-tape and paper work in running the whole bloody country. The sooner they become independent, the better!"

His anger rising, Van der Mewre's English grew more gutteral and the rough intonations of Afrikaans began to show through. He paused for a moment, then lowered his voice. "I'm going to tell you something, Arnold. For me, a good Kaffir is a dead Kaffir, so I'm not going to waste my time trying to figure out their loony stories. The more who die, the better! Alive, they only think up ways to kick us out!"

For once, Arnold lost his cool. "Van der Mewre," he said, looking him straight in the eye, "I know Reginald Howe very well, and I doubt he appreciates this kind of thinking. All it would take is a call on the radio to send an army detachment to inspect the village. If you like, I can take you there in my helicopter. I'll check with Howe later about the expenses, and you can see for yourself what's happened."

Behind his wide desk, Van der Mewre looked like he was about to have a stroke. His face with its close-set eyes and thick neck had turned bright red, and he looked ready to fly out of control.

Arnold knew what he was thinking. If he could have, he would have cheerfully strangled the foreign bugger who ordered him about. And worse, over filthy blacks! No question, the French bastard was one of those "Kaffir-booties," those white "Nigger-lovers" who betray their own race.

But Arnold felt he had the upper hand. Over the past few years he had rendered vital service to the South African Army, and he knew that Van der Mewre had to be aware of it. Especially the fact that he had carried off several discreet and delicate missions in Angola to rescue commandos who had parachuted too far inside during their sabotage operations. And he still had, he knew, a large reserve of goodwill with the military, and with Howe, Van der Mewre's boss.

The same thoughts evidentally crossed Van der Mewre's mind too. Instead of launching into another tirade, he thought for a moment, scratching his cheek. He finally spoke in a more moderate tone.

"O.k. Arnold, I'll look into this business of yours. It's no use bothering the army. They're in the middle of a search operation in the east. I don't have anybody on hand to go with you tomorrow and I'm busy all day. If you like, we can go up there early Wednesday morning."

Arnold was sure he wasn't all that busy, but decided to let it drop. In any case, he was just as glad to wait for the results of du Toit's tests before taking off again.

"That's fine with me," he said. "With the heat, the bodies aren't going to be such a pretty sight when we get to the *kraal*, and I suggest protecting ourselves with gloves and masks. I'll call you tomorrow to settle the time for take-off."

"Fine. Ah, but there's one more thing, Arnold. It's best not to speak to anybody about all this until we know exactly what happened. No use to create unnecessary panic."

"Very considerate of you, but I doubt we can keep this under wraps for long."

"Let's wait at least until Wednesday morning. After that, we'll see."

"All right, if that makes you happy."

Arnold wasn't sure he'd keep his promise, but he didn't want to discuss it further with Van der Mewre.

He quickly left the general administration buildings under the sullen gaze of soldiers in reddish-brown uniforms standing motionless at the entrance. Ten minutes later he arrived in front of the comfortable little bungalow he rented in a newly established residential neighborhood at the western edge of the city.

Laura was waiting for him, anxious because he was late. He avoided kissing her, and turned away his son who ran to throw himself into his father's arms with all the enthusiasm of a five-year-old.

"Something wrong?" Laura asked.

"No, but I think we better not touch each other," he said after sending Pierre into his room. "I found this village in the north which was completely wiped out by an epidemic, or something like that, and I don't want to give you anything, in case I caught something myself. I saw du Toit, and he said theoretically I don't have anything, but you never know."

He poured himself a whisky before settling down to tell Laura in detail what had happened. She had the same reaction he did.

"It's absolutely unbelievable. Are you sure they were all dead?"

"No doubt about it. It was really horrible," he answered, seeing again the distorted faces of the Ovahissas.

Just before dinner, he checked his schedule to see what was coming up in the next few days, and one name caught his attention: Steve Denton. He was supposed to come in ten days. But he'd absolutely have to get here sooner—this story would certainly interest him. He got on the line to Paris right away.

That night he slept in the guest room, far from Laura. And he loved sleeping next to Laura, feeling the touch of her leg or her arm, burying his face in her neck . . .

When he awoke, she had already left for the bookstore on Kaiserstrasse where she worked. A little disappointed, he fixed a cup of tea and a few pieces of toast, before plunging voluptuously into bed again to listen to the news on the "world service" of the BBC. He had long ago quit listening to the government radio station, SABC, which only gave out garbled and ridiculously distorted bits of information.

He fell back asleep and didn't wake up until noon. Before jumping in the shower, he phoned Van der Mewre to confirm that they would leave the next morning around 8:00. Then he called his friend Johannes Viljoen, the editor-in-chief for the *Windhoek Examiner*, a very popular weekly in Namibia. But Viljoen wasn't there. He had just left for Swakopmund on the coast to look into some fiscal fraud and wouldn't be back until the next day. A pity, because it certainly would have been nice to tell Viljoen about what he had discovered.

He spent the afternoon fixing his radio and getting his helicopter ready for the trip. Choppers didn't like long trips, and he certainly didn't want to have any kind of breakdown with Van der Mewre next to him!

The dinner party at home that evening was very pleasant. For one thing, du Toit told him that the first results of the tests done the evening before indicated that nothing was out of line.

"Everything's negative," he whispered, when Laura went to check on something in the kitchen. Arnold took a deep breath. The idea that he had perhaps brought back a fatal virus from the bush had worried him a lot.

During dinner, they tried to forget the whole business for a little while and chatted about other things. Piet announced that he would leave next year for London to do a three month stint in a Hampstead Hospital. He was very excited by the prospect.

"Ah, my friends, for me Pinter, the Royal Opera House . . ."

"You have all the luck. Why don't you take me with you?" joked Laura, who adored theater and opera, pleasures practically unheard of in Windhoek.

Arnold looked at her. She really was very beautiful, even dressed simply in jeans and a crew-neck cashmere sweater. He suddenly realized that they almost never went out, just the two of them, and that his wife didn't live a very exciting life.

"Laura, how about if we take a week of vacation at the end of the year and make a little trip to Capetown? It'll be a nice change from being out here in the sticks."

". . . Arnold, I'm talking to you. Are you deaf, or what?" Van der Mewre's voice broke like thunder, shaking him from his thoughts. "So what are we going to do?," he bellowed. "We can't wait around here forever. I have things to do in Windhoek." He headed for the Jet Ranger.

Arnold, unable to believe his eyes, started to follow him, then turned to glance around once more.

It was no use protesting. Just a little while ago, as soon as the helicopter had landed, he hurried into the village and confirmed for himself that he hadn't been imagining things.

The *kraal* was completely empty. All the bodies he'd seen had completely disappeared, along with the sickening smells and the disgusting buzzing of the flies. All that was left was a village deserted by its inhabitants, strangely deserted, motionless, as though stopped in time. . . .

CHAPTER 5

Aboard the SAA Boeing 747 approaching Windhoek, December 1

Steve Denton looked out the window. The South African Airways 747 began its approach to Windhoek, flying over stretches of desert where only the rare plant sprang from the ochre-colored earth. An occasional farm, with a bouquet of scrawny trees clustered about its dwellings, was visible from time to time to break the monotony of the landscape. It had only been last night that they'd taken off from Frankfurt. God, it seemed like last year!

The plane was now very low, but there was no hint of city nearby. J.G. Strijdom International Airport was situated on a vast, desolate plateau forty km. from Windhoek. A dull thud accompanied the opening of the traps and the dropping of the wheels; within minutes the Jumbo had landed with astonishing ease.

Denton stood up and reached for the camera case which had slipped under his seat. A cup of coffee brought by a stewardess had opened his eyes, and he couldn't help feeling a little prick of excitement, sharpening his curiosity.

During the flight he'd been thinking over what Arnold had told him about this tribe. Now he couldn't wait to find out more. One thing he knew for sure—Arnold wasn't the type to make things up.

"Ach, Windhoek . . ."

His neighbor, a German woman of copious proportions who spoke no English and had spent the better part of the trip drinking beer with her husband, crushed him against the seat trying to

29

look out the window. Not wanting to spoil her pleasure, he said nothing.

The plane would continue on to Johannesburg, but a good number of the passengers got off in Namibia. Like his seatmates, they were mostly Germans of a certain age, who, caught up in nostalgia for the past, came to this old colony of the Kaiser which had been lost in 1915, but remained German in atmosphere and mentality.

As soon as he stepped off the plane, a blast of dry desert air stuck in his throat. Southern Africa was just as he remembered it! But still he was happy to be back in this part of the world where he had so often come while posted at Johannesburg with A.P.

He was now only a few yards from the vast windows of the terminal and tried to make out Arnold's face among the dozens of heads turned toward the passengers coming down from the 747. But there was no sign of the familiar profile of his friend.

He shivered stepping into the huge hall; the air conditioning gave a glacial chill to the interior. Getting through the passport line, as usual, took forever. The South African immigration officials, dressed in their olive-green uniforms, questioned each arrival with suspicion, asking everyone systematically why he had come to Namibia. There was the general sense of distrust that comes with an occupied country.

After getting permission to stay for a month, Denton pushed open the gate and plunged into the crowd that filled the waiting room. Shouts of welcome in German and Afrikaans came from every direction. Denton looked once more for the deeply lined face of his friend, but in vain. Remembering Arnold's distaste for mobs, Denton decided he must be waiting outside, or on the first floor. Clearing a path for himself in the midst of the crush of people, he managed somehow to get to the spot where the black porters with sullen looks on their faces had just brought the baggage.

Seeing the stairs to the first floor and the bar, he ran up them. But after a quick check of the tables, he still didn't see Arnold.

"So, the lazy cuss is waiting for me in his car. So much for emotional reunions!"

Denton was a little let down. He loved to be met at the end of a long trip, especially a plane trip. He went back down the stairs, and stepped outside into the furnace. A few taxis waited in front of the airport, and several dozen private cars were parked in the lot, unprotected from the sun. He made himself inspect them all, one by one. Five minutes later, he was forced to admit it: Arnold hadn't come to meet him despite his promise.

Annoyed, his jacket and shirt already soaked with sweat, he pulled his address book from his sack and began to look for a phone.

He dialed his friend's home number and let it ring five or six times before anybody answered. At first he thought he'd dialed the wrong number; the voice on the other end sounded so faint it nearly disappeared over the wire.

Still he knew that it was Laura—and sensed instantly that something had happened.

"Laura, hello. This is Steve Denton. I'm at the airport . . . What's going on? Yves wasn't able to come meet me?"

There was a silence which seemed to last forever before Laura answered. "Steve . . . It's . . . it's terrible. Yves died yesterday morning."

Denton was speechless. All about him, noisy groups of people were leaving the airport, chatting happily together.

"Oh, Laura, look, I'm so sorry. I'll jump in a taxi and be right there."

He hung up, stunned, and not even having thought to ask how it had happened. Only a few minutes before, he'd gotten off the plane full of enthusiasm and curiosity. Now he wondered what he was doing here in the middle of nowhere, suddenly so alone.

CHAPTER 6

Windhoek, December 1

"**B**ut how could an accident like this have happened?"

Sitting in the living room of Arnold's small house, Denton couldn't think what to say. Dressed in a simple turquoise house-dress, with her grief-swollen face and beautiful green eyes red from tears and lack of sleep, Laura was hardly recognizable.

"I don't know, Steve, I don't know. Yves had completely checked out his helicopter. He took such good care of that machine . . ."

Laura told him about the accident which had taken place in late morning on the day before. Yves had wanted to test the new radio he'd just installed. He'd begun to gain altitude after take-off when one of the blades suddenly came off. There was absolutely nothing he could do. The Jet Ranger dropped like a stone and crashed at the end of the runway.

"You know, Steve, he didn't have time to suffer, I'm sure of that. It all happened so fast . . . barely a few seconds, according to what they told me at the airport."

"Yes, I'm sure that's true," Denton answered, thinking that even a virtuoso like Arnold couldn't do anything about this kind of accident. "And this tribe in the north? What happened to them? It's because of them that Yves asked me to come early."

Dying of curiosity, he couldn't help asking the question, even if it wasn't the right moment.

"The tribe? Oh yes, the Ovahissas. But didn't you know?"

"Didn't I know what?"

"Well, they all disappeared, you see. All the bodies had disappeared two days later when Yves went back up there with some guy from the general administration office."

"What?"

"Yes. The village was empty. Yves meant to tell you all about it. Probably he didn't have time."

"But that's incredible. You mean, one day he sees I don't know how many bodies, and two days later, none at all . . ."

"That's right. And he didn't know what could have happened. He came back from Kaokeveld a bundle of nerves. And this administration guy was furious over being inconvenienced for nothing—which didn't help either."

"So what did he say about this disappearance? Had the bodies somehow been buried?"

"No, he didn't see any sign of burial. It was as if nothing had happened, as if the village had suddenly been abandoned by its inhabitants. But Yves hadn't imagined it, he really did see the bodies. The whole business was really getting to him. Besides, he had the feeling he was being followed. He told me so the night before last."

"Followed? By whom?"

"I don't have any idea, Steve, no idea at all . . . Oh, it's so horrible. Yesterday, at this very same time, he was still living, he was with me, like you . . ."

Laura broke down in sobs, her face buried in her hands. Denton, who didn't know how to act or what to say in the face of someone else's grief, approached her and awkwardly laid his hand on her shoulder. He felt weak himself. This death had changed all his plans, and he didn't know what to do next.

She lifted her head, trying to smile.

"Thanks, Steve, you're very kind. I'm sorry to be like this . . . You know what you could do is to go see Johannes Viljoen, the editor of the *Windhoek Examiner*. You remember, you met him here one night for dinner. I think that Yves saw him at the end of his second trip north, and that he's heard the whole story."

"Viljoen? Sure I remember him. How could anybody forget a character like that? He really knows what's going on, doesn't he?"

"Yes. He *is* a bit crazy, but you can trust him. He came to see me as soon as he heard about the accident. He and Yves were close friends."

Of course Denton remembered Viljoen very well, and knew his reputation for being the best-informed journalist in Namibia. Seven years earlier, he had founded the *Windhoek Examiner*, which came out every Friday in English. It was a curious mix of Windhoek's juiciest gossip, uncompromising political tracts, often lively reporting . . . and photos of naked women.

"Good idea, Laura. I'm going to try to find him as soon as I get a hotel room and rent a car."

The doorbell interrupted them. Laura went to open the door and came back with a man of about forty with an open, intelligent face, whom she introduced as Dr. du Toit, a friend of Arnold's.

They talked briefly, and the doctor offered to take him to a hotel. Denton accepted, and the two men went off toward the Furstenhoff, a charming old hotel with good specialties of the house right in the center of town.

Du Toit also found the story of the Ovahissas very bizarre. "Yves was afraid he had caught their disease, but he didn't have a thing. The symptoms he described didn't tell me anything at all. A sort of curious mix of plague, boils and cholera. But no epidemic has been reported in the region. And why did the bodies disappear? I'm sure Yves didn't make it up, and I'm ready to help if you want to investigate any of this."

Denton told him that he would call on him. But for the moment he needed to talk to Viljoen.

Arriving at the Furstenhoff, he jumped into the shower and let the warm water run over him for several minutes. The flight and the news of Arnold's death had exhausted him.

An hour later, he went down to get a bite in the small dining room where the walls were decorated with cheap pictures of the German and Austrian countryside. The room captured perfectly the absurdity of Namibia, a country deep in Africa where the descendants of the first German colonists were mentally still in Bavaria.

Denton wolfed down two or three sandwiches, then left to find Viljoen's office. The quarters where Viljoen composed his masterpiece on the second floor of a small gallery of shops in the center of town were easy to locate. Everybody knew Viljoen. And just in case somebody overlooked his operation, there was the large sign over his door which announced in capital letters: WINDHOEK EXAMINER—PICTURES, REPORTING, EDITORIALS. Truly a one man show!

It was a real *tour de force* to bring out a weekly that was full of information and often carried exclusives. And the General Administrator devoured every word from the first to the last page, while South African President Pieter Botha had it flown in every week to get an idea about what was really going on in Namibia.

God only knew if the South Africans really wanted to suppress it, which they tried to do from time to time. "Bad Viljoen"— Viljoen the screwball in Afrikaans—had in fact embraced most of the ideas of SWAPO and took no pains to hide his beliefs, as Denton found out when he met him at Arnold's.

He took pot-shots at Pretoria's policies toward the former German colony, and openly advertised his hostility toward the South African "occupation forces" as well as the huge foreign mining interests, such as De Beers, Rio Tinto or Cullum, all accused of looting Namibia despite virtuous resolutions of the United Nations.

Denton pushed open the door and found himself in a small reception room with ghastly vinyl armchairs and an ancient desk, all seemingly for a secretary. As there wasn't anybody there, he wondered briefly what to do when he heard noises from one of the other two rooms leading from the entry. He cocked his ear and came closer to the door; then he heard a weak groaning and noticed a sign on the door-knob, "Do Not Disturb."

"Hello, anybody there?" he asked, knocking twice lightly on the door.

Suddenly there was silence from the other side. After a long pause, the voice of an irritated man called out, "Who is it?"

"Steve Denton, I'd like to speak with Viljoen."

"Later. I'm busy. Didn't you see the sign. Come back tomorrow."

"I'm an American journalist, a friend of Yves Arnold's. We met at his place last month."

"Hmmm . . . Right. Hang on a minute. Take a seat. I'll be right there."

Denton sat in one of the chairs. He was sweating, and it was stiffling in the little office without airconditioning. Africa in all its splendor! Automatically he reached for a copy of the *Windhoek Examiner* and stared wide-eyed at the page he'd opened to quite by chance.

A voluptuous British beauty on her knees and wearing only a G-string offered up to the readers her two enormous breasts which she held, with an air of mock innocence, in her hands. Beneath the photo in capital letters, was the improbable caption, "Shiela says, if its hot, make love."

"It's really too much," Denton frowned. At that moment the door opened, and he suddenly understood what was going on in Viljoen's office.

A statuesque black beauty, almost as endowed as the blond in the photo, sauntered nonchalantly from the office, sat down in the secretary's place, and motioned for Denton to go in, looking him right in the eyes.

Well, at least there's one person who practices what he preaches, Denton thought, trying not to smile as he entered Viljoen's office.

With his delicate glasses perched on his nose and his hair disheveled, Viljoen looked distinctly out of sorts.

"Sorry to have disturbed you, I know that you are a very busy man," Denton said, offering his hand.

Viljoen scowled for a moment, the brusquely got up and offered his hand and a very wide smile.

"Come on Denton, no bullshit. It's true you might have arrived a tad later, but I can always pick up where I left off. Arnold told me you were coming. On that score, you arrived too late, if you don't mind my saying so. Happy to see you anyway." While speaking, he switched on a fan that whirred like an airplane motor.

"Ah, right," Denton answered, a bit thrown by Viljoen's special brand of humor. "I saw Laura this morning, and she told me to see you."

"She did right. Yves was a friend, and I can't accept yet that he's dead, all the more so since I feel a bit guilty about it."

"How come?" Denton lowered himself into a chair half full of holes.

"Well, he came to see me just after getting back from his trip north with Van der Mewre, that jerk from the administration. He was all excited—and this story of a tribe who all died and then disappeared is pretty interesting, even if he didn't have any proof. No way, really, to write anything about it without proof."

Pushing his hair back from his forehead, Viljoen revealed a babyish face with a fine, narrow nose, bright eyes and the lips of a gourmand. "Besides," he went on, "I had an article on Swakopmund to finish and the deadline for the paper, so I wasn't as interested in his story as no doubt I should have been. . . ."

"What are you saying?"

"Yves also told me that he felt he was being followed, that somebody was watching him ever since his first trip to the north. He even had the sensation of being watched in the village . . . when everybody was dead. I confess I really didn't pay too much attention. I have a lot of enemies here, and I'm used to such things. I get death threats every week—and they've already poisoned two of my dogs."

"But do you think Yves was in danger?"

"I don't know. I guess I ought to have taken what he told me a bit more seriously. Thinking about the helicopter accident, it is a bit strange, after all . . ."

"You think the chopper might have been sabotaged?"

"It's not out of the question. But you have to look closely and not jump to any conclusions. I'm going to see what the police and the aviation experts conclude before starting any investigation of my own. In the meantime, I'm completely in the dark."

Denton also had a funny feeling that there was something out of the ordinary, something mysterious, about Arnold's death. Perhaps he'd have to go north to see if he could find an answer.

"And what if we went to this Ohissa village?"

"Ovahissa," Viljoen corrected him, vigorously picking his nose. "Why not? The dirt road to the village is good and we could easily get there in my Land Cruiser. The only problem is the mines. This route isn't used by the army every morning like the main roads are."

"How big is the risk?"

"Pretty small. That part of Namibia has been calm for months. I'll bet we could chance it without necessarily being turned into heat and light."

"Into what?"

"Heat and light. It's sort of a sacred term to describe stepping on a mine. Denton, if you've forgotten your classics, it's time you took a refresher course. In any case, don't worry, I know the score because I do thousands of kilometers every month just crossing this fucking country."

"O.k., o.k., I trust you. Maybe we could leave in a couple of days. I think Yves' funeral is tomorrow."

"Right. But are you sure you want to do this? You're here for the *Geographic*, not to look into this affair. It's possible the authorities won't appreciate a foreigner messing about, and if Arnold was a victim of sabotage, it could become dangerous."

"Viljoen, now it's your turn to bullshit me. Yves was my friend, and I want to know what happened to him. Besides, nothing can keep me from taking pictures in the Kaokoveld."

"Very well then, Denton, I haven't uttered a word. I'll see you tomorrow at the services, and we'll leave very early the day after." Viljoen adjusted the glasses that had slid down his nose, and got up.

"Fine. I'll go now to get a little rest. I'm whipped," said Denton, pulling himself slowly out of the chair.

"On your way out, would you mind telling the secretary to come in. I've got some business to finish with her."

Viljoen gave a slight smile to Denton, who couldn't help admiring his South African colleague. The man had style.

It was still hot when he left the shopping gallery. He wiped his forehead with a handkerchief and began to follow the road back to the hotel, when he noticed on the other side of the street a parked Land Rover whose driver, a white man, seemed to be watching him. Denton stopped, trying to make out the man's features, but he turned his head abruptly, stepped on the gas, and took off. Denton followed the car with his eyes until it got lost in the traffic. Then he turned briskly in the direction of the Furstenhoff.

CHAPTER 7

Kaokoveld, December 3

"**O**.K., Steve, we're getting close to Etosha. This is where it gets dangerous. Let's stop for a drink. I'm sick of swallowing sand."

Viljoen had to shout to be heard over the deafening noise inside the vehicle. With all the doors open because of the heat, the Land Cruiser got up to 80 kph on the road which undulated like a wash-board, leaving behind a long plume of white dust.

They'd left Windhoek at 4:00 in the morning and had rapidly crossed the paved road to the north—a road kept in good condition by the authorities for strategic reasons.

Only the sunrise, always of a savage beauty in the bush, had broken the monotony of the road on this immense plateau sparsely strewn with scruffy thorn bushes, solitary baobabs and "koppies," those flat mounds of southern Africa generally infested with mambas and other poisonous snakes.

A little way past Otjiwarango they had left the paved road and taken the gravel track that went toward the Cunene.

Denton had taken the wheel, as ever finding real pleasure in driving the rutted African road. In Africa he had caught the bug of the road, that desire to drive hundreds or even thousands of miles on pot-holed tracks of dirt or sand, sometimes without any particular direction.

He stopped near Etosha National Park, that impressive preserve protected from tourists by the nearby guerrillas. In silence they drank down several beers, not daring to bring up what lay ahead.

Viljoen took a last swallow, pitched his beer can as far as he

40

could into the bush and ran his hands through his disheveled hair to shake out some of the dust. "Let's get going. It's no use sitting around here torturing ourselves with worry. The less we think about it, the better."

Then he got behind the wheel and started the Land Cruiser, this time taking off at full speed onto the dirt track that opened endlessly in front of them. It was the beginning of the most dangerous leg of the trip.

As if hypnotized, they stared, eyes fixed on the road a few feet from the hood, fearing a fatal explosion at any moment. In spite of the cease-fire, the SWAPO freedom fighters were masters at the art of hiding mines on the hundreds of tracks which wound through Ovamboland and Kavangoland along the Angolan border. The South African Army had neglected to sweep them, content with a daily clean up the Tsumeb-Ondangwa-Oshakati axis which was vital for the provisioning of bases along the border.

The only way to avoid the mines was to stay in the recent tracks of another vehicle and pray that nothing would happen.

It had taken more than four hours to go a little over 100 km. Drenched in sweat and covered with dust, by the time they neared the Ovahissa village, they were a pair of wrecks with frayed nerves.

Denton pulled some binoculars from the side-pocket of the vehicle and turned them toward the wooden stockade and the huts of the *kraal*.

"Not a soul. The place looks completely dead."

"All right. Let's not hang around here forever," Viljoen replied. "Let's have a look inside. Let's leave the car and go by foot."

Denton agreed and got out.

Viljoen lifted the Winchester 40/40 from the hooks attached to the backseat of the Land Cruiser, put a bullet in the chamber, and stuffed his pockets with extra shells.

They ran the 500 yards that separated them from the entrance, then stepped inside the village. Viljoen took the lead, then stopped suddenly, motioning Denton to do the same.

"Shh . . . you hear it?"

Denton cocked his ear and heard a strange noise, which seemed to come from the center of the *kraal* about fifty yards away. It sounded like somebody scraping the ground.

"What's that?"

"I haven't a clue," Viljoen whispered, "but lets find out. Here, take my pistol. You never know." And he passed his companion the Colt 45 he carried in his belt."

"But I . . ."

Denton didn't have time to finish his sentence. A sort of piercing laugh, almost a jeer, exploded the quiet.

Frozen with fear, neither dared move. Then it was silent again, but for only a moment before another screeching outburst.

"Shit, what *is* that?" Viljoen clutched his rifle in front of him.

"I have no fucking idea . . ."

"Look out!" Viljoen yelled.

A brown-colored mass came flying out from between two huts and went straight for Denton. By reflex he pulled the trigger. At the same moment he heard a shot from Viljoen's gun, and the beast, stopped in mid-air, landed at their feet.

After a moment of shock, Viljoen raised his gun again and burst out laughing. "A hyena . . . A bloody moth-eaten hyena! God what a couple of fools to be taken in like that. And she was no doubt ten times more frightened than we were, poor devil."

"But what was she doing here?"

"Maybe she smelled death? It's a lingering odor, you know, and these animals are scavengers—specialists, if you like. Let's see what we can find in the village. It looks completely deserted."

They began to search the place methodically, looking for some sign inside every enclosure and hut, but finding none. The village was clinically clean, as though nobody had ever lived there. It had the look of one of those "authentically reconstructed native villages" for tourists in the national parks in South Africa.

"It's really weird. Just like Yves said. I understand how astonished he must have been if only two days before he'd found dozens of bodies . . ."

Viljoen swatted at a mosquito and looked around at the neighboring hills, as if he hoped to find some key to the mystery there. There, on the other side of the slimy green Cunene, lay Angola.

"No. No way Arnold was seeing things and the tribe simply crossed to the other side of the river. Something happened here. But what?"

"And what if it was SWAPO who massacred the villagers and took away the bodies?" asked Denton. It was impossible to even count the villages that had been razed by Namibian nationalists as punishment for collaborating with the whites.

"Not very likely," Viljoen replied. "They would have left some trace. The Freedom Fighters use firearms or machetes and they usually burn down a village once they attack it. Besides, the Ovahissas were so isolated, they hardly had any contact with the outside . . ."

"And the South African Army? According to what they told me last month, the atrocities of the Namibian auxillaries are every bit as bad as SWAPO's."

"A fuck-up by the army? I don't think so. They're so busy messing up other things, they wouldn't bother to exterminate a poor tribe stuck in a God-forsaken region nobody ever goes to. And then what about those symptoms Yves described? And the business of the yellow airplane? It doesn't add up. . . ."

The afternoon began to fade into rapidly falling night. A light breeze rose and blew in gently from Angola, bringing in a sensation of freshness. But it couldn't quite blow away the oppressive silence that hung like a threat covering the village.

"Let's get back to the car. This place give me the creeps,"

Denton said as he left for the Land Cruiser. They were supposed
to spend the night in a Lutheran mission run by some of Viljoen's
friends.

Viljoen climbed into the driver's seat, then stopped, looking
carefully behind the Land Cruiser.

"Steve, did you notice something?"

"No, why?"

"Look, behind the car there, on the road, there are tire tracks.
And they look new. In fact, those are the ones we followed to
get here."

"You're right. And they're from a truck—with pretty big tires
at that."

"At first it didn't strike me as anything important. But if you
think about it, why would a truck have been here recently? Nobody ever sets foot in this part of the Kaokoveld unless its the
army or some geologist. In any case, not by that route . . ."

"Maybe an army car came to see the village after the Ovahissas
disappeared?"

"Maybe. But it would surprise me. First of all, the military is
nervous about the mines and they prefer to go by helicopter—
usually the Alouette 3 or the Puma. Besides, those tracks are
larger than the wheels of army trucks. And it looks like there
might have been several trucks. Strange isn't it? . . . Well, let's
get going before dark."

About an hour later, they reached the first buildings of the
Lutheran mission. Like so many others along the border on both
the Namibian and Angolan sides, it contained a little school, a
tiny bush hospital and a chapel.

A Finnish couple and their three children, friends of Viljoen,
lived in two mud-brick houses, while a half-dozen nurses and
black attendants shared a few huts with their families.

Altogether there were about thirty Finnish missionaries in
northern Namibia from the Kaokoveld to Kavangoland. Every-

body knew that their sympathies lay with SWAPO and not the South African Army, and it was with them that Sam Nujoma, the tough, stubborn leader of the nationalist movement, had learned to read and write. Pretoria would have loved to get rid of them, but as the first Lutheran missionaries had arrived in the 1870's, their expulsion would have caused a general uprising.

Pietari Weikkolin came out of the house just as they were parking the Land Cruiser. Of medium height but a strapping build and white-blond hair which fell in his eyes, he was jovial and exuberant, nothing like a traditional missionary, if such even existed anymore.

"I'll be damned if it isn't Johannes! How's everything?" he boomed, thumping him on the back before squeezing Denton's fingers in a bone-crunching handshake. For all the world he looked more like a Viking conqueror than a modest messenger of God.

His wife, Anni, her serious face beneath a cap of short blond hair, à la Joan of Arc, was a doctor and kept very busy in the little hospital where she tended the victims of the war.

Another guest was with them for the evening too. Hilma Ranttila lived at Ongandjera, the biggest Lutheran mission in Namibia, next to the large military base at Oshakati. Risking her life, she served as the link between the different missions, carrying mail, medicines or supplies. Small, plumpish and near fifty, she accepted her role with a kind of good humor and fatalism, keeping her mischievous look well hidden behind thick tortoise shell glasses.

They all headed to the table for a frugal meal. Weikkolin and his wife were terribly upset to learn that Arnold had been killed, because they knew him well. Viljoen told his hosts that he had been with Denton in the Ovahissa village, but didn't mention Arnold's macabre discovery. Representatives of the administration in Ruacana had explained the sudden disappearance of the tribe by its passing into Angola.

"Everyone around here knows about it," said Weikkolin. "The

news spread like wildfire, but nobody was too upset because the Ovahissas really lived in isolation. Nobody would be surprised if they did go back to Angola. They've been jumping across the Cunene since the days of the Portuguese."

The two journalists exchanged glances. They had agreed not to contradict the official story in order to avoid suspicion and to carry out their investigation discreetly.

"And you, Sister, have you been traveling much lately? Have you been near the *kraal* of the Ovahissas?" Viljoen asked, smiling broadly at Hilma Ranttila.

"No, to tell the truth. I only went there once a long time ago. A couple of weeks ago I only got near the vicinity, going to visit a Catholic priest about sixty km. further south, not far from Etosha."

"And did you notice anything, uh, abnormal or unusual?"

"Heavens no! Everything was just fine, *Deo Gratias*," she answered with a laugh. "Of course, one does think of mines and one never knows when the Lord is going to call you to come to Him. But the track between Ruacana and Otjovasandu seemed safe enough. In fact, there were even a lot of vehicles on the road, if I remember right."

"What did you say?" Denton broke in, suddenly paying attention.

"Well, I passed quite a number of trucks which were going north. Maybe seven or eight . . . it was toward the end of the afternoon."

"Trucks? What sort of trucks, Sister? What color?"

"You know, to me, a truck's a truck, and I didn't pay too much attention. As best as I can recall, they were those big ones like you see in the mines, sort of an orange color. At the time I figured they were going to get gravel or sand on the banks of the Cunene."

"And do you remember what day you saw them?"

"Not exactly. But I can find out from my record book."

The missionary gave a wry smile and interrupted, "Tell me, you seem curiously interested in this story. . . ."

"You know, Pietari, I don't like to like to leave any stone unturned when it comes to something happening in Namibia," Viljoen replied.

"Good. Now, if we're going to experience one of life's great pleasures, I'm sure our friend Steve will come with us," Weikkolin winked at Viljoen.

"What's this all about?"

"It's a surprise," Viljoen answered while rising from the table. "You coming, Sister?"

"*Vade retro satana!*" she laughed. "Pietari told me to watch out for you. Maybe I'll go later with Anni."

Puzzled, Denton followed the other two out towards a construction which resembled a giant tool shed. Arriving first, the missionary flipped on a switch and motioned Denton to come inside. Blinded by the bright light, at first he couldn't see exactly where he was.

But his eyes adjusted, and then he understood where he'd been taken: to a sauna! There, in the middle of the bush, in one of the hottest countries in the world . . . those Finns were really incorrigible. He wanted to back out, but Viljoen pushed him gently back in.

"Come on, come on, you'll see. It'll do you a world of good, and you'll steam away all the grime from the trip."

The three men stripped and five minutes later sat on a plain wooden plank, while Weikkolin emptied an enormous bucket of water over a charcoal pan filled with red-hot coals. Denton thought he was going to faint when the little enclosure was buffeted by a blast of burning steam.

"Good. Now let's talk seriously," the missionary said when the steam had evaporated a little.

"What do you mean?" Viljoen replied with a touch of defensiveness in his voice.

"I didn't want to make too much of it earlier, but I'm sure you didn't say all you know about the village. Why so many questions about it? Johannes, you know you can trust me."

The two journalists glanced at each other for a couple of seconds, wondering what they should do. Viljoen was the first to break the silence.

"Look, Pietari, we'll tell you everything that happened, but we're doing it in complete confidence."

Ten minutes later the missionary shook his head in disbelief.

"It's incredible, but you're absolutely right. There's something very strange about the whole story. In any case, if it's the South Africans who have done this we simply must expose them."

"Hey, take it easy Pietari. That's not my job and we can't just go around making accusations without proof. We're going to continue looking into it, but we've got to get back to Windhoek pretty soon. Maybe you can do some investigating from here, you know, ask around, go over to the village, see if anybody saw anything. You will attract a lot less attention than we would."

"Sure. I'll see what I can do."

"Good. Call me at Windhoek if you turn up anything. Let's get out of this oven. I can offer you a beer—I've got some in the Land Cruiser."

They took a cold shower, then went to relax on the porch of the main house. Denton enjoyed the peaceful moment after three grueling days. He felt a familiar stirring of emotion to be once again in the savage, scented twilight of the bush, the welcome freshness of the African night setting in after the oppressive heat of the day.

A feeble chant, coming from the direction of the hospital, broke the perfect calm of nightfall. Flickering red shadows meant a fire had been built.

"What's that?" Denton asked.

"It's probably the Ovambos who came in this morning with a young boy. His leg was almost blown off by an anti-personnel mine. No doubt they've brought in a witch-doctor, and they're chanting to make him better."

"Is it o.k. to take pictures?"

"Why not? But you'll have to get permission first. I'll come with you."

Denton went to the car to get one of his cameras, then approached a group gathered around a dying fire.

The witch-doctor, an old man outfitted with a curious straw hat, kept his eyes half-closed while chanting in a low voice making animal-like sounds, which a dozen other tribesmen repeated in a hypnotic rhythm.

Weikkolin, who got along in the main Ovambo dialect called Kwanyama, leaned toward the witch-doctor and whispered a few words in his ear. The man nodded his head without interrupting his chant. Then he opened his eyes wide and stared at Denton, who snapped some pictures. Despite the flash which punctuated the night with weak bursts of light, the man barely blinked.

Denton, troubled by the fixed stare, but not wanting to disturb the group, signaled thanks by a nod of the head and turned to go back to the house, when the witch-doctor raised his hand and gave out a gutteral cry that stopped all the chanting. Then, looking straight at Denton, he spoke several dry phrases in a threatening tone.

"What's he saying?" Denton asked Weikkolin, slightly nervously.

"It's a bit difficult to interpret," Weikkolin answered, listening intently. "Yes, I've got it, though it's a little bizarre. He's saying something like: PICTURE-MAN, YOU WIELD LIGHT AND ATTRACT THE STORM. BEWARE THE MAN-WITH-RED-HAIR. HE WATCHES YOU IS NOT YOUR FRIEND. YOU WILL FEEL THE WIND OF DEATH IF YOU DO NOT FLEE . . . Does this mean anything to you?"

"No," Denton replied, feeling acutely uneasy. He stared back at the old man, trying to understand what he meant.

"Don't pay too much attention—he's no doubt in a trance and says whatever comes into his head."

"Yeah, probably . . ." Denton murmured, with little conviction.

Weikkolin took him by the arm and led him from the fire, when the witch-doctor shouted a new phrase.

"What's he saying now?"

The missionary himself seemed a little shaken when he translated the witch-doctor's last words: "THE WIND OF DEATH ARE FOLLOWING YOU, GO HOME PICTURE-MAN."

CHAPTER 8

Palm Beach, December 4

A light breeze rustled through the stately row of palm trees at the end of the garden, facing the ocean. Dressed in immaculate white slacks and a navy blazer, his elegance a kind of sixth sense, David Cullum slowly looked over the vast lawn which separated his house from the Atlantic.

Looking up, he glanced toward the house to see if the three men he was waiting for had arrived. No sign yet. Patience, he told himself.

He had always loved this house, one of the most beautiful in Palm Beach. It was an impressive sprawling villa with white walls, a red tile roof, and bedrooms overlooking the ocean, where he used to fall asleep to the rhythmic sound of the waves. Nowadays, though, he couldn't sleep and the house seemed like a vast, empty hotel, deserted during the off-season.

"David, Joe is here," Elizabeth called him from the top of the stairs that led gently to the garden.

At forty-five, she was still beautiful, her natural Mediterranean looks heightened by a semi-permanent tan. A lovely oval face crowned with lustrous dark hair, a straight nose, well-formed lips concealing brilliant white teeth, a slim body always elegantly dressed: Elizabeth was the perfect rich hostess, somebody right out of the pages of *Vogue* or *Town and Country*.

But her eyes gave lie to her self-assurance: nervous and darting, always moving, they showed deep-seated anxieties.

"O.k., Liz, thanks. I'm coming." Cullum moved toward the house with resolve.

"I'm going out. I've got a few things to pick up."

She moved away quickly, waving to the two men in passing.

"Hello, Joe, how are things?" said Cullum when at last he reached his guest. Joseph Kramer, lanky, with thinning hair, and the slightly sad face of a Buster Keaton, stood when Cullum came in.

"Everything's fine, David," Kramer answered. A financial counsellor with an apartment in West Palm Beach, he came regularly to his winter quarters in Florida, where, he claimed, he could work as easily as he did in New York.

"How's the market doing? I haven't been watching closely these past few days, but I suppose it's continuing to go down."

"That's right. But I'm expecting a small technical rise soon, so I recommend staying put for the moment."

Kramer was considered one of the wizards of Wall Street, a mysterious and discreet man who religiously avoided all publicity and worked out of modest offices on Gold St. with only a computer terminal and a secretary. He wasn't one of these "gurus" of the New York Stock Exchange, whose so-called "confidential" letters sold for a fortune and one time out of two gave the wrong tip. Many sought his advice, but few were chosen, because Kramer only gave it out to a few select friends, or to people whom he liked for completely arbitrary reasons. Cullum was among them.

"You know, I have complete confidence in you, Joe. Besides, that hasn't interested me much lately."

"Don't worry, the market will end up back on track."

Kramer had helped Cullum a lot when the British millionaire had decided to leave London in the late sixties—he was stifling in the City—to move to the U.S. where he wanted to manage the commercial and mining empire left to him by his father.

When Cullum arrived in New York, he had more than $300 million in his pocket, revenue from the sale of several lucrative properties and subsidiaries of Cullum, Ltd., in England. He had only retained the international trade interests and maritime shipping in London. These he supervised from New York, as he did the heart of the vast conglomerate he controlled: the gold, diamond, copper and uranium mines in South Africa and Namibia.

"David, how about a little golf tomorrow?" asked Kramer, already dressed the part in linen slacks and a short-sleeved cotton shirt. It was 3:00 in the afternoon and 85° beneath a brilliant sun.

"I'd better not, Joe. I don't feel in top form."

"Mr. Chambers and Mr. von Lassen have arrived, Sir." A butler with a slight Cuban accent leaned against the foot of the door, interrupting their brief conversation.

"Oh, good. Let's go, Joe," Cullum answered, taking Kramer by the arm.

"Hello, Ken. Greetings, Kurt. It's been a long time."

"Yes. I've just been to Brazil to see what's going on," answered Kurt von Lassen, an athletic looking man of fifty whose blue eyes gave away his German heritage.

"And how are things?"

"Not terrific. The economy isn't very strong and they're bleeding themselves dry to pay the foreign debt. I wonder if it isn't all going to blow up pretty soon. Luckily my investments there are all very long term."

Von Lassen, heir to one of the great German industrial families, had also come to settle in the U.S. several years after Cullum. A refined, elegant man of aristocratic bearing and good humor, he had fled Germany after a miraculous escape from a kidnapping.

He thought about it so often—his car suddenly blocked in a street in Dusseldorf, the procession of terrorists, the shot that exploded the skull of his chauffeur, the doors of the Mercedes locked shut by an electrical system, the police car appearing by chance out of a side street, blood trickling down the length of the seat. . . .

It was the end of 1977. The Red Army had just assassinated Hans Marin Schleyer, the kingpin of West German industrialists.

A few days later, Von Lassen left to live in America. He could no longer believe in Europe.

In the States he felt secure. And not only in Palm Beach, a watering hole for the super-rich and protected by veritable moats where "suspicious" strangers were quickly questioned by the police.

"In any case, it's always pleasant to go to Rio," Kenneth Chambers was saying. Chambers a tall, spare man of forty-five with the face of a diplomat sporting a thin mustache was the head of the prestigious New York firm Chambers and Mulligan, which specialized in international risk analysis.

"Yes and no, Ken. Rio has become pretty cut-throat. You can't even walk peacefully on Copacabana in the evening anymore. People are more and more nervous because of the economic crisis and the sense of insecurity. There are lynchings almost every day . . ."

"Popular justice sometimes becomes necessary when the authorities can't maintain control themselves." Chambers picked up the glass of orange juice passed to him by the Cuban steward.

"Yes. But I wonder what's going to happen. You never know what's going to happen in these countries. Just look at Iran. Who would have thought that the Shah could have been dumped so quickly by a ragtag band of religious fanatics?"

"Not I, that's for sure," sighed Chambers, who had bet on the Shah. With his fall, the reputation of Chamber's company had suffered. And then the hostages were taken at the American Embassy, damaging it even more. What humiliation!

He turned to Cullum with a questioning look.

"David, shall we talk business? I imagine that's the reason you asked us here today."

"Yes, Ken. I'd like to go over some things with you and ask your opinion about one specific aspect of our project. The preparation phase seems to be going all right. Only one little problem, it seems we had a troublesome witness and were obliged to take measures that you might call. . . . extreme."

"Are you telling me somebody was rubbed out?"

"Yes. That's what I've been led to believe."

"Who was it?"

"Some chap who lived in Windhoek. I don't have the details for the moment. Marais called me several times but was quite vague over the phone. He should be coming to New York soon and we'll know more then."

"And does this bother you, David?" Chambers asked.

"Not a bit. I gave a free hand to Marais and I think he did what he had to."

"You're right," Chambers went on. "You can't take a plunge without making waves. I only hope there weren't other witnesses."

"No, but we've had two journalists on our trail for several days. More or less by chance as I understand it. Luckily they haven't gotten far yet. One is a local journalist, and we can handle him. The other's an American, a reporter for *National Geographic* who's preparing an article on Namibia. They both knew the fellow from Windhoek."

"Yeah, that's trouble. You never know with the press. And if something happens to them that could be big trouble. But once again, we'd better take precautions. Once these reporters start sticking their noses into things, they're certain to start coming apart. In any case, the fewer journalists there are in this world, the better."

"You're exaggerating a bit, Ken," answered Cullum, who had his own bones to pick with the British press at the time he left London. "Here's what I propose. Let's continue to follow and observe these two, especially the American. If they get too close and seem on the verge of discovering something, we'll intervene. If not, we'll leave it alone, which would obviously be best. What do you think, Joe?"

Kramer remained silent a few moments, being a man in the habit of measuring his words carefully. "I think that sounds reasonable. But we mustn't hesitate if we have the least suspicion. Do we agree?"

"Agreed," von Lassen answered before turning to Cullum. "How's everything else then? All right?"

"Yes. But I hope there won't be too many unfortunate episodes of this sort."

"Me too, obviously. But we can't stop now. We've got only a few weeks left at best. And you know you can count on us, David."

"In the final analysis, it's the end which counts and not the means," Chambers said, his voice filled with urgency. "Just keep our objectives in mind. I'm sure we all agree on this point. And a couple of half-baked journalists aren't going to ruin it."

"That's right, David. It's *got* to work," Kramer added. "You won't forget what happened, will you? You won't forget?"

"No. I won't forget, Joe. I'll never forget. You know that as well as I do . . ."

CHAPTER 9

On the road to Luderitz, December 7

"**T**HE WIND OF DEATH IS FOLLOWING YOU. GO HOME, PICTURE MAN. . . ."

For three days Denton had been obsessed by the warning of the Ovambo witch-doctor. Of course he tried not to take him literally, but he couldn't stop thinking about the threat laid on him by the old sage with the chilling stare.

Ever since his stay in Brazil, he took certain things seriously, things he would have scoffed at before. The Brazilian mediums, the priestesses of Candomble, the Mothers of the Saints he had consulted on the hills overlooking Bahia—all had convinced him of the power of spirit and faith over simple Cartesian reason.

"Hey! Look out . . ." He yelled and swerved violently to avoid the zebra which practically threw itself under the wheels of his small rented Datsun. Eyes fixed on the road, he hardly noticed the desolate mountains and huge waves of red sand blotting out the horizon.

After coming back from the *kraal*, Denton spent two days going around in circles, thinking about the words of the old witch-doctor over and over again. Wouldn't it be best to follow his advice and go back to France as soon as possible? To go back to the peace of his life in Paris . . . to Caroline, who had been on his mind constantly for days.

Then it hit him quite suddenly that he had almost forgotten his story for the *Geographic*. He decided to go to Luderitz to take pictures of the ghost town at Kolmanskop. From there it

57

was easy to get to the uranium mine at Naukluft, one of the biggest in the world.

Swerving again to avoid a huge rock in the middle of the road, Denton grabbed a paper towel and wiped his forehead. After hours of driving on the dirt track, at last he was close to Luderitz, the curious little port on the Atlantic southwest of Windhoek which was completely encircled by the Namibian Desert and its immense red dunes.

A few kilometers before the first houses appeared, the road became paved and in generally good condition. After seeing the ruined houses and shops of Kolmanskop from a distance, he passed by the small Luderwitz airport, composed of two hangars, a control tower that had seen better days, and two decrepid buildings.

Following the road to the Strand, his hotel next to the sea, an image suddenly appeared to him with terrible clarity. He slammed on the brake without even bothering to check if there was a car behind and made a quick half-turn beneath the astonished eyes of a small group of half-caste fishermen.

Going slowly back along the road to the airport, he convinced himself that he hadn't been seeing things the first time. Off to the side of the dozen or so single-engine planes parked on the tarmac, in front of the hangars, a small company biplane stood out in the fading twilight. The plane was bright yellow . . .

Denton stopped the car and stared open-mouthed at the plane, hypnotized by his discovery. With Viljoen he had scoured the two airports at Windhoek for the airplane described to Arnold by the last Ovahissa. And then to find it at Luderitz!

It was rapidly getting dark, but he was still able to make out the registration mark on the plane: the black letters on the fusilage, ZS-EVS. He jotted them in his notebook and took the road back to the hotel, jittery with nervous excitement.

As soon as he arrived, he called Viljoen. "I'm going to try to find out who owns the plane, but I'm kind of anxious about going to the airport. I don't want to attract attention and Luderitz

looks to me like the kind of hole where everybody knows everything as soon as it happens."

"Yeah, you've got it. Better take care. Listen, I've got an idea.
Use my name and go see a girl I adore and who knows everybody
in that corner of the world. I don't know why I forgot to tell
you about her before you left. She works at the city's tourist
bureau. Since they get about fifty tourists a year, it goes without
saying she's got plenty of free time on her hands. Besides anything
that breaths in that town, she knows about."

"Can I trust her?"

"Yes. But tell her right away that you've been sent by me,
otherwise she'll send you packing."

"Ok., I'll go see her tomorrow morning," Denton answered,
before collapsing on his bed. The trip and now this development
had wiped him out.

At first blush, Gudrun von Bach didn't appear to be a very
easy character to deal with. The tourist bureau seemed an odd
sort of place for somebody to work who had the maddening habit
of dismissing people whose faces she didn't like. A forceful-looking
woman of forty, dressed in austere good taste, she had the habit
of answering in German when visitors asked her questions in
English or Afrikaans, just to remind them that Namibia had been
a colony of the Kaiser before it became a South-African province.

The name of Viljoen got a magical response. Gudrun von Bach
suddenly became all charm.

"Welcome to the desert of the Tartars," she said, flashing a
wide smile. "Here nothing happens, absolutely nothing, and we
pass our days waiting for the invasion."

"Invasion?"

"Right. SWAPO and all that. With independence coming up,
the whites are leaving the ship like rats. Nobody's investing and
businesses are drying up one after the other. Even the fishermen
are starving to death because there aren't any fish. Luckily, there

are still the mining companies. But how long will they last? Besides, they live in   . Well, I don't want to bore you any longer with my gripes, especially since I'm not supposed to be "selling out" the town. . . . What can I do for you?"

Denton explained briefly that he wanted to finish up a piece for the *Geographic* by visiting Kolmanskop and Naukluft.

"No problem for the ghost town. The people from de Beers will give you a guide. But Naukluft could be difficult. The Cullum boys aren't exactly friendly and they aren't keen on people seeing what goes on there. But anyway, you can try Colin Davis, the local administrative rep. You never know."

"Thanks. You've been very kind," Denton replied with his most winning smile. "By the way, there's one more little thing," he added in a deliberately off-hand way. "Last night coming in I noticed a little yellow biplane at the airport. Do you know who it belongs to?"

"No, but I can find out."

"I was wondering if it belonged to someone I used to know pretty well in Johannesburg. The registration number is ZS-EVS."

"Right. I'll call you at your hotel this afternoon."

Denton set off right away for the headquarters of Consolidated Diamond Mines, the local branch of de Beers, where he easily got permission to visit Kolmanskop, located in the diamond-cutting district. Then he went to see Colin Davis in the Cullum offices, not far from the port.

A frail sort of man of about forty-five, he gave a polite but firm no to Denton's request, going strictly by the book. "The orders are quite clear. I'm sorry, but you'll have to go to Jo'burg to get the green light from our Director General, Piet Marais. It's the only thing you can do, because he won't give you a pass unless he's seen you."

"I understand. It's no problem. I'd already counted on spending a few days in the Golden City to see some friends. So I'll kill two birds with one stone."

The Cullum agent seemed extremely relieved that Denton hadn't insisted.

Denton left and ate a quick lobster in a small port restaurant. Then went to see the ghost town. Once a flourishing city of southwest Africa, Kolmanskop was nothing more than an empty carcass, half-buried in the dunes of the Namib.

He visited several houses, their windows opening onto the immensity of the desert. Springing out of the sand during the diamond boom at the turn of the century, Kolmanskop, like Elizabeth Bay, had, little by little, returned to sand between the two wars. The annexation of the territory by South Africa and the deposits in the Orange River—much easier to exploit—sounded the death knell for mining towns clinging tenuously to life in the southern Klondike.

Feeling depressed, as though he'd stumbled into the end of the world, Denton quickly snapped about fifty pictures. On the way back, he decided to swing by the Naukluft mine to try for some pictures of the exterior. But 500 yards from the entrance he was stopped by two tough-looking guards who sent him back to Luderitz.

A bit surprised by such unusual security, he quickly looked over the mine before setting off. Like a prison or military base, it was surrounded by metal stakes with barbed wire and the guards at the entrance appeared heavily armed. This seemed like overkill; the SWAPO guerrillas would never come in this area.

Of course, certain precautions made sense, Naukluft being the second largest uranium mine of the territory, after the one in Rossing by Rio Tinto between Windhoek and Swakopmund. But to turn the thing into a fortified camp. . . .

Back in Luderitz, he spent the rest of the afternoon photographing the old structures built at the turn of the century by German ship owners and merchants who followed the footsteps of Alfred Luderitz, an adventurous businessman from Bremen, to settle in the ends of the earth.

The houses were for the most part built on the hills overlooking the port, one of the most beautiful in Africa. Once thriving, now it was almost empty. Leaning over the open balcony of one of the houses, he was able to see a half-dozen old rusty trawlers and only two other ships: a South-African tug, probably putting into port between Capetown and Walis Bay, and another, curious vessel, a sort of modified tuna trawler about 100 feet long, with a derrick and a helicopter platform on the back.

Puzzled, Denton watched it for several minutes. Anchored in the southern part of the port, it was obviously well kept-up and sheltered from the winds and swells of the open sea. It carried no national flag and no name was visible. Denton promised himself to go take a closer look later.

Returning to his hotel, he found Gudrun von Bach waiting for him in the lobby. In a light cotton dress with her tight chignon undone, the tough, unyielding secretary of the tourist bureau had changed into a full-bodied woman. The effect was altogether enticing.

"I didn't know Luderitz was also famous for beautiful women," Denton said.

"Thanks for the compliment. You're not bad yourself," she answered with a smile. "I have the information you wanted. It isn't what you think. The yellow plane you saw yesterday doesn't belong to anybody from Jo'berg."

"It surprised me a little that he'd be here. So who does it belong to, anyway?"

"To the Cullum Corporation, which brought it down here about six months ago."

"Cullum?"

"Right. In fact the plane's used mostly to ferry Dr. Schlammer about. He's an old German physician who's lived a long time in

Luderitz. He's in charge of the health and hygiene services for the company, but also plays flying doctor for other firms or isolated farms in case of emergency. I know him. A courteous sort, but a bit strange, and something of a loner. He rarely goes out and always has this sad look about him."

"Well, thanks for having tried. You really know everything that goes on around here."

"It's true. But I can tell you everything tonight. I imagine you don't have anything planned for dinner. So I'm going to cook up a little something at my place. I trust you aren't a loner yourself. . . ."

"No, but . . ."

"Come, come, don't stand on ceremony with me, Mr. Denton. If you're a friend of Viljoen's, you can't refuse. Besides, I have lots of things to tell you. Some strange things have been going on around here these last few months. I'll come around to pick you up at 8:30," she said, the peremptory bureaucrat again.

Curious about what he had just learned, Denton couldn't figure out what link there might be between a doctor for the Cullum Company and the Ovahissa village. Maybe this was a dead end? There were surely other yellow planes in Namibia and South Africa.

He decided to go see the doctor immediately. It was 5:30, so maybe he was already home. As soon as Denton found out from the hotel receptionist that Schlammer lived in one of the old houses he'd photographed that afternoon, he went over right away.

A black steward opened the door. Denton identified himself and was led into a salon filled with massive furniture where the windows were half-hidden behind heavy green velvet drapes. Carefully studying an old poster for German railroads, he didn't hear the doctor come in. A discreet cough announced his presence, and Denton turned, caught a little off-guard.

Facing him was a round-shouldered man of medium height wearing a white short-sleeved shirt and slightly old-fashioned beige pants. He looked to be about seventy. Beneath gray hair and mustache, his blue eyes stared out from an angular, worn-looking face and fixed unblinking on his visitor. Denton was struck first by how sad he looked, by how his thin lips were tightly drawn.

"And what may I do for you?" he asked in a low voice. He spoke English touched with an accent difficult to define.

Denton introduced himself and explained that he was writing an article for the *National Geographic Magazine* and had just come back from a two week trip in the north.

"I just spent a few days in a little village in Ovamboland, near Oshakati, and on several occasions we noticed a yellow plane which flew over us. It looked very much like the one here at your airport, and which you use, I believe, when you travel yourself. Being curious by nature and by profession, I just wondered if it's the same plane. Can it be that the Cullum Company is also interested in that part of the country?"

Schlammer waited a long moment before speaking.

"You must be mistaken. This plane rarely goes north of Windhoek. Besides, what would we do in Ovamboland, where there's nothing but sand and terrorists?"

"But it seems to have the same registration number. ZS-EVS, I believe. Maybe one of your company pilots borrowed it to buzz up to Oshakati and say hello to some friends?"

His answer fell like a sword. Now Schlammer gave up all pretense of smiling. "I repeat, you are mistaken. That plane has hardly left Luderitz for two months. I really don't see what you're getting at and I don't understand why you're pressing this. Is this the only thing you wished to speak to me about?"

Denton quickly changed the subject, trying to prolong the conversation with Schlammer, who now seemed nervous. He told him that he wanted to visit Naukluft soon, then asked some harmless questions about his work and life at Luderitz.

Schlammer relaxed a little, but still maintained a wary reserve. He seemed defensive, as though afraid to say too much. He ended the conversation abruptly, giving the excuse of an appointment. Denton got up and headed for the door, when he saw the converted trawler out the salon window. The boat was anchored not far from the house and pulled against its chain, its bow pointed toward the other side of the port. He leaned over to see if he could read the ship's name. Schlammer intercepted him.

"It's a research vessel that belongs to the company. It helps us locate polymetallic nodules and diamond deposits in sediment. A very useful tool for our work."

"No doubt. It looks to be in very good condition," Denton remarked.

Schlammer didn't reply.

Denton left and started down the stairs. Glimpsing the research vessel again, he stopped and got out his camera to take a picture. This was complicated by the uncertain light of the fading sun, an enormous orange ball ready to plunge into the ocean.

A man leaning against the rails of the trawler stared at Denton while he adjusted his telephoto 300 mm. lens. The man wore a canvas military-style jacket. Denton watched him for a moment, then whipped himself around suddenly to see the doctor, who spied on him from the salon window. It was only a fleeting image before the heavy curtain fell without warning.

Beyond the house, overshadowing the town, the red dunes of the Namib rose up, threatening, like so many giant waves, to unfurl themselves against this little port at the end of the world.

Turning toward the ship once more, Denton saw that the canvas-clad man was pointing him out to a second man, who had come to join the first one on the bridge. He was suddenly overcome by a strange sensation of anxiety.

He quickly took two pictures of the ship, whose name, "*Sarah* . . ." he could partially make out with the telephoto.

Then he put the camera away, and ran fast down the street

leading to the port and his nearby hotel. Going into his room, a strange feeling seized him: his bag was open on the table. Hadn't he left it on the floor next to the bed, locked?

Moving close to the window, he gingerly parted the curtains to look down at the street, barely visible in the last light of day. Two men were just getting out of a Land Rover parked behind his car. They approached the black porter near the hotel entrance and spoke to him a couple of seconds, glancing nervously about.

The men had a military bearing, but they weren't soldiers. Denton had the impression that the porter pointed out his rented Datsun to them. They examined it briefly before climbing back in the Land Rover and speeding away.

All at once Denton felt danger, and he knew he had to leave Luderitz immediately. He gathered his things, went to the desk to pay his bill, left a brief note making his excuses to Gudrun von Bach, got in his car and tore into the night, heading for Windhoek.

CHAPTER 10

Windhoek, December 8

Sitting in a half-collapsed chair in Viljoen's office, Denton tried to explain his precipitous departure from Luderitz. After driving for two or three hours, he'd stopped to sleep beside the road, then took off again to arrive, a bit out of it, just past noon in Windhoek.

He quickly recounted everything that had happened. At first Viljoen was incredulous. Then he began listening attentively and raised an astonished eyebrow when Denton told him about the Cullum Company and Dr. Schlammer.

"It's incredible! Could the plane be Schlammer's? Well, well, that's really bizarre."

"Why?"

"That bloke arrived in Namibia just after the war, and his real name isn't Schlammer, if my sources are correct."

He turned toward a metal file cabinet behind him and rapidly retrieved a small white file. "There it is. His name is really Helmut Sorge. He changed names before entering the territory in 1945."

"What for?"

"I have no idea. No doubt he had something to hide like many of the Germans who came about that time via South America. For a long time Pretoria had a weakness for them, and the rare ones who've stayed on, like Sorge, seem to be untouchable."

"That's interesting. But what connection is there to the Ovahissas?"

"None, off-hand. At least there doesn't seem to be any personal connection—unless the Cullum Company is involved. I don't trust

67

these mining companies that plunder the country without returning anything to the people. They're capable of doing anything to make money and protect their interests."

Viljoen began taking off then putting on his glasses with a rapid non-stop motion—a sure sign that he was agitated.

"But what reason would they have had for destroying the village?" Denton asked, taking a sip of ice water. "To get rid of a troublesome tribe? To attack SWAPO? That seems very unlikely."

"The army's taking care of SWAPO and these big miners' groups entered into discreet negotiations with Nujoma a long time ago. They're ready for independence and will probably suffer minimum loss. Now the old boy isn't very smart, but at least he knows it's in his interest to talk with them."

"So what do you make of this?"

"I don't know what to think," Viljoen answered, raising his arms to the ceiling. "All I know is that Schlammer has a suspicious past and I don't like Cullum."

"And don't forget that our German doctor seemed anxious when I started questioning him. You know, I've had this feeling of being threatened ever since leaving his place."

"I'll bet you've been thinking about the Ovambo witch-doctor," Viljoen laughed. "No, seriously, the mining trusts are very powerful here. They decide when the sun rises and sets." Viljoen got up and paced a little in the small space. "I think you'd better come sleep at my place tonight. They're going to think twice about attacking journalists, and I know how to defend myself. So what do you think you'll do now?"

"Schlammer, excuse me, Sorge, maintained that his plane hadn't left Luderitz for two months. Can you find out if the Cullum offices have asked for a flight plan for Ovamboland over the past, say, four weeks? Because I expect one doesn't fly over the border zone without authorization."

"Exactly. The South Africans watch it like a hawk because they're afraid of Angolan pilots flying suicide missions." Viljoen thought for a moment. "I think I can get that information. But it might take a few days . . ."

"No rush. I was thinking of going to Jo'burg to get permission to visit Naukluft. I have to see a certain Piet Marais."

"Marais! Ah the Director of Cullum. Now there's an unstable character. There isn't a greater extremist, anybody more *verkrampte* than he among all the Afrikaners. He's already threatened to shut down my paper, and he has the means to do it. You didn't run into him when you were in South Africa?"

"No, never. I've only vaguely heard of him. Do you think he could be mixed up in all this?"

"I have no bloody idea. But it would certainly be interesting to go see him and have a little chat. You'll be able to tell if something's going on by his reaction. But you'll have to be careful—he's dangerous, and very well connected with the government. He keeps a low profile, but he carries a lot of weight. Don't forget that Cullum, along with the others, has contributed to financing South African war efforts. . . ."

"I'll be careful. Think I'll leave tomorrow."

"Right. In the meantime, I'll do some digging about that flight plan and Arnold's accident. The police investigation doesn't seem to be moving very fast, and I'm going to check out the shop that worked on the helicopter for myself. As for Schlammer-Sorge, I'll be surprised if my contacts tell me much more."

"Hey, I've got an idea. Do you think you could get ahold of a picture of him?"

"Yeah, probably. He must be in photos of luncheon meetings I've published in the paper."

"If there's a good, clear one, I'll show it to this guy I know in Paris. He specializes in research on Nazi war criminals and he's worked a long time with Simon Wiesenthal. You never know, he might have something in his archives."

"Fine. I'll see if I can dig something out tomorrow. For the moment, I've got to go defend myself in front of the administration.

Those bastards on the publications board are pressing me again to give up running the nudes. They say I'm inciting the public to debauchery!"

"How dare they!"

"Oh, they play these little tricks all the time," Viljoen went on, pretending not to notice Denton's smile. "They seize an issue of the *Examiner* and threaten to stop publication. But this is obviously just a pretext to shut me up. All kinds of German magazines with ten times more sex than mine sell on the open market here. But they don't get harrassed, because they're too powerful."

Viljoen looked genuinely disheartened and began nervously shuffling the folders on his desk covered with an incredible mess of paper.

"They left me alone for several months, but they suddenly jumped all over me again yesterday. I'm really getting fed up. I'm going to fight this for another six months, but if they keep it up, I'll close shop. Meantime, there's no question of letting up. If you want, we can go see Laura tonight. I've got the feeling she's beginning to come out of her shock, with the help of du Toit, who has a certain weakness for her. I don't expect she'll be a widow for long."

"Right. Let's go. It'll be a pleasure."

"If you want to wait for me here, I have some things to do for an hour or two. In fact, my secretary said she found you very attractive, if you get the drift. . . ."

"Uh . . . I think I'll take a little walk," Denton answered quickly. He could hardly believe his ears.

He left the office, careful to avoid even glancing at the secretary. Stepping onto the street, he stretched and instinctively looked around, but didn't see anything suspicious.

What if they were just getting themselves all worked up over nothing? he asked himself harshly. After all, nothing had really confirmed Arnold's story nor the theory of the helicopter's being sabotaged. And maybe the yellow airplane was just a coincidence. . . .

But then where had the sensation that he was being followed come from, the feeling of panic that had seized him at Luderitz?

Denton walked around for a few minutes in the center of Windhoek, where the old German-style buildings mixed curiously with ultra-modern construction. He stopped in a jewelry store and bought a necklace with round pieces of ivory strung on elephant hair.

He wanted to give it to Caroline. It would make a lovely Christmas present. Or maybe for another occasion. . . . She'd been constantly in his thoughts since his arrival in Namibia. He would have given anything to have her with him in Windhoek that night.

CHAPTER 11

Palm Beach, December 10

"David, you didn't forget about tonight, I hope?"

"Tonight? Something's on for tonight?"

"Only the Red Cross Ball, the most important event of the season. But you know all this. The Davises are coming by so we can go together."

"I'm not sure I want to go, Liz. I'm really a bit tired this evening."

"Oh, David, honestly! How about making an effort for once. It'll do you good to get out. Besides, you can't just let me go all by myself."

Her voice vibrated with an anxiety, a kind of impatience that Cullum had trouble understanding. He watched his wife, who wore a soft white cotton dress that showed off her tan as she leaned against the doorway to the living room. She had just come back from another shopping trip on Worth Ave. and would no doubt dash into her room any minute to begin making herself up and getting ready.

"Liz, let's not discuss this again. You know I just can't stand that type of party and the imbecilic conversations of pretentious money."

"But, David, that's ridiculous. All your friends are rich, and you can't spend your whole life locked up. You should go out, see people."

Cullum couldn't begin to understand her perpetual need to "go out," to go to restaurants, to get invited to these parties, or even to give them herself when she had the chance. Besides, he could no longer stand the pitying and pointed, "How are you, David?" which sprang from the lips of the diamond encrusted matrons who accosted him every time he showed up at one of those awful parties. Only three days ago, he had almost smashed Marjorie Whitmanson in the face—a gossip of the worst sort who interrogated him with oozing concern and false sympathy.

"Listen, Liz, this time I don't even want to talk about it. I'm not going to the Red Cross Ball, and that's it. The Davises can take you, and I'm sure you'll find no end of charming partners who will invite you to dance."

Elizabeth's mouth drew into a pucker of bitterness. Without a word, she turned her heels and dashed toward the marble staircase to go up to her room.

Cullum expected this reaction, but it still bothered him. He never got used to these flashes of bad temper. Why could she never accept his point of view and respect his desire to be left in peace? Why this atmosphere of endless confrontation?

It was true that their relationship had deteriorated over the years, as it became more apparent with passing time that they didn't share the same interests, nor even, really, the same view of life. Was it his fault? He had often asked himself that question without really finding an answer.

But how had they gotten there, to this withering of a love that had once so completely transformed his life? Wasn't this the same woman whom he had met twenty years ago in London, whom he had married so quickly, who had given him Melissa and those years of happiness?

He would never forget the wild sexual abandon of their honeymoon in Paris and on the Riviera. He, a timid and slightly awkward Englishman, had found in her body, her mouth, her hips a piercing physical pleasure he had never known before. He could still smell the scent of her flesh, of her sweat; he could still hear the words in English and French that spilled forth from her to excite him, inflaming his desire to a point he had never dared even imagine.

They had stayed in a little hotel on the Left Bank, in a city he then thought the most beautiful and sensual in the world. Twenty years already! Now he preferred to never think of Paris . . .

When Melissa had announced her intention of spending a year in Paris studying art at the Ecole du Louvre, at first he had reacted negatively. He didn't like the idea of having her go off like that for so many months. But Elizabeth supported the idea, figuring that her daughter should spend at least a few months in France to improve her French and that she was big enough to take care of herself alone for a while in Paris. Besides, there were lots of relatives to look after her.

So he gave in, not wanting everybody to think he meant to keep Melissa caged in, cut-off from the realities of life.

When she had been around ten or eleven, just on the brink of adolescence, he had watched her intensively, wondering often what she would become. After all the years he had spent at her side, he never knew exactly what she was thinking: little girls always hold back a bit from confiding everything to their fathers.

In her clear, smooth face he saw all the potentiality, and all the fragility, of happiness. He had seen the lives of so many friends' children prematurely broken by drugs or alcohol that he was willing to pay any price to keep Melissa from falling in these traps. Especially drugs, which seemed to be everywhere in New York and Florida. The Davises' son, whom Melissa knew well, was, at 23, a wreck, dragging his wasted body from one "detox" center to another.

While wanting to protect Melissa, at the same time he had forced himself to strengthen her the best he could, to teach her everything he knew, all the while reinforcing the natural bond of sympathy that existed between them. Secretly he hoped one day she would come work with him. But he didn't want to force her, and he felt strongly her desire for freedom and independence that had pushed her to go to Paris, far from the cocoon of the family.

A door slammed suddenly upstairs. Cullum looked up for a moment, then covered his ears with his hands. Tomorrow he would leave for New York. There were still things he needed to do.

CHAPTER 12

Johannesburg, December 11

"**N**o, Mr. Denton, what you ask is impossible. The mine at Naukluft is closed to the press. I'm sorry . . ."

Piet Jocobus Marais settled deeply into his leather armchair. Steve Denton found himself on the thirtieth floor of the Carlton Center in the middle of Johannesburg staring across at this ruddy giant. Fiftyish, Marais showed the beginnings of a slight paunch which protruded beneath his sombre, well-cut suit. What impressed Denton the most was his unflinching toughness.

"I'm sorry too," he replied, "because my story won't be complete without one or two pictures of Naukluft. Just a quick visit would do. I didn't have any trouble visiting Rossing."

Marais' small, gray, crafty eyes observed his visitor carefully from behind narrow gold frames. Denton moved uncomfortably in his chair.

"The people at Rio Tinto can do as they like," Marais answered. "That's their business. But there's no reason we should do the same. Besides, Mr. Denton, your magazine doesn't have a very good reputation in industrial circles around here."

"What do you mean? My magazine is completely honest and apolitical . . ."

"—it supports the terrorists of the ANC and preaches more or less openly about the departure of whites. That's not what I call apolitical. The *Geographic's* article on South Africa a few years ago has not been forgotten by anybody in Pretoria. I'm frankly surprised that you were able to obtain another visa."

The vehemence of the attack surprised Denton. Up to that point the exchange had been courteous enough, even though it ended by the categoric denial of permission to go to Naukluft. He made a conscious effort to remain calm.

"Your accusations stun me, and I frankly don't see where you're getting all this. The *Geographic* has a good reputation everywhere in the world. As for the article you mentioned, it's very difficult to report on South Africa without interviewing some colored or Indian leaders. After all, whites make up only a fifth of the population."

"Denton, you're just like all the other foreign correspondents who're always trying to teach us lessons and tell us how to treat our blacks . . . But we know them ten times better than any of you, because we're true Africans. White Africans, to be sure, but Africans nevertheless. We arrived in this country before any of the filthy Kaffirs, and we made South Africa what it is, not they!"

Marais flushed with anger and punctuated his speech by banging his fists on the majestic yellow-wood desk, a wood the color of butter and soft to the touch. Denton was astonished. Piet Marais, one of the most powerful men in the country, was acting like some knee-jerk Afrikaner militant at a political meeting in a remote corner of the Orange Free State.

"Listen, Marais, I don't want to give lessons to anybody. It's not my country and I don't take sides . . ."

"—but you never stop taking sides," Marais interrupted, hitting the desk once again. "From the time of your first stay in Johannesburg for the Associated Press, you were already the most anti-white of the foreign correspondents, gobbling up all that marxist propaganda from the ANC terrorists. Like the ones who are here now, those vultures who wish for and predict our end. But the joke's on them. They'll have vanished from South Africa long before we do. Just like the rest of them, you only associate with people who are hostile to us. Did you even try to meet with the administration officials responsible for Southwest Africa when you were there a few days ago?"

Denton felt anger rise through him. He stiffened in his chair, running his hands through his hair as he tried to get control of himself.

"I came to Namibia mainly to take pictures. I had made all the necessary contacts my first time through, and contrary to what you seem to think, my relations with the officials in Windhoek are good. Besides, why all the mystery about Naukluft? Do you have something to hide?"

Marais narrowed his eyes and clenched his fists, as if he, too, were ready to explode.

"Denton, hear me out. We have nothing to hide, and your suggestions are ridiculous. I've heard that you were asking some strange questions when you went through Luderitz, and your association with Viljoen, and the fact that he accompanied you on your trip north, strike me as very bizarre. I caution you to stop nosing around. It will lead nowhere."

Denton stood erect against the chair, unable to contain himself any longer. "Marais, it's not for you to tell me what I should do. I don't have to report to you. . . ." He stopped himself, realizing suddenly Marais knew far too much about what he'd been doing these past few days in Namibia.

Marais also stood up. Behind him the huge windows looked down on Rissik St., one of the busiest in Johannesburg.

"Denton, I'm telling you once more to listen to me. If I were you, I wouldn't stay any longer in this country. I'd take the first plane tomorrow for Europe or the States."

"Would you be threatening me, Marais?"

"Take it however you like, but keep in mind what I've told you. You have absolutely nothing to gain by staying, Denton."

He decided not to respond, but grabbed his bag and left the room without saying good-bye.

As soon as Denton was gone, Marais picked up the phone and called his secretary. "Doris, get me Hobson fast. It's urgent."

Five minutes later, Denton was in the street, feeling much better than he had in the sumptuous, air-conditioned offices of the Cullum Company. He hadn't foreseen such a rough meeting.

The sun shone brightly in a pale blue sky, but the extremely dry air, so typical of Johannesburg, made the heat bearable. He decided to walk a bit toward the residential areas north of town. He had promised his friend Philippe Bramant, the South-African correspondent for a French daily, that he would come by for lunch, and it wasn't quite noon.

A crowd of black office workers and laborers filled the sidewalks, taking advantage of the lunchbreak to swallow a sandwich washed down with a coke. But this evening, like every evening, they would leave white Johannesburg to go back to black Soweto.

He soon reached the top of the hill overlooking the northern part of the city. This was Hillbrow, home of most artists, musicians and such fringe types as Johannesburg could boast, a place where old apartment buildings were mixed in with seedy villas and little shops. It was an offbeat neighborhood where you could sit on the sidewalk of the Vienna Cafe and almost imagine you were in a normal country, in a city where the weather was always sublime. It would be easy to give in to this . . . if only you didn't *think* too much about the clouds that were gathering, about the recent explosions of violence.

A few minutes later, a taxi dropped him off in the posh Rosebank section, at Bramant's house, which was surrounded by imposing residences all protected by high walls. The French journalist had put an office in the garage, only a few yards from his pool. Denton found him just sending off an article over the telex. The two old friends hugged each other with affection.

"God it's good to see you, you old son of a bitch. Still sending out the same old crap, I see."

"*Voyons*, Steve, truth is only an illusion, as you know well. We seek it relentlessly, but only the editors-in-chief know where to find it," he said wryly before bursting into laughter. "I've just got to finish this bit. Hang on and I'll be right with you. Wait for me in the garden."

A confirmed bachelor, Bramant lived alone and was looked after by Rita, an ancient Venda servant. Now she brought Denton a whisky out by the pool, where he had sat beneath the jacaranda trees.

Bramant soon came out to join him. Tall and well built, he looked a little like Cary Grant in his heyday.

"Things are really heating up in the townships," he said sitting next to Denton. "Paris is on me all the time for stories."

"What's going to come of all this?"

"I don't know. After 600 deaths in Soweto in 1976, they said it couldn't go on, and still nothing has happened. Believe me, the whites have no intention of giving up. So, what brings you here, anyway? Not a pleasure trip, I presume . . ."

"No, Philippe, it's business, if you can call it that. I'm just finishing a piece for the *Geographic* on Namibia. It's only missing pictures of Naukluft."

"And I imagine Cullum isn't having anything to do with you."

"Exactly. In fact, I just came from a very ugly go-round with Piet Marais."

"That doesn't surprise me. Not exactly a very engaging fellow. But, *voyons*, you ought to be wearing a tie. You know they're pretty formal around here."

"I don't care. The day I quit AP, I promised myself never to put one on again." Denton wore a white short-sleeved shirt and beige slacks.

"Bravo for you! As if there weren't already a rope around your neck," Bramant broke into a wide grin. "I see your little

Hemingway act is still intact. But all things considered, tie or no tie, they never let any journalists into Naukluft anyway."

"Doesn't that seem a little fishy to you?"

"*Bof!* This is South Africa, remember? But I'll tell you in confidence that Marais is no friend of mine."

"I can believe that. He's not like the Anglo-American types you see hanging around the pool at Wanderers. He actually warned me to get my ass out of South Africa right away. Is he really as influential as they say? Johannes Viljoen told me up in Windhoek to watch out for him."

"Good old Viljoen is right. Marais is very powerful because David Cullum hardly ever comes here and has given him a free hand to run the mines. He knows everybody in government and the security forces. And his political views aren't hard to imagine. He's very close to Eugene Terreblance, the leader of the Afrikaner neo-Nazi group Weerstant-Beweging."

"I figured as much in his office."

"He's also tried out a few dubious business ventures. For instance, he bought up the houses of English-speaking whites for a song when they sold out *en masse* after the riots in Soweto. Then, when everything calmed down again, he resold them for three or four times as much. You can say they were fair game. But still, it gives you an idea of the man."

"Look, say no more."

"Wait. Something that somebody said recently just occurred to me. Something about him contacting the ex-members of Mike Hoare's mercenary band. You know, he's the guy who completely fucked up an attempted *coup d'etat* in the Seychelles. I'm not sure exactly what Marais did, but I can find out more. Are you interested?"

Bramant gave a tight smile, and Denton was tempted to tell him everything. But he thought better of it, and said nothing.

"Why not? I'd like to know what somebody like Marais has in mind when he begins to keep company with the Affreux."

"Let me make a couple of phone calls, and I'll get back to you when I know more."

They headed for the table set by Rita under a little veranda near the pool. It was still hot, but the little clouds which would bring the 5:00 o'clock rains—a sign for all the civil servants to go home—had already made their appearance. Except for the cries of bulbu's and weavers, birds that swarm in the gardens of Johannesburg, the only noise disturbing the quiet of the summer afternoon was that of a tennis match on a lot nearby.

"You playing much these days? You know the latest fad around here is to have two courts, so you can invite friends over and organize tournaments."

"It really is the good life, isn't it?" Denton answered.

"I know what you're thinking, Steve. By seeing this, you understand better why they'll fight to the death. Anyway, I haven't heard much about what you're doing in Paris. Tell me more . . ."

They stayed together until the middle of the afternoon. Denton wanted to check out the bookstores to find some books on Namibia that he couldn't get in Europe or the U.S. Bramant called a cab, and ten minutes later an old Opel parked in front of him.

"I'll get in touch with you at the hotel as soon as I have something new on Marais. In the meantime, don't get too excited over that filthy redhead."

Denton, who was just climbing in the car, stopped suddenly and turned toward Bramant, looking astonished, as though he had just heard a profound revelation.

"Redhead, you said redhead . . . but it's true. Marais does have red hair," he stammered.

"So, have you got something against redheads?" Bramant asked, looking at his friend with both amusement and alarm.

"Uh, nothing actually, . . . well, that is, I do. I think I just don't like them in general. Bad memories I guess. I'll tell you about it one of these days," Denton spoke while wiping big drops of sweat off his forehead. He suddenly saw himself again next to the fire under the penetrating stare of the witch-doctor.

"*Bon* . . . Look, just relax. I'll call you tonight or tomorrow morning."

Denton climbed in the taxi without having any idea what to do next. All of a sudden he had no desire at all to go for a stroll.

CHAPTER 13

Soweto, December 13

"**W**hat a mess! We'll be lucky if we don't kill somebody!"

Philippe Bramant slammed on the brakes to avoid hitting an old woman who had literally thrown herself in front of the car. It was 7:00 P.M. and things moved on the Soweto road as they always did at dusk—chaotically, like a Breugel painting redone African-style.

The Peugeot 504 threaded its way gingerly through the potholed street, amongst the broken-down cars, wobbling trucks, endless motorbikes and the local Putco minibuses, pale blue wrecks over-flowing with passengers. The shoulders of the road crumbled under the weight of pedestrians.

The open windows of the car let in the familiar smell of charcoal fires. In winter, their fumes covered the immense bedroom town with a thick gray coat. Denton felt a shiver of recognition; since he had left South Africa in 1977, nothing had changed in Soweto.

"You're sure this isn't dangerous with all the unrest now?" he asked.

"No, no. You're not supposed to come here at night, but nobody pays any attention," Bramant answered, his eyes glued to the road. "Besides, it was the only thing we could do. He wouldn't even discuss meeting in town. Relax. I know my way around very well and I'm not about to take chances."

"And this guy, you know him well?"

"Well enough. He's a Rhodesian who served with the Selous, Ian Smith's commandos. We have target practice together, and he trusts me. He's ready to tell us more of the story on the mercenaries recruited by Marais. But he'll be very cautious. We're getting close—I see the spires of Regina Mundi."

Denton felt his heart catch as he saw the church, which had become, over the years, the symbol of resistance to the "white power" of Pretoria. There he had often heard the moving speeches of the Anglican Bishop Desmond Tutu or the brilliant and popular community leader, Nthato Motlana.

Night had fallen completely now, and there were fewer people outdoors. After passing Regina Mundi, Bramant left the Potchefstroom road and angled right down a small, poorly lit street. Here the houses were all alike: the famous "matchbox houses" where a dozen or more people crowded into two miniscule, shabby rooms. It was in this promiscuous squalor that black hatred and frustration fermented.

"*Zut!* I think I'm lost. Never mind, I know this fucking Sheebeen by heart." Bramant poked along for a good ten minutes, trying to keep an eye out for the spot they were looking for, one of the hundreds of clandestine bars in the black town."

"Ah! *Le voila.* I see Jim's car."

They got out and went toward the entrance. Near the door they were greeted by the sharp, wailing notes of a saxophone inside. Braman gave three brisk knocks. The music stopped abruptly. From behind a parted curtain two eyes stared at them for a few seconds. Then the door opened wide.

A short man of about 50 with a comical face and long hair came out. He wore velvet burgundy pants which were too big and an old checkered shirt.

"Evening Frenchie. I got your message. Wondered what kept you. Your other friend's already here."

"The traffic was terrible, Masoja, and I had to be careful not to run over anybody."

"Right you are," the host replied, smiling. "Come on in and make yourselves at home."

He stepped aside to let the two men pass, then carefully closed the door behind him. They followed into a long room with three old couches shoved against the wall, a few low wooden tables and beaten up arm chairs. Four or five men sat in the smoke-filled half-light drinking beer and listening to the sax player and a guitarist.

Masoja led the two journalists to one of the couches where a man was waiting. About thirty-five, he had short brown hair and wore faded jeans with a brown leather jacket.

"Jim, this is Steve Denton," Bramant said to the mercenary. He merely nodded his head as an invitation to sit. Masoja, who had ducked into the little room behind the musicians, came back with a tray and three beers.

"I even found you some glasses," he winked at Bramant. "Whites like you can't very well guzzle it down like poor Kaffirs . . ." He burst out laughing.

"Masoja, you'll never change," Bramant replied. "It's really good to see you. And its good to be here. How's the family?"

"Very well. I just had my eighth—a boy. Well, I'll leave you to the music. Be back to chat in a little bit," he answered before slipping toward the back of the room.

The sax player, a tall, muscular black, did a slightly choppy improvisation on the theme of "Round about Midnight." Denton, a great jazz fan, adored this piece by Thelonius Monk.

They listened religiously for a quarter of an hour, then Bramant leaned over toward the Rhodesian. "Jim, I want you to give us some details on what we spoke about."

The mercenary looked at the two of them before glancing rapidly around the room.

"It goes without saying that everything must stay just between us. Where to begin?"

"Tell us everything you know. We'll stop you if we don't follow."

"Ok. Like I said, Philippe, Jack Hobson's a tough bastard who's pretty well known in the business, and maybe two or three months ago he recruited about three dozen mercenaries. Old Selous, like me, buddies of Mike Hoare now out of the slammer or guys from the Buffalo Batallion."

"How did you learn about it?" Denton asked, at last breaking his silence.

Jim paused for a moment. "Let's say I was also contacted."

"And you refused?"

Bramant shot a look at Denton. He didn't want to put Jim off with too many direct questions. But Jim seemed unperturbed and went on talking in a calm voice.

"Right. It was an interesting proposition, but I turned it down in spite of the good money. I've risked my ass enough on crazy jobs like that, you know?"

Suddenly they heard two loud knocks at the door. Masoja dashed across the room and ran to the window to see what it was. After what seemed an eternity to Denton, he finally opened up. Three black men entered and talked urgently for a moment with Masoja. He pointed to some seats, then, looking anxious, left to get drinks.

Jim continued his story. "Hobson was pretty careful not to give away too much to people who might end up saying no. That's normal. He simply said it had something to do with going to Namibia to protect Cullum property."

"You couldn't find out anything more than that?" Bramant asked.

The sound of breaking glass made them turn with a start. One of the new patrons had just tipped over the beer brought in by Masoja a minute before. Another took a drag on a slim dagga cigarette, the local marijuana, whose odor began to fill the room. Denton suddenly felt the eyes of the three men on him; their stares felt like threats. Bramant watched what was going on for a minute, shrugged, and turned back toward Jim.

"I got some more details," the mercenary was saying. "You know, you don't belong to the Selous for three years without keeping some contacts. One of my friends who did accept gave me a rough outline of what it's all about."

Denton hunched forward to hear him better. Caught up in the conversation, at first he didn't notice that the man with the dagga had planted himself in front of them and was saying something. The music swallowed his words, and Denton, all of a sudden realizing he was there, cupped his ear in vain, not hearing a word. He glanced at his two companions and saw they hadn't heard anything either. He smiled up at the man, then saw that his face was filled with hate. Alarmed, he tried to catch what the man was now repeating in a louder voice.

"Whites like you have no fucking business here. You don't live in Soweto . . . Go back to your rich neighborhoods . . ."

Bramant had finally grasped what the black man was saying, but didn't seem particularly disturbed. He waved his hand as if to smooth things over. "Look, we're friends of Masoja. I often go to his house, and if he invites me, it's because he knows who I am and what I think."

This seemed to make no impression on the man, who was short and rather frail and looked to be around forty. "I told you to get the hell out. As for you, Frenchie, we know who you are. But we don't want whites in Soweto. Especially not American spies." He glowered at Denton.

Surprised, Denton glanced around the room trying to spot Masoja. The other patrons pretended not to hear, and the musicians continued to play as if nothing were going on. The two other blacks then got up and came over to stand in front of the three whites. The short man began his harangue again.

"My friends and me want you to get out fast. We're not going to say it again. So come on, get out." He lifted his arm in threat. His speech was slow, laboured like that of an alcoholic trying to make a point. The dagga was taking effect.

"I'm going to go look for Masoja in the back-room," Jim said softly, after watching what was going on without betraying any sign of nervousness. He would be able to get to that room better than his friends, whose path was blocked by the three blacks.

He got up without taking his eyes off them, and walked toward the end of the room. But as soon as he got close, the little one caught him by the shoulder and pulled him half-way around.

"I said OUT. Don't you understand, you dirty white!"

The mercenary turned around suddenly, and without saying a word, stuck out his leg, lowered his head and gave a karate chop of such violence that Denton saw the man fold up like a leaf. Stunned by the blow, the black man collapsed on the wooden table. The musicians had stopped playing. Surprised, Denton looked down at the man sprawled on the ground, then heard Bramant yell.

"Look out, Jim . . . !"

Denton looked up to see a metallic flash in the dim light, followed by a violent, deafening crash. The body and head of the Rhodesian were thrown forward with a brutal jerk, as though he'd been overcome by an enormous hiccup.

But he didn't fall. A huge machete blade thrust deep in his skull held him back; the biggest of the blacks held it with both hands and tried with wild, frenzied movements, to pull it out. Blood spirted everywhere. There was a moment of silence—a disbelieving, stunned silence—and then pandemonium.

The patrons ran toward the exit, in their rush knocking into Denton and Bramant who had just gotten on their feet. Masoja, who had come out from the back room, was pushed back inside by the musicians fleeing out the back in panic.

Barely on his feet again, Bramant saw the second black coming at him with a screw-driver sharpened to a fine point, the favorite weapon of the *tsotsies*, the thugs of Soweto. He barely jumped aside in time, throwing his attacker off balance. They fell together.

Denton hesitated a moment, paralysed and unable to react; then he rushed for the door. But it was too late. The black with the machete had finally gotten it free and leapt up, blocking Denton's path. He stood in front of him, a crazed look on his face, waving the bloody weapon like a gigantic butcher knife.

My God, this isn't possible. It can't be true, Denton said to himself, suddenly having the incongruous impression of finding himself in the middle of a movie scene—a horror film that he'd soon forget.

Then the black stepped forward.

Denton moved back slowly, tripping over the legs of an armchair. The black, gripping the machete in both hands like an axe, struck a blow at Denton, who regained his balance at the last moment and jumped aside. The blade grazed his shoulder and landed in the back of the armchair. Denton rolled on the floor and grabbed a bottle of beer. He looked over to see Bramant still struggling, barely able to fend off the arm brandishing the screw-driver. He thought about going to help him, but there was no time. His own attacker, the machete once more pulled free, came at him again, sweeping away the space between them with his weapon.

Denton suddenly felt that it was over: he would die a stupid death in this dive in a back-alley God only knew where in Africa, butchered by a raving madman . . .

Seized by despair, his shoulders began to tremble. Then he heard a muffled sound from Bramant's direction, but didn't dare take his eyes off the machete. He suddenly felt the wall behind him and aimed the bottle at his attacker's head. The black dodged it by taking one step to the side, then raised his arm behind him again to strike. Denton was ready to dive out of the way, when he heard a gunshot. Then another. His attacker froze, arm still above his head, an expression of surprise and pain on his face. The weapon fell from his hand, then, slowly, he swayed back and forth.

Dazed and groggy, Denton stood up again, trying to figure out what had happened. Glancing around the torn-up room, he saw Bramant who in turn was anxiously looking at him, a pistol in his hand. Next to him was Masoja holding a bucket, an astonished expression on his face, and the other black, who lay stretched out on the floor. The musicians and the other customers had all fled.

"You o.k., Steve? You had a narrow escape, *mon vieux.*"

"Yes. Thank you, Philippe," Denton belched after finally managing to swallow. "But what . . ."

"You better thank Masoja. He came in and beat that guy over the head with his bucket when I was nearly finished. I pulled out my pistol as fast as I could and shot the other one just in time. You weren't afraid, were you?"

"Are you kidding me, or what? I thought I was done for. Kaput!"

"Masoja, you know them?"

"No, Frenchie, and that's what bothered me when they first came in. I couldn't keep them out, or they would have made trouble. I don't understand why they attacked you like that."

"I've been mixed up in this kind of thing before, but I've always talked my way out of it," Bramant answered, scratching his scalp. "Jim must have thought the same and didn't pay too much attention. That tall one just pulled the machete out of his jacket very quick. I saw it too late. It was totally unexpected."

"I have to say that Jim went after them good. He must have killed the first one with his karate chop," said Denton.

He went over toward the body stretched out on the floor, then stopped short. The black whom Masoja had hit over the head was just trying to get up.

"Watch out Steve! Don't move."

Bramant approached, his gun ready. The man looked around, trying to figure out what had happened.

"Drop that and tell us your name," Bramant ordered in Zulu, aiming his gun at him.

The man didn't answer and began to slip toward the door.

Wearing a dirty T-shirt and torn cotton pants, he looked like a wild animal at bay, ready to bite if anyone got near.

"Stop or I'll shoot," Bramant yelled.

But the man continued to move forward without uttering a word. He too had the slightly mad look of a dagga user.

"What shall we do with this one?" Denton moved aside to let him pass as he approached.

"Watch out, he's going . . ."

Bramant didn't even finish the sentence. The black man made a dash for the door. Bramant calmly took aim and fired as soon as the man tied to turn the door handle. Hit right in the neck, he stopped suddenly before falling over backwards with a loud crash.

Denton was shocked. "What did you do that for?"

"Steve, around here you never hesitate to fire. If that guy had gone out the door, we would never have gotten out of Soweto alive and Masoja would have had big trouble."

"But . . ."

"Look, we'll talk about it later. Right now we have to get out of here fast and decide what we're going to do about these bodies. Masoja, is the third one really dead?"

"Yes," he answered, leaning over the mangled corpse. "What are you going to do with your friend? Take him back to Jo'burg?" He motioned toward the mercenary mired in a pool of blood face down, his skull split in two.

"Out of the question," Bramant answered. "I doubt Jim had any family, and I can hardly see us going to the police. Do you know any spot where we could get rid of them quietly?"

"Hang on, Frenchie, let me think a minute. I'm sure we'll be able to figure something out."

Denton admired Bramant's *sang froid*. Even just after personally killing two of the three blacks, he didn't seem unduly upset. Then he remembered that whites in South Africa were rarely prosecuted for this kind of "incident." Most often it was enough for them to plead legitimate self-defense.

"Right," Masoja spoke again. "I think we can try to get rid of them in a place about twenty minutes from here on the Eldorado road. It's the colored township. I can take them in my "bakkie" and cover them up with a tarp. My brother, who lives nearby, can come with me and leave your friend's car somewhere. It won't be abandonned for long . . . As for you, you better get back to Jo'burg quick."

"This will be all right with you?"

"Fine. Don't worry. I'll hide the bodies and they won't be found for days. Nobody around here will talk. And tomorrow I'll leave for Lesotho to spend a few weeks with my wife's family."

"Thanks, Masoja. I'll pay you back for this," said Bramant, putting away his gun. "*Allez*, let's get going. We can't stay around here forever."

A half-hour later, they left the Shebeen after helping Masoja load his small truck, while his wife began to clean up the mess of bloodstains. The darkening streets were nearly deserted. At that time of day, even the police stayed inside their stations, which became veritable armed camps with barricades, barbed wire fences and bags of sand in front of the doors and windows.

An hour later, they were back at Bramant's place in Rosebank. During the trip back, Denton had decided to tell his friend everything that had happened to him since he'd arrived in Namibia. Bramant kept shaking his head in disbelief and pouring himself another whisky.

"Do you really believe it was Marais who sent them to get rid of you, or to keep Jim from talking? It's really too much, isn't it?"

"I'm sure it wasn't just bad luck. Those guys were watching me from across the room from the moment they came in. And didn't you notice what they said just before the fun began?"

"I don't remember."

"They called me an American spy. They knew who I was ahead of time and were out to get me."

"You're right. Too bad everything began the very minute Jim started to tell us what Marais is up to."

"Whatever that is, it's big enough for him to play hardball to protect."

"*Bon.* Under these conditions you ought to leave here as soon as possible. Marais won't miss the second time. I'm going to get you a seat for tomorrow on one of the flights to Europe. I've got some connections at KLM and Alitalia. For now though, you absolutely can't go back to the hotel. I'll send my driver over tomorrow morning to pay your bill and pick up your things."

"Thanks, but I hate to put you out."

"Don't worry. The essential thing is to get you out of here. Don't think about me, I'll manage."

"O.k. We'll stay in touch. I'll see what I can do in Paris."

Denton sank back in his chair, suddenly exhausted. The trip was ending as badly as it had started.

CHAPTER 14

"**W**ait, Steve, not too fast. I've got a stitch in my side."

Caroline stopped, winded, and held her sides. They'd almost finished going around the lake and were approaching a small pier, deserted at this time of year. Denton came close to her, grabbing her around the waist. She straightened, smiling, and leaned her head on his shoulder. Then they started down the path again, walking this time.

A pale winter sun tried to break through the morning fog over the Bois de Boulogne. Other runners passed them, some in silence, some breathing heavily, some in flashy two-tone running clothes, others in outfits for the perfect athlete. The French had come in their own time to jogging—once they called it "footing," but that had become quickly dated—and Denton had watched the ranks of runners grow regularly during the five years he'd been running around the lake. That's where he'd first met Caroline. Since then, they'd made a habit of jogging every Saturday, summer and winter.

"I have the feeling this trip to Namibia did you some good. Am I right? You're running around here like a jackrabbit this morning," she said, letting go of him.

"Yeah. I feel great. Maybe it's just the rest I've gotten these last few days," he said, wiping the sweat off his forehead with the bandana he had around his neck.

Rest and a certain peacefulness. After the endless plane ride and his sudden departure from Jòburg, he'd had time to think long and hard and had decided to drop the whole thing.

Not that he was a coward, or lazy—far from it—but he felt, after Soweto, that he'd been drawn into a spiral of violence and hate that he had to get away from before it was too late.

In his whole career as a journalist, he'd rarely felt in danger. He'd hardly even felt a shiver of anxiety the day some slightly drunk soldiers threatened him on the Mozambique/South Africa border. He'd never been to Viet-Nam or the Middle East. Many of his friends, who had sometimes covered "the war" from the bar of the Continental in Saigon or the Commodore in Beirut, were always telling him that he didn't know what he was missing, that there was nothing more exciting than "seeing death up close" according to the cliche so dear to his profession. He just shrugged it off. That kind of thrill didn't interest him.

But he had seen death in the crazed look of the black man with the machete in Soweto, and one week after his return to Paris, he couldn't stop thinking about the killings in the Shebeen.

"Steve, you're daydreaming again. What's on your mind?"

He leaned over to Caroline and kissed her on the forehead. He had come back from Africa more in love with her than ever. When he gave her the ivory necklace he'd bought in Windhoek, he felt for the first time that he wanted to spend the rest of his life with her. He had nearly even spoken of marriage, a word he thought he'd banished from his vocabulary forever after his first, disastrous experience in New York. But he'd held back at the last minute. She, after all, was very independent. What if she didn't want to marry him?

"You're thinking about this South-African business, aren't you?"

"Yes and no. Actually, as little as possible."

He hadn't forgotten Yves Arnold and the Ovahissa village and did feel a twinge of guilt. But what else could he do? He'd called Viljoen and told him everything. But Viljoen, who was struggling with the authorities to prevent them from closing down his

Windhoek Examiner for good, didn't have time to take up anything else just now. Bramant had promised to keep on investigating. But after the killings in Soweto, he felt very uneasy and decided to lay low for a couple of weeks and take a trip to the Seychelles.

Denton had talked this all over with Caroline many times and she agreed that he was well out of the whole mess. Still, she brought it up again from time to time, as if she weren't completely convinced it was the right decision. As if there were something else at the back of her mind.

"Me too. I've been thinking about it. I'm just positive something's brewing down there. But what?" she said.

"Look, there's not much we can do about it at the moment."

"And this German doctor? Have you tried to find out more about him?"

"No, and I swear I'm not getting involved."

"But you ought to do it anyway. With that sort, you never know what they did during the war. Maybe he was one of those torturers in the death camps. For a bastard like that, there should never be one minute of peace."

There was an urgency in her voice that surprised Denton. He'd never heard her speak that way.

"You're right of course. But I never knew you were interested in war criminals."

Caroline stopped for a moment, puckering her eyebrows as though she were hesitating about saying something. Then she began walking again, her arms crossed over her chest.

"Steve, I'm going to tell you something that will make you understand why this interests me. Maybe I've told you that my mother's mother died during the war. What I didn't tell you was how she died. My grandmother was a very beautiful and very brave woman who worked for the resistance during the German occupation. She was picked up during a sweep in Paris, and they sent her to Auschwitz where she fell into the hands of an assistant of Mengele. He used her for his personal medical experiments. I won't give you the details, but she died a terrible death."

"God, that's horrible. Why didn't you ever tell me this before?"

"I don't like to talk about it. I never knew my grandmother— obviously—and my family didn't learn about it until a long time after. My mother was only ten when she disappeared for good, and she never really got over it. And that's why she's always so worried about me. She's repeated that story God only knows how many times, always telling me never to forget. Of course I can't forget, and everytime I hear about somebody like this doctor who might have been associated with the Nazis, I think of my grandmother on the operating table, getting cut-up by that horrible butcher . . ."

She was nearly in tears, and Denton drew her to him. But she soon pulled away.

"Steve, don't let it drop. I can understand that you don't want to get into this any farther, but at least try to find out some more about the doctor. You told me that you knew Marc Rosenberg. I'm sure he'll be able to help you. He probably has something in his archives."

Rosenberg was a survivor of the death camps where he had been taken, while still a child, near the end of the war. Since then, he'd dedicated his life to researching war criminals. Denton had met him in Brazil, where he had come to follow the story of the former prison warden of Sobibor who was found near Sao Paulo. The two men had taken to each other, and Denton had gone to see him from time to time in his small apartment in the Marais.

"All right, I'll go see him. But maybe he won't come up with anything—it wasn't only Nazis who fled Germany after the war."

Viljoen had given him a picture of Schlammer before he left Windhoek and he could always show that to Rosenberg.

"Yes, that's true," Caroline answered. "But it can't hurt to try. Who knows what he might be up to in Namibia?"

"O.k., I'll call Marc next week, after Christmas."

They had decided to spend the holidays in Paris and he'd put off his trip to Washington until early January.

"Come on. Let's do one more short lap . . ."

They went back through the pine trees. Denton turned to look back over his shoulder. Ever since he'd come back from Johannesburg, he did that from time to time almost automatically, just to make sure nobody was following him. Even if it was really most unlikely.

There wasn't anybody behind them. Only the chilling quiet of the Parisian winter.

CHAPTER 15

New York, December 21

"No, it can't be true, Marais! It can't be true!"

Cullum got up from his armchair, red with anger, and shot a look of disbelieving scorn at his South African visitor. Marais sat across from him in the living room of his elegant apartment at the corner of 72nd St. and 5th Avenue. The contrast between the two was striking: the graying patrician squared off against the massive, full-blooded shark. But their roles were reversed. It was Marais who remained calm, while Cullum was beside himself.

"I'm afraid it is, sir. Unfortunately, there were a few casualties. You see the wind pushed the gas toward the village, and there was nothing we could do. It was too late . . ."

"How many died?"

Marais, still cool, looked directly at Cullum an instant before answering. "About twenty. It was a small village. And the animals were all killed."

"My God, Marais, what you did is completely insane. And we agreed that you'd try this on animals only. You should have taken precautions. You're going to ruin everything with your stupidities. And you might have told me right away."

"It was impossible. I could hardly mention it on the phone, or write about it in a letter. Besides, I frankly don't see why the disappearance of a few savages should make the slightest difference . . ."

"Marais!"

"Calm down, David. What's done is done. No use to make a mountain out of a molehill."

Kenneth Chambers, who sat next to Cullum, took him by the arm and pulled him back into his chair under the watchful eyes of Kurt van Lassen and Joseph Kramer.

Kramer had carefully taken in everything. Marais didn't inspire much confidence. Almost some off-putting physical quality he couldn't name.

"All right, let's get to the point. Marais, you said you left *no* trace, including the unwelcome witness . . ."

"Precisely. From that point of view, we're covered."

"That's absolutely essential," Cullum broke in, a threatening tone in his voice. "Nothing must compromise the plan, you understand, Marais? How do we stand on these journalists? Are they still on our tail?"

"I'm afraid so. An unhappy set of circumstances led them to uncover a couple of things which could be very troublesome for us. The South African is no problem. We can take care of him. But the American is more worrisome. We absolutely must silence him just in case. I'd hoped to take care of that in Johannesburg last week, but it didn't work out."

"So what are you going to do?"

"I don't know exactly. The problem with the American is that he's in Paris. That makes taking care of him a bit difficult to arrange. We're not sure just what he's found out, but my sense is that he'll keep on pursuing this. We'd better not take any useless risks. Don't worry, we'll succeed in keeping him quiet one way or another. Hobson's in charge—he's got good contacts in France."

"All right, Marais," Cullum replied after a pause, "but I don't want any more mistakes. Is everything else going all right?"

"Fine. The men are well trained and know what they're supposed to do. The boat should leave tomorrow or the day after. Will everything be ready?" Marais turned toward von Lassen.

"I don't think there should be any problems," he answered,

lighting a slim cigar. "I was just there last week to take care of all the details."

"Good," said Cullum, straightening in his chair. "And as for the money, you've taken care of that, Ken? A week ago I put $5 million in the account in Luxembourg."

"One of my contacts went to get out what we need and took it to Zurich for us whenever we want it. There'll be no way to trace it, or the purchase of the planes either. Marais, will you need any right away?"

"No. I've already made the advance payments. The rest gets paid afterwards."

"As you like. I suppose you arranged all that with Hobson?"

"Yes, you can rely on me."

"We *are relying* on you, Marais," Kramer cut in with an insistant edge to his soft voice. "But watch out for any more slip-ups of the sort David spoke about earlier. Outside Namibia or South Africa, they'll be much harder to control or cover up."

"Right," Marais answered, feeling uncomfortable under the sharp gaze of the financial specialist. "We'll be careful."

Cullum stood up and glanced out the window. It was miserable out, with heavy clouds blowing swiftly over Central Park. A violent wind whirled the last dead leaves of autumn. Winter had come quickly over the city, without transition, after a wonderfully long Indian summer.

Elizabeth had been waiting for him for two days in Palm Beach, where they were supposed to spend Christmas and New Year's. But he had no desire to go.

He turned back to the living room, its large space filled with white Italian couches and green plants. On the walls, pictures by Warhol and a huge painting by Pollack accentuated the modernism of the decor. Cullum found it a bit cold. He hadn't wanted to object in any way to his wife's selections—after all, she did have very good taste. But still he preferred a more traditional feeling, like he had in his office, with old English mahogany furniture, leather armchairs and hunting scenes hung over the wainscotting. Von Lassen, who possessed one of the most beautiful collections of 18th and 19th Century paintings in the world, had the same sort of taste. He always smiled knowingly when he entered the 5th Ave. apartment.

A Filipino servant brought tea to the four guests. Cullum had decided against a meeting in his office because he didn't want to arouse the suspicions of his secretary. It seemed to him that Kay had been observing him in a rather curious fashion lately, and he didn't like it.

He suddenly remembered another meeting just like this one, only eight months ago, when they had made the definitive decision to go forward. Who had had the idea first? It was difficult to say. They'd talked about it so often! In fact, the idea grew slowly until it seemed to impose itself on them as something necessary, something unavoidable. After hesitating a long time, he'd finally spoken to Marais, who had enthusiastically agreed.

Cullum had often questioned the wisdom of his choice, and the story of the dead villagers planted more seeds of doubt. He'd kept Marais on after his father's death, because it was practical: Marais seemed to manage and control the mines well enough. But he didn't actually like the fat man with the little mustache very much.

He himself rarely went to South Africa, and it was only on his last trip that he'd discovered with alarm the extremism of some of Marais' friends—the sorts who cocked their guns and hounded blacks for the slightest provocation, and took no pains to hide their actions. They seemed to live in a completely unreal world. But were they really representative? The men at other mining companies struck him as much more moderate. But for the moment, his headache was that he was stuck with Marais.

Marais turned to him now. "If it's all right with you, I'll leave tomorrow to go back to Johannesburg so I can spend the holidays with my family. Will you be in Florida?"

"Probably," Cullum answered, sitting down again.

In just a little more than a month, it would all be over. There was nothing more to do but wait patiently, to go to Palm Beach. He detested this time of year.

CHAPTER 16

Paris, December 30

"**W**hat can I say, Steve? You know, I love the holidays. They always make me feel so alive, if you see what I mean. Here, have a chocolate. They give you strength."

Marc Rosenberg, with his graying mustache, bushy eyebrows and disheveled hair gave Steve Denton a wicked look from behind his thick glasses. He held out a box of Nihoul chocolates, no doubt sent to him by one of his Belgian contacts. Everybody knew about his passion for chocolate and he received dozens of boxes from all over the world every year at Christmastime.

Denton picked a chocolate and smiled. Everytime he saw his friend, he was struck by his external cheerfulness and *joie de vivre*. Rosenberg had come back after more than a year in Buchenwald and often said that every day of his life was like a second-helping which he ought to enjoy to the fullest. But he also dedicated his life to what he considered his mission: there were still dozens, if not hundreds, of Nazi criminals around the world, and he had sworn to track them down to the very last man.

"O.k., Marc, I'll take one just to please you, but don't forget that we're going to have dinner with Caroline soon. She's dying to meet you, since I talk about you all the time. We'll go pick her up at my place—she had some papers to correct."

"Fine," said Rosenberg, closing the box which he carefully balanced on the table covered by books and folders. His little apartment on rue des Tournelles, in the heart of the Marais district, was hidden under a confusion of papers and documents.

"You said you'd found something on the German doctor?"

"Yes. I didn't have anything in my file-box, so I asked the Wiesenthal Center in Vienna. That took a bit of time, but they just sent me what they have."

"Great. So he was a war criminal!"

"Well, it's a rather special case. Wait while I have a look." He took a folder and lowered his glasses. The look of relaxed cheerfulness gave way to the hard-nosed gaze of an investigator who let nothing slip.

"There it is. Helmut Sorge was a young and brilliant student at the University of Hamburg. He had two majors at once, medicine and industrial chemistry and had done some pretty advanced research on toxic gas. When the war broke out, Sorge started to practice medicine after mildly protesting the Nazi regime. Then suddenly, in 1941, we find him in Luneburg, near Hamburg, where he took part in research on gas for use in warfare in an ultra-secret lab."

"Is that right? My God! Go on, this is fascinating." Denton turned around in his chair.

"O.k., but a little history first, if I don't bore you. You know how I love to show off my knowledge of the Nazis. Have you ever heard of the Tomka Project?"

"Never."

"Well, that doesn't surprise me. You may remember that during World War II the Nazis didn't resort to chemical gas, contrary to what they'd done in 1914–18. They were deterred by the fear of the massive reprisals promised by Churchill—a nice piece of disinformation, by the way, because the Allies certainly didn't have the means to reply in kind. The Nazis had done some pretty high-powered research and had come up with some terrible gases which attack the nervous system like *tabun*, *sarin* or worse, *soman*. Also they started up again on some research they'd begun with the Russians in the late twenties under the provisions of a super-secret agreement, the Tomka Project."

"With the Russians?"

"No. The joint work with Moscow ended in the beginning of the thirties. The Germans took it by themselves again a little before thirty-nine in a new facility in Luneburg, but by then they were working alone. They concentrated especially on *Yperite*, the famous mustard gas, the terror of the trenches in the first War."

"I did know about that. It was the stinking gas, wasn't it?"

"Yes. And it caused more than a million deaths during the war. Poor devils were sent to the slaughter then asphyxiated like rats—really horrible."

"So why did Sorge work at Luneburg?"

"I have no idea. All that they can figure out is that, after the war, he appeared briefly in Hamburg before disappearing from sight altogether. He had a wife and a young son, but nobody knows what became of them. Well, whatever happened to him, he was seen quite by chance by one of Wiesenthal's informers in Namibia. That was two years ago. His whereabouts was pointed out to the South African authorities, but with little hope that anything would come of it. In any case, he's far from top of the list of war criminals."

"But was he one? Maybe he was forced to work on that research. Besides, in the end the gas was never used."

"True. Nobody knows exactly what he did; the case against him is fairly slight. But we mustn't forget that the gases developed in those research labs, at Luneburg and others, were tested in the death camps."

"I see! Then maybe that's how the tribe was exterminated. Shit!"

"What are you talking about?"

"The reason I wanted the information on Sorge—I didn't have time to tell you before—he could be mixed up in some very nasty business in Namibia. All the inhabitants of a village in the north were killed by some mysterious epidemic."

"And what makes you think he had anything to do with it?"

"A lot of signs point in his direction. I'll give you all the details later."

"But why would he have done that?"

"I don't know any more than you do. He appears to be involved in some sort of plot that's in the making down there."

"Not that again! Even you've gotten caught in that tired old trap, 'Former Nazis plot to reconquer the world.' You know perfectly well such a thing never existed. Maybe they had a network to help each other escape, but nothing more. Those guys want only to be forgotten and left alone in whatever obscure corner they've crawled off to. Remember what we said about Wagner when we were in Brazil?"

Franz Wagner, a warden who was nicknamed the "butcher of Sobibor," had been found near Sao Paulo in the seventies. He'd fallen to pieces after his arrest, and had tried suicide several times in his prison cell. The Brazilians had refused to extradite him and had let him go free, but he died a few months later anyway.

"Believe me, those bastards don't think of anything except keeping out of sight and finding a little peace. There's no way they're going to get mixed up in any damn plot."

Rosenberg got up to go revive the fire in the small fireplace of his living room. Denton watched him while he poked the dying embers, lost in thought.

"I'm thinking of what you said once about Mengele. You remember that story about gas or defoliants dropped on a tribe in some far-off part of Paraguay? That made a big impression on me at the time."

"Yeah, that's right," Rosenburg answered, coming back to his chair. "His name was brought up sometimes in connection with that story. Something about him wanting to appropriate the place where it happened for the local authorities. . . . But it doesn't add up to me. There've been so many stories about Mengele."

"And if Sorge did something of the sort in Namibia? He works for a mining company. Maybe it wants to get rid of some bothersome local tribes."

"That would be absolutely outrageous. What could possibly push them to do such a thing?"

"I haven't the foggiest idea. I had decided to drop the whole investigation. It was nothing but a pain in the ass. But now, after what you've told me, I think I'll go ahead with it."

Rosenberg shook his head and leaned over to take another chocolate. Denton put his hand out to stop him.

"Hey, Marc, remember we're going to eat in just a little bit. Come on, let's go. We'll pick up Caroline, then head for Lipp or la Coupole."

"O.k. o.k. let's go!" The Nazi chaser got out of his chair. "Wait, I'm going to bring her a little something. Let's see . . ."

With all the concentration of a connoisseur, he studied the assortment of candies spread out on the table in front of him. Godiva, Lindt, Cotes d'Or, huge bars of Hersey's and Nestles'.

"Corne de la Toison d'Or? No, the Belgians are too rich. Bernachon de Lyon? Umm, too provincial. Charbonnel et Walker? The British claim that these are the finest in the world, but I find that they lack body. Ah voila! Perugina of course! Women adore the Italians . . ."

"They like the Americans all right too."

"Oh, I have no doubt, even if they are a bit crude. I'm speaking only of chocolate, mind you. So, you better tell me all about Caroline. I don't want to make any gaffes. She's been your girlfriend for a long time? You planning to get married?"

"We've been together for two years. Up to now, marriage obviously hasn't been part of the picture. But I've been thinking about it lately. She's really a fantastic girl. Actually, I was thinking I might propose tomorrow night after a good bottle of champagne."

"Traitor!" Rosenberg said, slipping on his overcoat. "You and your grand theories against marriage!"

"All right, all right. Let's get going. Take an umbrella. I think it's going to rain all night."

"On the town, perhaps, but never in my heart," Rosenberg winked. "Nothing like dinner with a pretty woman. She is pretty, isn't she?"

CHAPTER 17

Paris, December 30

The man in crepe-soled shoes walked slowly along the wet sidewalk of l'avenue Henri Martin, going up from the Trocadero toward rue de la Pompe.

Paul Lavagne, with his close-cropped hair, well-defined jaw and broad shoulders, kept his eye to the ground. An envelope left under his door had given him the green light; he knew exactly what to do from there on out. At first he'd hesitated, because he'd never done it before. But the pay was so good that in the end he'd decided to go with it. It had been six months since his return from Gabon, and his money was running dangerously low.

He was finished with Africa. No more going down there to throw his weight around for local tyrants and their little kingdoms. Besides, Libreville was too boring, a real back-water where he'd already wasted too much time. Now Kinshasha was something else. The problem was he couldn't go back there. He'd already fucked up too many times, broken too many heads in the Congo in the sixties. Those were the days! Wherever they went, women at their feet. And the ones who weren't willing, they took by force. Cleaning out villages with grenades and machine-guns with Jean Schramme and the Katangans . . .

Nothing quite like it since. Certainly not the Comores. That been a small-time little venture, practically without opposition. But at least it had succeeded, which is more than you could say for the Seychelles, where those idiot South Africans had made fools of themselves. How was it possible to blow such an operation?

111

All you had to do was to rush in there and shoot whatever moved without thinking about it . . .

Before coming back, he'd gone down to South Africa to spend a little time and see if he could find something to do. But they were too serious down there. It was difficult to get along with those beer drinkers who thought they were the last defenders of the white race and Western civilization. At least he'd made a few contacts which had gotten him this job.

After passing rue de la Pompe, Lavagne arrived at the building and raised his eyes up toward the third floor. All the apartments had lights on. It was 7:00, the night before New Year's Eve, and there was every chance he'd find who he was looking for. The instructions were short and simple: liquidate the occupant of apartment 3C in as discrete a manner as possible. That suited him perfectly. He hated getting bogged down in details.

He pulled leather gloves from his pocket and put them on carefully, one finger at a time, his eyes fixed on the apartment entrance. There was a code system to open the door, but it was disconnected at this time of day and the doors opened automatically. He also noticed a service entrance near the garage exit, on rue de la Pompe.

After making sure there was nobody else in the well-lit entrance, Lavagne slipped toward the glass door and quickly opened it. Once in the hallway, he skipped the elevator and went straight to the stairs to get to the third floor. So far, nobody had seen him.

In front of the door of apartment 3C, he hesitated a moment before ringing the bell. He had an explanation all ready in case the tenant asked questions before opening. But he didn't need it. The door opened wide. So did his mouth. He hadn't expected a woman. Petite, short haired, and dressed in a bathrobe, she just looked at him with an expression of surprise. He pulled himself together quickly.

"Steve Denton, please. I believe this is the right apartment."

"Yes, this is the right place. But he isn't home at the moment. He should be back any minute."

"I'm an old friend of his. We knew each other in South Africa. I was just passing through the neighborhood, and thought I'd stop by and say hello. Would it be all right if I waited here? With all the rain, it's not much fun outside."

Caroline wasn't sure what to say, and played nervously with the ivory necklace around her neck.

"Well that is, I don't know if . . ."

That was all she had time to say. Lavagne lunged for her, putting one hand over her mouth and holding her with the other. She tried to fight him off, but was helpless against his strength. He reached out with his foot and quietly closed the door.

Glancing quickly around the apartment, he took in the kitchen on the left, the living room on the right and the hall opposite which led to the bedrooms. Going down the hall, he pushed the half-open door of a well-lit room with a double bed. He laid Caroline down, and sat astride her, pinning her arms with his weight. Then he took a large handkerchief from his pocket and carefully gagged her before taking the belt off his raincoat to tie her hands behind her back. Finally he grabbed a scarf from a chair next to the bed and tied her legs together.

After getting up, Lavagne looked down at her for a minute, annoyed. Nobody had told him there would be a woman in the place. Now what was he supposed to do? Denton could arrive at any moment, and he'd have to make a decision fast.

He went through the apartment quickly, put the security chain on the door, and went to find the service door in the kitchen and unbolt the lock. Back in the living room, he sat for a moment on one of the couches, listening to the Brazilian music that was playing on the stereo. Outside the window, rain still fell in an icy drizzle that promised to last all night.

Just then he heard a loud noise from the back of the apartment. He lept up and ran into the bedroom. Caroline was leaning toward the nightstand and had knocked over a lamp trying to reach the telephone. Her movements had caused her robe to slip open, exposing her thighs and part of her panties.

"What do you think you're doing, bitch. I told you to lay still," Lavagne yelled at her.

Then his expression changed as he came closer to the bed. He smiled uncertainly as he grabbed Caroline to pull her up. "Say, you're not bad, you know. Not much meat, but it's in the right places."

Slowly he opened her robe. Paralyzed with fear, Caroline didn't dare move while the mercenary ran his enormous, gloved hands down her body. He stood up and untied the scarf around her legs.

"We're going to have a little fun, sweetheart. Don't worry. If you're nice, everything will be all right and you won't mind a bit."

He unbuttoned his trousers and leaned down toward her. Caroline, curling up in a ball, kicked both feet into his crotch. Caught by surprise and doubled with pain, Lavagne lay on the bed to catch his breath for a couple of minutes. When he got up again, his hardened face froze under an angry glaze.

"You slut, you asked for it," he said, and threw himself on top of her. One hand tore off her underpants, while the other spread open her legs. Still gagged with her hands tied behind her back, Caroline could do nothing to defend herself and shook as Lavagne brutally entered her, his face, straining and sweaty, distorted by an inhuman smile. Pinned to the bed by his mass, Caroline struggled in vain; he, in turn, leaned down closer to come in her more deeply. Torn and in pain, Caroline lurched forward violently with her head, hitting him hard on the nose and mouth with her forehead. Surprised once again, Lavagne rose up and slowly wiped his upper lip which had begun to bleed.

A look of hatred flashed across his face. He seized Caroline by her ivory necklace and began twisting it as he pushed into her again and again. Slowly, she felt the air go out of her as the ivory balls squeezed her throat. Lavagne had lost all control of himself, half-crazed with the double joy of coming and the desire to kill, to crush this woman who had dared resist him. It had been the same in Africa. He had never been able to stop himself, never . . .

Two minutes later, he got up, completely drained. Without bothering to even look back at his victim, he dressed himself and, stoney-eyed, made his way to the kitchen to clean up the blood running from his lip.

As he approached the sink, the doorbell rang. He stopped and quickly put his hand in the pocket of his raincoat. A key turned in the lock and the door jerked open before being stopped by the security chain.

Then a voice called out, "Caroline, it's us. I'm with Marc. Come open the door for us. It's chained."

Lavagne hesitated a second, tiptoed to the service door, opened and shut it silently before disappearing down the stairs. . . .

CHAPTER 18

Gulf of Guinea, January 2

The boat had reached its cruising speed of about 12 knots, and a light breeze, created by the movement of the ship, caressed the face of Kurt Schwager. He badly needed a shave. Leaning over the starbord rails of the big trawler, he watched the shoreline, thick with tropical growth. Now maybe six miles away, he could barely make it out under the layer of steamy heat that covered the entire coast.

"Stinking country, glad we got our asses out of there," he thought to himself, lighting a cigarette. Every time he heard the word Lagos, he remembered what happened to his friend Sosic, the Yugoslav. One day he'd taken his motorcycle into town, and as usual he'd gotten stuck in a "go-slow," one of those endless Lagos bottlenecks. He was sitting in traffic, when these two Nigerians approached him. One had gotten his attention by pulling out an ivory bracelet, while the other, without warning pulled out a machete and cut off his hand clean at the wrist before ripping off his gold Rolex and disappearing in the crowd . . .

Savages! Schwager arched himself, stretching, in hopes of getting rid of the pain in his lower back which always came if he bent over too much. A miserable little reminder of a nasty wound he'd gotten in Angola. The bullet fired by the hidden militiaman hadn't injured any vital organ, but it had bruised the nerves. From time to time a twinge made him remember . . .

The boat had reached the long swell of the Atlantic; Schwager could feel it as they began to roll gently from side to side. Behind them waved the "Red Ensign," the flag flown by British merchant ships.

Officially the *"Sarah of Man,"* which had recently left Luderitz, was based at Douglas on the Isle of Man and carried engineers and experts in oceanographic research.

Schwager, a blond giant with hair cropped like a Marine's, was one of the best bargains in the mercenary market-place, a real hot-head always on the lookout for a suicide mission and a few thousand bucks. He had seen a lot of action in the seventies with the South African forces, especially the "Recos," short for Reconnaissance Commandos, the elite unit of the South African Defense Forces. Parachuting far into Angolan territory to cause havock—and making surprise attacks look like the work of Jonas Savimbi's UNITA—the Recos destroyed whatever crossed their path. The Benguela rail line was a favorite target, but they also systemmatically killed any human being they ran into. No prisoners, no witnesses . . .

The steady drumming of the diesel engine together with the gentle pitching of the *Sarah* lulled Schwager into a pleasant daydream.

"Kurt, are you deaf or what?"

The small, withered man with dark skin who called to him from the bridge could hardly hide his origins. Although his family had been in South Africa for several generations, he was Italian to the tips of his toes.

"What's going on? That's the third time I've offered you a beer. Are you dozing or dreaming of your girl-friend?"

"Stupid bugger, I haven't got a girl-friend. But yes, I'll have a beer, if you'll stop talking like a damn fool."

A beer can flew to Schwager who caught it with one hand. He actually liked Venardi, who was without doubt the best shot he'd ever met. He'd known him since the days of the 32nd Battalion. When a friend had told him about the existence of this secret unit which had even more freedom than the Recos, he leapt instantly. Within the space of six weeks, he asked for and got a transfer to the 32nd—better known as the "Buffalo Battalion."

As a mercenary, he thought he had seen everything, still, he was impressed: never had he encountered such a crop of killers. Quite a few of them were black, mostly Angolan expartisans of Roberto Holden and his FNLA. It was a first-class collection of all the mercenaries seen in Africa over the last years: former Selous from Rhodesia, the hired guns of Bob Denard, Mike Hoare and Jean Schramme. All top professionals with no scruples. Men for whom human life had absolutely no value, especially not the lives of the Angolans.

Their role was to spread terror, and they were very good at it. They often razed whole villages, massacring every man, woman and child before burning the huts and crops. Thousands of southern Angolans had fled north, turning the area near the Namibian border into a lifeless no-man's land, and of little use to the SWAPO guerrillas.

It had been good work, but after two years in the 32nd, Schwager had decided to return to civilian life, where it was very easy to find body guard jobs which paid plenty.

Hobson had contacted him in his comfortable studio apartment in Durban and had made this offer which he couldn't refuse. He'd thought it over, but not for long. It wasn't everyday somebody put $60,000 on the table. The truth was, the operation was highly unusual, and they'd already gotten themselves into a sticky mess in the Kaokeveld village. But the idea appealed to Schwager, as it evidentally had to many other veterans of the 32nd, who were also on board with him.

The coast had now almost completely disappeared and he decided to go up on the bridge. A small group of mercenaries played cards in the prow, sitting or lying on the deck. Others were aft, talking under the platform holding the Alouette-3 helicopter. For the rest, it was a time to sleep in the hammocks hanging aft in the former hold for fish.

Schwager scrambled nimbly up the ladder and reached the bridge. He nodded to the watch and entered the wheelhouse. The room was crammed with a dozen people and filled with smoke. For a minute he was tempted to go out again, but, a bit bored, decided to stay after all. Venardi was in a heavy discussion with the captain, a tall, thin fellow of about fifty who was known to the crew as Commander, and who seemed to have Hobson's full confidence.

Inside the windows, the heat was suffocating and beers kept coming in rapid succession from the refrigerator next to the card table. Schwager was about to go for a second can when the watch burst into the room.

"Commander, two launches starbord aft. They're heading straight for us, full-speed."

Conversation stopped instantly. Captain Johan Vogels went over to the radar screen positioned left of the lookout, turned a dial to change the focus and shook his head. Without a word, he grabbed a pair of binoculars from the table and went out on the bridge. Pointing with his finger, the watch showed him the two spots that were rapidly widening behind the ship. Vogels watched them for a long time before going back into the wheelhouse. "We're going to have a visit. One of them seems to be a police launch, the other could well be a pilot ship. I haven't got any idea what they want."

He turned toward the little radio behind the card table. "Jim are they trying to contact us?"

"No, Commander. I haven't received any message. Maybe they're transmitting on a special frequency."

"Switch to 2182. That's the international distress frequency. They must know it."

The radio operator nodded and did as told. The captain went

to an intercom and rang three times. A voice answered almost immediately.

"Who's there?"

"Hobson? Vogels here. I'd like you to come see me right away. Two unidentified small craft are bearing down on us. One could be the police. I think they'll reach us in ten minutes at the most . . ."

He put down the intercom and went to look at the map. The trawler was heading straight west, toward 275. Vogels had enough problems. What if they intended to examine the cargo!

Hobson flew in like a bat out of hell. Stocky and square, he was very well preserved for a man just under fifty. The creased face, straight nose and blue eyes made him look like a mercenary right out of central casting. But he was the real article, and nobody liked to cross him. He had been all over Africa, and everywhere there were stories about him. Stories to make your hair curl.

"What do these jackasses want? You've paid your port tax haven't you?"

"Of course. You know I'm not taking any chances. And our men never set foot on land."

"You're telling me!" said Hobson, who had had his hands full guarding the mercenaries shut in for three days on the anchored ship. Even worse, it had been just at New Year's. He cursed himself for ever having put in at Lagos—the most rotten city in all of Africa in his opinion. Besides, he hated Nigerians, whom he had fought with Ojukwu in the Biafran War. But he hadn't really had a choice: a key part in the propulsion system had slowly died at sea, and they had to stop as soon as possible for repairs. The closest port which had spare parts was Lagos, and they had hauled in there at reduced speed.

The breakdown had cost them three or four days which they absolutely had to make up. When Marais heard about this over the radio, he'd had a fit, and ordered, once the repairs were finished, for Hobson to push full-steam ahead to try to reach Omega on time.

Hobson had his reputation to defend and he knew that his financial future was assured if he succeeded in carrying out this mission—never mind that it was unlike any operation he'd ever been in before. There was no way he was going to let some two-bit Nigerian in a police uniform throw a monkey wrench in the works.

"Hobson, they're here. Come look. They're signaling us to cut our engines."

The commando chief crossed over the bridge. The two launches were low in the water and about thirty meters long. One was black and had the word "pilot" written on the starboard side. The other was a kind of gray, with a small 20 mm. cannon on the forecastle. Both were bearing in from the portside, about fifty yards from the trawler.

Besides Vogels, Hobson and the helmsman, about fifteen mercenaries, including Schwager and Venardi, watched the scene impassively, leaning over the rails or the bridge.

"In fact," Vogels whispered to Hobson," they first gave us the order to stop with their Scott, but I pretended not to get it."

"You did the right thing. But now we have to obey and find out what they want. Fast. This isn't a pleasure cruise and I'm not going to palaver for hours with these niggers."

Vogels shouted an order to the helmsman, and the *Sarah* slowed up almost immediately. Then he gestured to the other boats, letting them know what he had done.

"Tell me, Vogels, don't you think there's something funny about these guys? I know that the Nigerian sea patrol doesn't exactly compare to the Royal Navy, but I still think something looks weird about them . . ."

The *Sarah* was still on course, but barely moving. Like Hobson,

Vogels was also watching these two launches very closely, and he, too, was surprised by their delapidated condition. No word had been exchanged between the trawler and the two boats in pursuit, and Hobson really began to wonder what they wanted.

Suddenly the gray boat widened its berth, putting fifty meters between itself, the other launch and the trawler. A man stood behind the small cannon and aimed squarely at the *Sarah*. The Nigerians weren't taking any chances. It was an inspection strictly by the books.

At the same time, the pilot-boat approached the trawler, and the captain, dressed in greasy beige work clothes, came on deck and called out that he wanted to put some men aboard. Three sailors began to drop some tires for bumpers to prevent crashing, while two others got the hawsers ready fore and aft.

"What's going on?" asked Vogels. "Why do you want to come on board? Our sailing documents are all in order, and we're leaving from the port at Lagos."

"Anti-drug control," answered the man in the work clothes, while the two boats kept coming closer, ever so slowly.

"What's all this about? I don't like this at all. Look, Vogels, see those two in the wheelhouse with Kalachnikovs . . . since when did pilot-boats come equipped with AK-49's?"

Hobson's old fighting instincts rose up in him. He felt in his bones something was funny about this interception. Some of the men must have been thinking the same thing, because they searched his face, waiting for an order. He ran into the wheelhouse and dialed a number on the intercom.

"Frank, tell the men still in the hold to get the lead out. Two Nigerian launches have intercepted us and it's not clear what they want. Look out the porthole and you'll get the picture. Then grab the rocket launcher, load it, and get ready to drop a load on that little tin gun there on the gray boat. Shoot when you hear our foghorn. And to make doubly sure, put another one in their wheelhouse, o.k.?"

Hobson had spoken without pause. He then turned, and with a broad smile, addressed Schwager, who had followed him into the wheelhouse.

"Did you hear all that? Great, we're going to let them have it in five minutes. I just know these bastards are pirates. Absolutely certain. They watched us leave Lagos, and waited until we got far enough away to move in. That happens a lot around here . . ."

"What are we going to do?"

"You go give this message quietly to the others. Every man should get a gun, automatic or otherwise. Uzi's are best; they can hide them under their jackets. Tell everyone to mark a man and when I give the order, to blow him away. Also, do try to not shoot each other. Frank's in charge of taking care of the second boat."

"But what about the ones who stay aboard the first boat?"

"For them, my dear fellow, there's a free demonstration of offensive grenades. There are some in this closet for just this sort of emergency."

Hobson opened a small cupboard in the wooden bulkhead of the wheelhouse, grabbed two grenades and gave two to Schwager.

"I'm not telling you how they work," he added with a slight, crooked smile. Schwager disappeared and Hobson joined Vogels again on the bridge.

"My dear Commander, take a good look at these brave men while they're still alive, because they won't be for long."

"What are you saying? Are we going to kill them?"

"Exactly. I'm putting everything on the line because I'm positive they're pirates. Once they're on board, and covered by the 20 mm. cannon, they're going to try to take control of the *Sarah*. Then they'll throw us overboard and take some potshots at those who are still afloat.

"Trust me, Vogels, I can smell trouble miles away. That's the reason I'm still alive today. My advice to you is to take shelter because this is going to blow any minute . . . Ah, yes. Keep your hand on the foghorn, will you? As soon as I give a shout, blow it, o.k.?"

Vogels took a deep breath and shook his head. He didn't like violence. But Hobson was no doubt right. Acts of piracy were pretty common along the Gulf of Guinea. It would be plain stupidity to let themselves be taken.

Suddenly he thought about the aluminum gas containers carefully stowed in a water-tight, cooled compartment in the forward part of the hold. Perhaps he should go check and make sure they were all right.

A thumping sound shook him from his thoughts. The black launch had come alongside and two Nigerians quickly jumped on board to secure the hawsers. The dozen or so mercenaries on deck spread themselves out across the *Sarah* with a kind of leisurely indifference. At the same time they took in every detail of the maneuver. Hobson looked them all over to make sure that no gun was showing.

The captain of the launch himself now came aboard, followed by seven men who looked odd for sailors, probably because they weren't. Their leader had a Colt at his belt, but the others carried new flaming Kalaschinov assault rifles, which hung from their chests on straps slung around their necks.

Having barely set foot on the *Sarah*, they lined up along the rails, aimed at the commandos and ordered them to put their hands up. The mercenaries obeyed, pretending to be surprised. Meanwhile, their leader scaled the ladder to the bridge, his gun in hand.

Standing in front of Hobson, the Nigerian signaled him to stick his hands up like the others, and threatened him with his gun. "We are taking charge of this ship," he said in singsong English. "Don't resist unless we shoot. Everybody kill. The other boat has a cannon aimed at you. One false move and we shoot."

A half-dozen armed men had erupted onto the deck of the gray launch, spilling out of the hatches and the cabin.

"I . . . I protest," Hobson pretended to stutter. "We are researchers and our ship contains only scientific material."

"Shut your mouth. I'm not interested in your talk. You are going to do just what I tell you. Then everything be fine."

Acting confused, Hobson turned his head toward the door, as though looking for help from inside. Actually, he just wanted to make sure that everybody was ready and that Vogels was within reach of the foghorn.

"NOW," he screamed, turning again. In a flash he lowered his right arm and grabbed a pirate's gun at the same moment the foghorn blew.

Surprised by the attack, the Nigerian tried desperately to get back his gun to shoot Hobson in the stomach. But Schwager jumped him first, kneeing him ferociously in the groin before delivering a karate chop to the neck.

A long flame shot out from one of the portholes in the forward forecastle. The man on the intercom whom Hobson had called Frank was getting into the action: his first rocket slammed into the second pirate boat at the line where the bridge joins the hull. Reeling as though slapped, the launch rolled violently in the other direction. Vogels had not taken his eyes off the Nigerian ship, and now saw the gunner of the 20 mm. cannon blown several yards in the air and thrown in the sea by the explosion.

A thick brown smoke came out from the boat. For good measure, Frank fired another rocket immediately, this one into the wheelhouse of the launch. Its windows had already all been shattered into a thousand pieces.

A ball of fire rose over the launch, and bits of wood, scrap metal and plexiglass were blown for yards in every direction, some even landing on the deck of the *Sarah*. On board the trawler, the mercenaries had taken advantage of the confusion caused by the rocket explosion, seized their guns and shot the pirates who had followed their captain at point blank range. Only one of them had time to pull the trigger and release a burst of shots before falling. A bullet hit one of the mercenaries in the head, exploding his brain.

The men who stayed on board the launch tied to the *Sarah* had no time to react nor even to understand what had happened. Hobson as calm as though on a picnic, had thrown his two grenades on the deck of the boat. Schwager hadn't even had to use his: the destruction was total. Three mercenaries from the *Sarah* jumped aboard the launch anyway, to check for any possible survivors. A few shots rang out from the interior.

Hobson grabbed the pirate chief by his work shirt, and hauled him upright. The man was still stunned and held both hands over his crotch.

"So, you filthy bastard. You want to play soldier. This time it didn't work. At least after this you won't attack any other cargo ships which pass through here. Look at the blood. Not one man alive. Every one of them dead."

The pirate, a Yoruba with very black skin and an athletic build, straightened up slowly, staring at Hobson, his face contorted with pain and hate. Suddenly he threw his head back and spit at the white man.

"Dirty bugger . . . you're going to regret that you didn't die sooner with the rest of the lot," Hobson quickly glanced around.

"Schwager, I'm giving him to you. Do what you like just so long as you get rid of him."

Schwager nodded in agreement, grabbed the Nigerian by the shoulder and pushed him toward the ladder, wanting to get him to the deck, three yards below."

"Go down, you son of a bitch, we're going to settle this between us. There's not enough room up here. Get going, you bastard."

The Nigerian managed somehow to get down the rungs. A mercenary seized him on deck and forced him against the wall, his arms in the air. Hobson shouted orders from the top of the bridge.

"Throw the bodies of these pirates overboard and get some

explosives in the launch here alongside. And clean up this deck. It looks like a butcher shop."

"Moser took a shot right in the mouth. He's dead. What do you want to do?" Venardi asked.

"Too bad for Moser. Such are the risks of the business. Take all his papers off him and throw him over with all the others. The sharks are in charge of the funeral."

Venardi nodded, approving. That was the way it was. They all knew what they were getting into when they'd agreed to participate in the operation.

Schwager then came down the ladder and said to the mercenary who guarded the pirate with a certain healthy respect, "I'm going to have a little fun with this fellow here. Wait a minute, I'm going to show you something."

Two minutes later he came back with a pair of machetes, South African pongas, five inches wide. He grabbed the Nigerian by the collar and pushed him toward the forecastle. Passing under the wheelhouse, he threw him one of the two machetes. Several mercenaries stopped swabbing the deck and started to form a circle around them.

"Listen, mate," he called out to the pirate, "I ought to put a bullet in your brain after what you just did to Moser. I ought to give you to the sharks for supper. But I'm going to give you a chance. We're going to see if you know how to do anything but shoot people at close range—and spit on them. Watch out, or I'll cut you into ribbons."

Schwager took a step back, held his left arm out from his body, and stood ready to attack, the machete in his right hand, also clear of his body. Over six feet tall, he loomed above the Nigerian, who hesitated a moment before picking up the weapon thrown at his feet, fearing a plot. Stunned by what had happened to his men, he wondered what this meant. But after looking around for a minute, he saw he had no choice but to fight.

He quickly picked up the machete and took two steps back.

Leaning slightly forward, his knees bent, he appeared much more agile than Schwager, stiff on his long legs.

Hobson watched the two from on top of the bridge and suddenly wished he hadn't turned the Nigerian over to Schwager, who was probably less skillful in handling a machete than the Nigerian and might get hurt unnecessarily. Besides, they'd wasted enough time with this whole business and now they had to push on as fast as possible.

At that moment, the Nigerian rushed toward Schwager with a blood-curdling scream. The mercenary stepped aside effortlessly without bothering to strike when he had the chance, as though he wanted to play a cat-and-mouse game with his adversary.

The circle around the two grew larger as they faced each other off again, little rivers of sweat running off them both under the white heat of the tropical sun. Straining, the pirate never let his eyes wander from Schwager, who, in a surprise movement, began sweeping in front of him with the machete. But he only struck empty air; the pirate leapt backwards to avoid the blade.

He seemed very sure of himself, and Hobson began to think he should break up this duel which served no good purpose and was potentially very dangerous. He was about to call out when Schwager, who moved backwards slowly while raising his weapon, was suddenly thrown off balance by the swell of the sea. He knocked into a cover on the hold, and wishing to steady himself, had one knee on the ground and tried to grab hold of something with the hand that held the machete.

The pirate didn't hesitate a second. He rushed for Schwager, and aimed a blow across the top of his neck. Schwager instinctively lowered his head. The blade missed his scalp by inches and hit the metal cover of the hold, ringing loudly before flying from the pirate's hand. He landed flat on his face in front of Schwager.

The pirate lunged frantically for his machete, but at the very moment he gripped it, Schwager lifted his, and with an almost mechanical gesture, cut off his hand at the wrist. Convulsed with pain, the pirate rolled on his back, holding his bleeding stump with his other hand, while Schwager pulled his blade from the teakwood deck.

The Nigerian tried to get up when he saw the blond giant coming at him, ready to strike again. Terrified, he lifted his good hand up as if to protect himself, and, without hesitation, Schwager cut off the second hand, which flew in the air before falling near the first one.

Disgusted, Hobson turned away, while the pirate screamed in agony, waving his two severed forearms which spurted with thick blood. Without any sign of emotion, Schwager threw down his machete and rushed over to the pirate, seized him by the collar of his work shirt, and pulled him up roughly. Then he turned the wounded man around and pushed him toward the rails.

Understanding what was about to happen, like a beast who smells death approaching the slaughterhouse, the Nigerian refused to move. But the blond giant gave a violent push, forcing him ahead. Then, seizing him by the collar and the seat of his pants, he lifted him like a sack of potatoes and threw him overboard with a satisfied grunt.

The pirate sank like a stone before surfacing again, trying desperately to keep his stumps above water. But it was too late. The sharks, already attracted by the other victims thrown in the sea, rushed for the new prey. Fascinated, Hobson watched their steel-like bellies glide silently toward the Nigerian, who quickly disappeared in a bubbling mass of foam and blood.

Schwager turned at last toward the others, who just stared at him, mouths hanging open. They thought they were used to violence. "I've wanted to get even for the Yugoslav for a long time. Now it's done. The second one, that was for Moser." He pulled out a handkerchief to wipe his forehead, before calmly walking over to pick up the two hands and throw them overboard.

"O.k., men, the party's over," Hobson called out. "Finish cleaning up this pigsty. And then get ready to set off some charges on the launches and loosen the ropes."

The mercenaries leapt up to obey. Going back into the wheelhouse, Hobson glanced at the second launch which was drifting completely wrecked, about fifty yards from the trawler. He spoke to one of the men on deck.

"Frank, put a final rocket into that junk heap, just about at the level of the waterline. I'm not eager for somebody to stumble across this and tell the authorities. Vogels, bring her around starboard a bit so we can come in closer."

Frank McLaird went to look for his rocket launcher in his quarters, then kneeled in front of the rails. When the target wasn't more than twenty yards away, he fired. Mortally wounded, the launch broke in two and sank.

"Well done, Frankie. You can put away the hardware now. I don't think we'll need it again. The rest of you, light the charges and loosen the ropes on that filthy tub. I've seen enough of it."

The men did as ordered, and the second boat moved away from the *Sarah*. A few minutes later, a huge explosion blew apart the launch, which went down under spirals of black smoke.

"A job well done," said Hobson. "Good, Vogels. I don't think my presence is needed anymore, and I'm going to finish my nap. There's no point in bothering Marais about all this. I don't want some nosey little swipe intercepting our radio message."

The trawler was back on course, the engine beating like a steady drum once again. The sun, still burning, began to lower a little on the horizon. Schwager, leaning over the railing, took a big swallow of beer, and looked back over the stern of the boat, its wake barely stirring the glassy surface of the ocean. Only a few bits of wood bobbed up. As though nothing—or almost nothing—had happened.

CHAPTER 19

Paris, January 4

Rain, endless rain . . . It wrapped itself like a cold, damp coat around the walkway of Père Lachaise Cemetary where the funeral procession climbed slowly in the morning gloom. Staring at the ground, Denton was like a robot tagging after the crowd surrounding the casket: Caroline's parents, her family, friends, teachers and students from Jeanson de Sailly.

For five days, since that terrible moment when he had forced the front door, then pushed open the door to the bedroom, he had been torn between rage and impotence, unable to reason clearly. He could not help thinking about that moment of hesitation he'd had when Arnold phoned him from Windhoek. Should he have accepted? Refused to push forward his trip to Namibia? It was a decision that had made the difference between life and death, love and hate. . . .

It was his fault that Caroline had been brutally murdered. He knew it in the farthest reaches of his being, even if the police were convinced it was a crime committed by a sex maniac. Fate had given him a second chance when the Ovambo witch-doctor warned him to leave Namibia. It was simple enough: all he had to do was catch a plane and go back to Paris. But no, he had to play it "smart," go to Johannesburg, and step right into the lion's den. After that, it was too late.

The funeral procession had just stopped by the Duval family crypt; they were Parisians from way back. Four men began to lower the coffin as the crowd pressed around the opening. Denton stayed slightly behind. He was uneasy, not only because he wasn't exactly sure what to do, but because he keenly felt the looks—some curious, some hostile—thrown at him.

Caroline's assassination had made front page news in the popular press and had quickly become an unsavoury, sensational sex crime. "The Crime of Avenue Henri Martin." Then the wild speculation about what had happened began. Denton intensely resented the police questioning him about his sexual habits and asking him intimate questions about his relations with Caroline.

Happily, Marc Rosenberg provided a foolproof alibi; otherwise, he would have been a suspect himself. The interrogations at Quai des Orfevres plus all the articles had worn him down. He'd tried to explain to Inspector Paul Le Febvre that he would have to look into Namibia and South Africa for clues, but the suggestions fell on deaf ears. Denton's theories were quickly dismissed as outlandish, or, at the very least, impossible to track down.

"And what is all that supposed to mean?" Le Febvre asked, exasperated, and looking at him with a new edge of suspicion. Was this guy really a journalist, or was he an agent of the CIA? Rosenberg and a spokesman from the American Embassy, whom Denton knew very well, cleared up any doubts about him. But the inspector still found the whole thing bizarre and concentrated on going through the files of sex maniacs with a fine tooth comb, especially the ones who lurked around the Bois at night, hoping to come up with the killer.

Denton had met briefly with Caroline's father after the murder, but her mother refused to see him. Now, at the church, she had acknowledged him with a polite nod, but he sensed her animosity beneath the black crepe veil.

The family had gone down into the vault for the final ceremony, while Denton waited at the top of the steps, feeling awkward and very much pushed aside. Yet who among them had been closest to her? Who had held her in his arms as he had, loved her as he had? Her parents of course, but who else? Lost in these thoughts, he didn't notice that the ceremony in the vault had just finished. He lifted his head to find himself face to face with Caroline's mother on the last steps of the stairs. Seeing him, she stopped abruptly and lifted her veil.

"What do you want now? Haven't you done enough harm already?"

"But, Madame. . ."

"If Caroline had never met you, she'd be alive now. I just knew it. I always felt it would turn out badly. I told her to be careful. . . ."

Her face, swollen by tears, reflected a deep pain, but also a deep hostility, which Denton also saw in many of the faces around him. As though they were all convinced that he was responsible for the horrible murder.

He opened his mouth to respond. But then he remembered the story Caroline had told him about her grandmother. There was no point, really . . . this woman had just lost her daughter, after having seen her own mother disappear into a concentration camp. Nobody could make her listen to reason.

"Damn you!"

Caroline's mother pulled down her veil and walked past him quickly. Stunned, he felt the crowd close around him, ready to revile him as she had.

A voice cried out, "*Oui, c'est vrai. Retourne chez toi, sale amerloque!*"

Then a hand landed on his shoulder, and he turned around fast, relieved to see the mustache and reassuring glasses of Marc Rosenberg, who was pushing away the people surrounding him.

"Come on, come on, let's be reasonable. This is a funeral, after all, and you're being a bit ridiculous. This man has lost the woman he loved. Don't you think he's suffered enough? Come on Steve, let's go."

His intervention relaxed the tension. He put his arm around Denton's shoulders, and the two of them walked away from the crypt.

A man of about thirty-five, under a black umbrella, came to

join them. "Monsieur Denton, again, my condolences," said Inspector Lefebvre. A lean six-footer, the policeman had the physique of a movie star.

Denton certainly hadn't expected to see him at the cemetary. "Thank you, inspector. I didn't know you'd attend the burial."

"I was observing, M. Denton, I was observing. You must know that murderers often come to the funerals of their victims. And besides, you were there. Perhaps he wanted to look you over. From what you've told me, you were the target, no?"

"You think so?" Denton answered, looking warily around. Since Caroline's murder, he'd not had an instant's peace.

"Anything new, Inspector?" Rosenberg broke in.

"Nothing at the moment. The investigation is going forward. Oh yes, I received some answers to the questions I sent down to South Africa. Negative. Nothing confirms what you told me, M. Denton. No tribe decimated in God knows what sinister circumstances. There was a French pilot who died recently in Namibia, but it was a simple helicopter accident. You really sent us on a goose chase. I hope it wasn't on purpose. . . ."

Lefebvre spoke in a superior, slightly irritated tone. Denton suddenly grabbed him by the collar of his rain coat, and pulled him close.

"Look, Inspector, I'm fed up discussing this with you. It's like beating my head against a wall. You don't believe me? That's your problem. Have you even tried to find out anything from any of the mercenaries in town? I really wonder what the hell you *are* doing."

Rosenberg jumped in to separate the two men. "Come on Steve, calm down. Excuse him, Inspector, it's just nerves . . . the burial, you understand."

Surprised, Lefebvre had taken a step back, trying to put his raincoat back on straight. He thought for a moment before speaking in a low voice. "M. Denton, I understand your grief. But I advise you not to start up again. It's not up to you to tell me how to do my job. We're checking out every avenue, I assure you. While waiting for answers, I'd like you to stay in Paris, just in case something turns up. Didn't you tell me you were going to the States soon?"

"Right. I can stay here a little while, but I'm not going to wait around forever. The way you're going, this could take months. . ."

Lefebvre hesitated a moment, then decided against saying more. "I'll see you soon, M. Denton."

Rosenberg took Denton by the arm and led him toward the car parked near one of the entrances to Père Lachaise. To Denton there was something mysterious about the cemetary. He'd visited it once or twice before, but never imagined coming back in such circumstances.

Without hat or umbrella, the rain had beaten down on him, turning the hair across his forehead into ringlets. He sank into the front seat of his friend's run-down Renault, closing his eyes for a second and trying hard not to think of anything. He didn't succeed. Caroline's face, contorted by pain, had haunted him ceaselessly for five days.

The sight of her body, stretched out on the bed, the ivory necklace pushed into her throat, had altered his life forever. Never again would he see her dreamy smile, her gentle, sweet glance. Never again would they plan trips to exotic corners of the world, hunched together over maps spread out on his office floor. Never again would she sleep against him in the night, her head against his shoulder, light as a bird. And never again. . . .

"You all right, old man?"

Denton opened his eyes and saw the anxious face of Rosenberg leaning over him.

"Yes, I'm o.k. Don't worry, it's just the tension of the last few days. And then that idiot inspector on top of everything else!"

"Don't think about what happened at the crypt anymore. It's

not very important. You know that all the French aren't like that—far from it, in fact. You're dealing with the *France-Dimanche* mentality here, the sort of people who hang around cemetaries and believe all the garbage they read in those trashy papers. What you need is a bit of rest. We'll go back to my place for a bite to eat, then you can try to take a nap."

The car streaked through the narrow, gray streets of the eastern section of Paris, drowned in a sad winter drizzle. Soon they arrived at rue des Tournelles and began climbing mechanically the two flights to the apartment.

Once inside, Rosenberg lit a fire inside the fireplace without saying a word. Denton went to look for a towel, and began slowly drying his hair. He glanced over at Rosenberg, still busy at the hearth, and suddenly thought once more about the burial.

"Damn it, that fucking inspector!" He lost all sense of restraint. "Marc, you should have left me alone. I could have made him sit up and listen. Well, I promise you, he's not seen the end of me, the bastard."

Rosenberg continued to poke the fire for a minute, before slowly straightening up. "Believe me, Steve, I understand what you mean, but that's not what you should do. . ."

"Yeah, what then, what should I do? Lie down and wait for everything to blow over? I can't believe you would be telling me that, Marc. You of all people."

"No, no. Look at me, Steve. When by some miracle I came out of Buchenwald, I was a twelve-year-old with very little flesh on my bones and a head full of such terrible memories you couldn't even imagine such things. I was an orphan, and it took me a long time just to figure out what had happened. And when I finally understood, I was ready to kill those bastards right away. And then, little by little, I saw that it was necessary to do things differently, to collect myself, to be patient. You see where that has led me. . ."

"Yes, but. . ."

"Now just listen to me, instead of getting yourself all worked up for nothing," Rosenberg said, reaching over to open a box of chocolates. "I can watch over the investigation here in Paris. Why don't you go back to Namibia and South Africa to see what else you can find out?"

"I'd like to, but they'll never let me back in."

"Right. That's possible. I hadn't thought of that. Can't somebody over there help you? I'm thinking, for example, about the German doctor. There must be some way to make him crack. His type is fragile, and psychologically at the breaking point. We talked about this the other day, remember?"

"Yes, but I don't see how . . . Wait! Yes, there is somebody who could help me. A South African journalist. Yes, of course. I'm going to tell him to go visit the doctor in Luderitz right away. God, what an idiot to not have thought of this sooner."

"See, there's something already. . ."

"And then I've got to go to Washington in a few days. I have to go to the Geographic to revise an article and look at the pictures. I'm going to ask an old friend to see what he can do to help me. One thing for sure, I'm not going to let this drop. Those bastards are going to pay for what they've done."

"You're right. Turning the other cheek gets you nothing. You just get hit again. Come on, let's have a bit to eat now."

Rosenberg led him to the kitchen. Then Denton got up and went over to the fireplace. He watched the flames for a few seconds, holding his hands over the hearth. He felt as though a glacial cold had penetrated his body. A cold so harsh and persistent, it felt like winter had moved inside his heart. . . .

CHAPTER 20

Kaokeveld, Northern Namibia, January 10

Oblivious to everything around him, the huge elephant staggered across the road, crushed a thornbush, then paused a moment before zigzagging forward again, like a drunk stumbling from a bar.

Pietari Weikkolin howled, then turned to Eunda, the Ovambo medic next to him. "My soul, but he's completely bombed."

"He eat too much fruit from 'Gin and Tonic tree'."

The missionary focused on the enormous animal with the 105 mm. telephoto lens attached to his Nikon. It was the first time he'd ever photographed an animal who'd gotten drunk from the maerola fruit, a kind of wild apricot whose taste hinted strongly of gin.

The elephant kept going west, his trunk sweeping the ground in front of his hesitant legs. A good bath in the Atlantic would sober him up. Namibian elephants had the curious habit of splashing in the surf all up and down the Skeleton Coast.

Weikkolin put his camera down, leaned against the open door of his pickup, and wiped his forehead with a handkerchief. The heat was still heavy under the leaden sky. It was the middle of summer in the southern hemisphere.

"Well, enough playing for today. We better keep going if we don't want to get back too late." He turned to his companion as he spoke.

The two men climbed back in the four-wheel-drive Toyota and began the jerky ride over the rough track. Taking advantage of a quiet day at the mission, the Finnish pastor had indulged his passion for photo-safaris and had headed west, toward a region with no human inhabitants and lots of animals. He usually took Eunda with him on these jaunts because the medic was very familiar with the plants and animals of the area.

An hour earlier, they had passed the *kraal* of the Ovahissas. The mystery of their disappearance remained unsolved. Weikkolin, just as he had promised Viljoen and Denton, had made discreet inquiries about what had happened. But he had come up with nothing, not the slightest hint.

"Ouch, my head!" A violent jerk had thrown Weikkolin against the roof of the car. Even at 15 mph., it was hard to keep a grip on the steering wheel. He decided to go along the shoulder, which was sandier but flatter.

A half-hour later, they came to a sort of crossroads of two dirt tracks. The main one continued along the river. The other, very sketchy, went south along the Zebra range. They stopped, and Weikkolin picked up the survey map next to him.

"Hmm. That's funny, this road isn't on here," he said to the medic.

"Maybe Ovahissa track, hunt for kudu, waterbuck," Eunda answered.

"Let's have a look. It can't go very far," Weikkolin said, turning the car.

It was hardly a road at all, and the rains had erased all trace of any recent travelers, if there had been any. Prickly bushes without leaves scratched furiously at the sides of the car and Weikkolin had to roll up the window so his arm wouldn't be cut by the long thorns.

It must have been about 2:00 in the afternoon when they noticed the vultures circling overhead. A few minutes later they came out in a kind of clearing and surprised a half-dozen spotted hyenas who scattered quickly, except for one who left reluctantly. The Toyota wasn't more than fifteen yards away when the animal pulled something out of the ground and trotted off to join the others. Just at the moment it disappeared into the scrub, Weikkolin realized with a start what it carried in its mouth. He slammed on the brake.

"I don't believe it. Did you see, Eunda? It looked like a leg, a human leg. . ."

"Yes. Black man foot." The medic was rigid in his seat, straining to see better.

Weikkolin drove a few yards before stopping his pick-up just in front of the hole, where the hyenas had gathered around the edge just a few minutes before. The soil looked to have been scratched in nearly every spot. The two men jumped from the car and immediately gagged. The stench was nauseating.

Weikkolin noticed a black lump covered with flies. Fighting his nausea, he got down to see what it was the vultures and hyenas were fighting over in this desolate clearing. It didn't take long. He went to get a shovel from the Toyota. Chasing off flies, he removed a bit of earth before standing upright again, faint from the smell. There was no longer any doubt.

"That was certainly a man those filthy hyenas were tearing up. What could have happened to the poor soul?" The missionary turned to Eunda, who had his hand over his nose.

"Maybe hunter die, bury there," he answered in a single breath.

Weikkolin now held his breath and tried to uncover a bit more of the cadaver buried less than two feet deep in the muddy soil. It was in an advanced state of decomposition. With only a few shovelfuls of dirt removed, the head appeared—a ghoulish vision of a fleshless face turned toward the sun, a white worm dancing in one of the eye sockets. Overwhelmed by the sight and the putrid smell, Weikkolin sprang back to vomit.

Eunda grabbed the shovel he'd let drop and began to cover the body with sand again. Weikkolin stood up, trembling.

"You're right. It's better to bury him. There's no way to identify him in any case. I'll go find some stones to cover him with."

He looked around and noticed for the first time how strange, how artificial the clearing looked, which was less than fifty yards from the road. There were no shrubs or rocks, only a stretch of sand rising in a slight mound and trampeled by the scavengers of the bush. About three yards from the hole where they'd just discovered the body, the hyenas had begun digging another.

He trembled again, this time with a sense of foreboding. Taking the shovel from the medic, he began digging in the second hole. It wasn't necessary to go far before reaching a small, rather soft mass. After a second's hesitation, he started shoveling like a fool. In less than five minutes the body of a child was exposed. He recoiled, wanting to get away from the worm-eaten corpse, when he heard a sharp cry behind him and jerked around, the shovel still in his hand. But it was only a roller with a superb lilac throat, who, like a model airplane, made an almost perfect loop in front of him.

Weikkolin watched for a moment as it flew into the distance, then turned toward Eunda, stunned. He had just understood. Bringing out his handkerchief, he slowly wiped his face, pushing back the blond hair that hung in damp strips across his creased forehead. Then he handed the shovel back to the medic and gestured for him to keep digging. He couldn't bring himself to do it; he already knew what lay beneath the drab stretch of sand.

CHAPTER 21

"**V**ery nice, Steve. The article on Medoc is just fine. It's already in the pipeline and ought to appear in three or four months. Check with Wilson about selecting the pictures. The whole thing about the wines is especially good. Our readers are connoisseurs, too, you know. I hope you brought some choice bottles back and kept a few for my next trip to Paris. Even though I'm hardly an expert, I can still appreciate . . . Steve, you listening to me?"

"Huh? Oh, yes. Sorry, Bob. Excuse me. I was thinking about something else."

Denton couldn't seem to keep his mind on the conversation with Robert Simmons, associate editor-in-chief of the *National Geographic* and a longtime friend. Seeing him was one of the pleasures of his trips to Washington. He liked to linger in his wood-paneled office, with maps and pictures all over the walls and shelves bulging with African and Indian carvings. Put politely, it was an eclectic mix which gave the room a comfortable feeling of informality. Like the big leather armchairs, where he could sit and flip through books on great expeditions and imagine himself as Stanley or Livingstone. It would be tough to match the big explorers of the 19th Century nowadays—there was hardly anything left on Earth to discover. But working for the Geographic made him feel in some way closer to the great explorers, and at least, after so many detours, realize his long-held childhood dream.

But this time he hadn't felt that sense of excitement that gripped him everytime he stepped inside the building on 17th St. He hadn't even stopped in Explorers' Hall to see what was new when he came in, hadn't bothered to thumb through the new books. . .

"Uh . . . sorry, Bob. My mind has really been wandering lately."

"I understand, Steve, and you know how terribly sorry we are about what's happened. How's the investigation going, by the way? Any news?"

"No. Never any news. I have the feeling that it's not going to be solved anytime soon."

"Probably not. I guess New York's not the only place with junkies and sexual weirdo's."

Denton had not mentioned his strange adventures in Namibia and South Africa and had done nothing to refute the official story about Caroline's murder. He didn't want to complicate his relations with the Geographic. It was better to work things out on his own, then, when it was all over, he would talk to them.

"Bob, do you think you could give me . . . oh, sorry. . ."

A man had just walked in the office. It was Walter Hayes, the man in charge of expeditions. Every year he financed and supervised several dozen trips, from the South Pole to the Australian desert, and his office was permanently under seige by applicants with crazy trip proposals in hand.

"Ah, Steve, how are you? Sorry to have interrupted. I'll be leaving in a few seconds."

"No, Walter, please stay," Denton replied. He was fond of the happy-go-lucky fellow who liked to spend a couple weeks out of every year in the Sahara or some other desert so he could shed a few pounds.

"It wasn't anything important anyway," Hayes said. "I've just got some guy in my office who claims he's seen a dinosaur in deepest Malawi. He wants us to pay for him to go back there and take a photographer. That can wait . . . Steve, I want to tell you how sorry I am. I hope the shock has worn off a bit."

"Yes. I'm o.k., Walter, thanks."

"And Namibia's coming along all right?"

"Yes. I'm almost finished."

"Say, speaking of Namibia, did you see that thing in the paper this morning?"

"What thing?"

"That story about the mass grave they found in the north."

"Mass grave?"

"Yeah. Look." He grabbed the *Washington Post* from Simmon's desk. Denton hadn't read it yet. Since leaving AP, he'd lost the habit of pouncing on the papers first thing in the morning—the *Times* and the *Post* when he'd been in New York. It had been like an addiction which was very hard to withdraw from. But now a haphazard look at the *Herald Tribune* by the end of morning was enough.

"Here it is. Have a look," Hayes was saying as he handed him the paper opened to the World News section. Denton quickly scanned the article entitled "Mystery Surrounds Mass Grave in Namibia," a summary of wire service dispatches.

Windhoek (Namibia)—A mass grave containing the bodies of approximately 200 members of the Ovahissa tribe was discovered last week in northwestern Namibia, local authorities announced Tuesday.

The bodies, buried in a huge pit about 30 miles from the Ovahissa village near the Cunene River and the Angola border, were found by Pietari Weikkolin, a Finnish missionary who lives in the area.

The bodies were badly decomposed according to Johan Van der Merwe, a representative of the administration in Windhoek, who declined to give other information about the cause or the possible date of the deaths.

The Ovahissas disappeared from their village toward the end of November, and at the time, Van der Mewre added, authorities believed they had crossed over into Angola. He further said that SWAPO guerrillas (Southwest Angola's Peoples' Organization—an armed movement opposing South Africa's presence in Namibia) are "without doubt" behind the massacre.

A SWAPO spokesman in Lusaka (Zambia) immediately refuted the accusation. "It was Namibian hirelings paid by Pretoria who committed this heinous act and who then tried to cover up their crime," he declared.

South African authorities declared the site of the discovery off-limits to the press until the investigation is completed. This prohibition has served to heighten the sense of mystery which surrounds the whole affair.

Denton read the article with growing excitement. It was an indirect confirmation of Arnold's story! So he hadn't been imagining things when he said he saw bodies in the *kraal*. But who could have taken them away and buried them that way? And Viljoen who hadn't found the time to go to Luderitz! He was still in Pretoria trying to get the powers that be to let him resume publishing the *Windhoek Examiner*. Maybe he finally moved his ass after they found the grave?

"God, this is incredible! I knew about this tribe suddenly disappearing. That happened just before my last trip down there. I even have some pictures of the empty village."

"You do?" asked Simmons.

"Yes. I went through there a few days later."

"We'll have to include this in your piece."

"Don't you think that'd be a little ghoulish?"

"No. You know we don't have to avoid delicate subjects like we did thirty years ago. You remember the reactions to your story on South Africa. They weren't very happy."

"You can say that again. By the way, don't forget to send the letter to Cullum to ask permission to visit the uranium mine."

"It's going out today."

"Good. Well, I'll be on my way. I'll come back sometime in the afternoon."

"Wouldn't you like a bite at Duke Ziebert's?"

Simmons loved the Connecticut Ave. restaurant. It was so

"in," so "right," so dependable in its straight American food seasoned for the unadventurous. For those whose tastes had converted to French, like Denton's, Ziebert's was a trial.

"No thanks, but you're kind to offer," he replied. "We'll go to Duke's another time. I have an appointment and I'm already a bit late."

Ten minutes later, Denton went into the Coffee Shop of the Hilton at the corner of 16th and K. After a quick glance, he found Thomas Aberder at an isolated table in the back of the room. He looked troubled and gazed at his plate with a distinct air of sadness.

"Hi, Tom, how's it going? Is something the matter?"

"Oh, hello, Steve. You got here just in time to witness the death of a great American institution."

"What are you talking about?" Denton sat down across from him.

"Well look. You can see for yourself," he answered, pushing his plate away with disdain. "Now I ask you. A club sandwich with a croissant!"

"Well, I have to admit it's different."

"Different! It's an atrocity. And you know what the waitress said when I complained? She looked at me like I was some kind of Martian and said, 'But sir, all the sandwiches here are served on croissants. Look at the menu. If you'd wanted plain white bread, you should have asked for it.' Can you believe this? This country is really going to the dogs when you can't even get a turkey club sandwich in a Hilton anymore. First it was brie, then quiche. Now its croissants. The French are taking over. Next we'll be eating snails for breakfast."

"Hey, take it easy. Don't you think you're overdoing it a bit?" Denton laughed out loud. It was the first time he'd laughed since Caroline died. "Anyway, it's poetic justice. Paris, after all has been invaded by McDonald's and Burger Kings."

"Watch it there. I'll turn you in to the Heritage Foundation for treason. I'm telling you, tradition is on the skids. Pretty soon there won't be any more Chevrolets and the Koreans will be the baseball champions of the world."

"O.k, o.k. You win. But don't worry too much. America still stands tall. Let me order something."

Denton signaled the waitress and asked for a hamburger and a coke. Aberder took the opportunity to send back his sandwich and get one on plain bread.

"So, let's talk. I expect you read the papers this morning."

"Of course. And I immediately thought about you," Aberder answered, his intelligent, craggy face becoming suddenly serious. "We asked for a complete investigation in Johannesburg, but it may take a lot of time."

Aberder, formerly with UPI and the *Washington Post*, had decided three years ago to cross to the other side and become an analyst for the C.I.A. He'd once told Denton how fed up he was with trying to weasle diplomatic or military information out of evasive, manipulating bureaucrats. Now he was the one keeping the secrets. He was through with begging for scraps and spending his week-ends chasing some goddam Arab sheik or African president who'd come to Washington to scrounge for arms or money.

Denton had known him a long time and had contacted him from Paris to see if he could get any information on Marais or Cullum.

"So at least you know I didn't make it up! Something funny is really going on over there, and my hunch is that those two I talked to you about are mixed up in it. I'm almost positive about Piet Marais. I really don't know about David Cullum. I'm going to try to see him in New York."

"We've got a file that thick on Marais," Aberder said, thumbing through a notebook. "A lot of the stuff you probably know already. He's an Afrikaner extremist, been mixed up in all sorts of shady business. Very good contacts in the government and with the secret service. As for this stuff about mercenaries—there were rumors that he'd hired about thirty or so for security operations, but nothing more. I asked them to do a little digging over there, and to do it discreetly. You have to be careful when you ask questions about Marais in South Africa."

"O.k. And what about Cullum?"

"Cullum. . . . that, my friend, is another story." Aberder rubbed his hand over his balding head in a worried gesture.

"What do you mean?"

"Listen, Steve, you know very well who David Cullum is. If you want me to spell it out, he's one of the most powerful men in the world. With his uranium and diamond mines in Southern Africa, his oil interests here, and his businesses around the globe, he's a key figure on the world scene."

"All right, all right. Enough. You're not working for the *Post* any longer. I already know all this crap. All I have to do is read *Who's Who*."

"Where you won't find a word about him. He's a very private man who detests publicity. Obviously we have a file on him. But it's a restricted file."

"How so, a restricted file?"

"You know, restricted. There are a certain number of people whose complete file can't be seen by anybody at the CIA. Top secret. Eyes of the Director only. You can add to these records and put in new goodies, but you can't read them or call them up without special authorization on grounds of urgent need. And in Cullum's case, this would have to be especially urgent, serious business."

"Why?"

"Because, from what I hear, he's a friend of the Director. They knew each other in New York when Moseley was still in business and came to Washington from time to time to do some lobbying. And there are more ties to the present administration that can't be overlooked. I'm telling you, Steve, when you're dealing with

Cullum, its like walking on eggshells. You have to handle him with kid gloves."

"A toast to the cliches." Denton lifted his coke glass. "You haven't lost your touch. But can't you tell me any more than that about him?"

"Nothing in particular. Only what's known publicly and what you read in the papers, which is to say, not much. There are some other billionaires like that who also are very private."

"And you can't even request the file?"

"But what reason could I give? Listen. I know Philip Carrington, the Assistant Director, pretty well. He owes me a couple of favors from my days at the *Post*, but I don't want to use them up without a damn good reason. And what have we got at the moment? Nothing except a vague suspicion."

"What? My fiancee was killed, two or three hundred Namibians were wiped out, and you call that nothing!"

"Look, Steve, there isn't any proof. From what you've told me, you really haven't got any established link, only hunches. That isn't to say I don't believe you. I simply have to have something more concrete before sticking my neck out. Now the story of the mass grave is a step in the right direction. But so far, there's no direct line leading to Marais or Cullum. Besides, there's no use kidding ourselves. If they're cooking up something in South Africa or Namibia, there's precious little we can do about it."

"It's a bummer. I was counting on you, Tom. I can't just let these bastards go if they're the ones who killed Caroline. I have a friend who's tracking the investigation in Namibia and I'm going to try to meet Cullum. Isn't there anything else you can do? I don't know, like put a tap on Cullum. . ."

"Tap Cullum? You know as well as I do that we don't have the authority to bug people here. Only the FBI can do that in the States," Aberder whispered, glancing around nervously.

Denton leaned forward and grabbed his arm. "Hey, Tom, wake up. Remember who you're talking to. It's me, Steve Denton. We used to cover State together. We've known each other for nearly twenty years. Are you through bullshitting me?"

Aberder, surprised, left his fork in midair without sticking it into his mouth. "All right, all right. I'll be honest with you. Yeah, we still do it from time to time. My boss doesn't get along very well with the Director and in certain cases he'd rather not ask him."

"So?"

"What do you mean, 'so'? You really want me to get my ass in a sling? O.k, o.k. I'll see what I can do. There's this guy I know pretty well in our telecommunication service. He used to work for AT&T."

"That would be great. . ."

"Look, I'll try to help you, but I've got to be very careful. I've only been working there for three years. If I fuck up I'll be out on my ear so fast, and they'll be on my tail for the rest of my days. You understand what I'm saying?"

"I understand."

"Good. Now I've got to get back to Langley. We'll stay in touch. When are you leaving for New York?"

"Tomorrow or the day after. I'm going to my mother's. Here's the number. Call me and let me know what's going on."

"Right. I'm off. You can pay. Journalists always have expense accounts, no such luck for us poor bureaucrats." Aberder winked, then got up.

Five minutes later, Denton was out on K St. He turned up 16th and headed for the Jefferson Hotel. It wasn't far, and he wanted to catch a cat nap before going back to the Geographic. An icy wind swept down the street toward the White House. Shivering, he pulled up the collar of his trench-coat. Winter seemed to be stalking him.

CHAPTER 22

Paris, January 15

The woman slowly removed her bra, freeing her large, firm breasts. Kneeling on the bed, she looked straight into the eyes of the well-built man across from her who sat in a chair against the wall. Running her hands down her hips, she touched the bikini pants which barely covered her, before moving them up her body again. Then, taking both breasts in her hands, she thrust them forward and began massaging them gently. Next she dipped her fingers in a saucer filled with an oily lotion and started rubbing it across her front. She repeated this motion several times until her breasts glistened beneath her fingers, which moved in a vigorous, kneading rhythm. One hand moved down her stomach and the fingers slipped beneath her pants, slowly spreading apart her legs. . .

The man then rose from the chair and approached the bed, removing his belt. Standing in front of her, he grabbed her hair roughly, twisting it behind her neck while he pulled her face forward. She watched him, her lips half-open. She knew what he wanted. For two weeks, it had always been the same. . .

"Come on, Duval, I think we should get in there." The inspector stuck an elbow in the ribs of his colleague, who was just finishing a ham and butter sandwich in the squad car. They were parked about ten yards from the hotel Mercure in rue Godot de Moroy, near place de la Madeleine. Since it was already about 2:00 in the afternoon, Inspector Duval was hungry. He looked up glowering, peeved at the untimely interruption.

"Wait a minute while I finish. You think this is the right time?"

"Yes. He went in forty-five minutes ago. He ought to be worn out by now."

"What if we just waited for him to come out?"

"No, not in the street. It's too dangerous. If he's armed and resists, that could mean trouble for people passing by. We've had too many problems like that recently. The chief says to be careful."

Inspector LeFebvre believed in following the orders of his superiors and not doing anything to jeopardize a promising career. Especially if he were able to solve the damned avenue Henri Martin affair, a fairly routine case, until the press got ahold of it—and, happily, they'd let up on their coverage a bit lately. But Desroches, his boss at the Criminal Division, wanted results—now! Checking out sex perverts in the Bois de Boulogne had been a dead end. In despair, he'd decided to ask around where the former mercenaries and legionnaires hung out, just like the American had suggested.

But that hadn't turned up anything. Another dead end. He'd had no idea where to turn next, when one of his colleagues had passed on a tip that he'd picked up from some prostitutes. Talk about some guy, an ex-fighter in fact, who suddenly had a lot of money to spend on his very unusual sexual tastes. Tailing him once and a quick check of the files had produced an identification. Now, the only thing left was to pick him up.

"You're sure that's him?" Duval asked, finishing his sandwich.

"Yeah. You saw that shaved head when he went in."

"What have you got on him?"

"This type doesn't usually hang around Paris. They prefer Marseille or the Cote d'Azur. He came a few months ago. Used to be a hired gun in the Congo and other places in black Africa. Very violent."

"What's he doing in Paris?"

"Nothing in particular. He came because he's got a brother

who lives in the 20th. He needed bread. Since the beginning of the year, he's been coming twice a week to this girl who's got a permanent room in the hotel. She's very expensive—3000 francs a crack—but she seems to be able to satisfy an animal like him. That's her specialty."

"I'm curious to see how she gets fucked."

"This isn't the moment for your fantasies. You finished? Let's go. And be careful. It may be a false lead, but the guy is dangerous. Really nuts like all these old mercenaries. You never know how they're going to react. Better get your gun out, and stick with me."

"You're not asking for reinforcements?"

"Nope. It's better if we move in alone for the kill. Otherwise it could just be a mess."

Exhausted, breathing heavily, hair sticking to her forehead with sweat, the woman lay on the bed, her hands tied behind her with string. Paul Lavagne, still undressed, had flopped back down on the chair and lit a cigarette, a Gitane, which made the dreary little room stink. Eyes half-closed, his face expressionless, he slumped into a stupor, as if he'd been drugged.

She lifted her head slightly to speak to him. "Come on, untie me. You really are too brutal. This is the last time for me. You're going to have to find yourself another girl."

Lavagne narrowed his eyes and looked disgusted. He was just about to put out his cigarette when somebody knocked hard twice. He jumped up.

"Who's there?"

"Police. Identity check."

"Hold on a minute." He leapt on the bed to untie the string.

"What's this about?" he whispered, untying the woman. "The cops come here often?"

"No. This is the first time," she whispered back. "The hotel manager is supposed to be protected."

"I don't like this. Maybe they'll try to squeeze us too," he said, keeping his voice down and picking up his pants from the floor.

He pulled them on quickly and went to the door, while the woman slipped on a peignoir.

"All right, all right. I'm coming." He pushed in the knob and opened the door, keeping the safety chain in place.

"Show me your i.d.'s."

LeFebvre pulled out a card and shoved it toward him.

"O.k., open up. This is a routine check. Everything will be fine if you've got your papers."

Lavagne hesitated, then decided it was better not to resist. He unlatched the chain and opened the door. The two policemen rushed in, LeFebvre first, Duval behind with a gun.

"Paul Lavagne?"

"That's me. What do you want?"

"We're taking you to Quai des Orfevres to ask you a few questions. Get dressed."

"Why? What's this all about? Do you have a warrant? What have I done?"

"You'll find out soon enough. Now get a move on," LeFebvre said. "You, too, honey. You're coming along for the ride."

"But I didn't do anything. . ."

"Shut up and throw some clothes on, will you?"

Without a word, while the two cops watched every move, Lavagne crossed to the chair where he'd left his clothes. He had an impressive build for a man of forty-five, and LeFebvre instinctively moved back to let him by. After that, everything was a blur.

Lavagne leaned over as if to pick up his shirt, grabbed the chair in his arms and threw it at the two policemen. They had no time to react. LeFebvre got the full blow and fell backwards, knocking Duval off balance. He managed not to fall and had just enough time to pull up his gun, when Lavagne leapt for him, his two enormous hands in front of him. Almost by reflex, Duval fired. Lavagne, hit in the chest, stopped short and fell on the floor head first.

LeFebvre, still dizzy, stumbled to his feet holding his forehead. Seeing Lavagne lying face down, he quickly turned him over and put his hand on the blood-covered chest. After about ten seconds, he got up, a pained look on his face.

"Shit. You killed him. Good reflexes, mind you. But this is going to complicate things."

He turned to the woman curled up on the bed.

"What's your name?"

"Regine."

"You know him long?"

"A little less than a month. He came twice a week. He was really brutal. I never saw anybody so vicious as this guy—and God knows, I've known some."

"And what did he ask you to do?" Duval inquired.

"Some pretty strange stuff. And always the same. Pretty kinky. But he paid full price."

"Explain a bit more. Just what did you do, exactly?"

"Come on, Duval. Let it alone. You can find out later. Call the Quai now, quick, and get an ambulance. Also, get ahold of the hotel manager and tell him. Say we're taking care of everything. As for you, honey, get dressed fast."

LeFebvre went to the window and lit a cigarette while his assistant used the phone. He inhaled two or three times before picking up the mercenary's jacket from the floor, then reached in the inside pocket and pulled out an alligator wallet which contained an i.d. card, a few metro tickets and some papers that he looked over one by one. He stopped after unfolding a small white piece of paper.

"Bingo!" he called out to Duval, who'd just hung up the phone.

"What? What'd you find?"

"Would you take a look at that!"

He handed over the slip of paper which had an address scratched on it:

125 av. Henri Martin
3e et C.

"So what?" Duval asked.

"So what? This means that he is the one who killed the girl on avenue Henri Martin, that's what. That's the American's address."

"Oh. Hey, good news. That means we've wrapped it up."

"Yes and no. It's a pain he's dead. The American said something about a conspiracy in South Africa with mercenaries and God knows what, and he's the one who could have sent us in the right direction. As a stiff he's no use to us. Besides, that eliminates the sex motive for the murder, and that's what we've been basing our investigation on up to this point."

LeFebvre rubbed his forehead and stared at the corpse, as if trying to see some way out of this bind.

"But how does this eliminate the sex motive?" Duval asked.

"How? What do you mean?"

"Well, look, this guy had all these obsessions—she's a witness to that," Duval continued, pointing out the bathroom where the prostitute was changing." He found out the address of the American's girlfriend and he followed her to her apartment and rang the bell. Once he got inside, he raped then killed her."

LeFebvre looked at his colleague for about ten seconds without saying anything, a smile playing on his lips.

"You know, that's a really good idea. You're absolutely right. We can tell Desroches that we followed a lead on a sex maniac and that he resisted when we began to question him. We can verify that later with clues from the apartment. I'm sure they'll match up. Then there will be nothing more to do but notify the press and call the American in New York to tell him we found the murderer and the case is closed."

"Bravo! Another case successfully solved. My congratulations, Commissioner."

LeFebvre smiled again. His chances for a promotion in the next few months were pretty good with this new success. . .

CHAPTER 23

"**N**o, Mr. Denton, Mr. Cullum is not able to see you."

"But two days ago you told me to call and make an appointment."

"I'm very sorry, Mr. Denton. You must understand that Mr. Cullum is a very busy man. He's leaving on a trip soon and has a lot of business to attend to. If you wish, one of his associates could see you. I could make an appointment for you next week."

"No. I want to see David Cullum. You told him I was with *National Geographic?* He must have gotten my letter about this."

"Yes, Mr. Cullum knows about you. He simply does not have the time to see you. Again, I'm terribly sorry. . . ."

Upset, Denton hung up the receiver without even saying good-bye to Cullum's secretary. For several days he'd been trying to make an appointment without any luck. This last call made it clear that Cullum had no intention of seeing him. He hesitated going directly to his office, fearing the door would be slammed in his face. Cullum was not a man who could be casually approached—and certainly would have a private exit to the garage.

Denton felt stumped. The phone call from the French police telling him about the death of Caroline's alleged killer had only partially satisfied him. The French clung to their sex crime theory, but Denton was convinced that was off the mark, that the murderer was only a hit man for somebody much higher up.

He wasn't happy about letting the case drop like this, but everyone seemed to be running in place. The blackout on the mass grave in Namibia was still on. Viljoen still hadn't gone to

Luderitz to see the doctor. Aberder had succeeded in getting Cullum's phone tapped, but so far that had yielded nothing of interest. . .

Obsessed by all this, Denton hadn't even given a thought to enjoying New York. He couldn't face visiting museums, calling his friends, or going to jazz clubs like he usually did. Restless in his mother's Central Park West apartment near Lincoln Center, he'd begun drinking and smoking again. He felt like an animal in a cage.

He got up and went to the window of the living room. It was 5:00. A bold sunset fell across the city, quickly turning the day into feverish evening.

He looked over toward the white General Motors building to the right, across Central Park. What was Cullum doing in his office? Was he also watching the city become enshrouded in night? Without knowing exactly why, Denton felt strangely drawn to the billionaire. He'd seen a recent photo of him in the *New York Times* archives, and had been struck by the tired-looking face and lifeless eyes. Had he really played a role in all this? Maybe not. What did a man like that have to gain from some dark conspiracy in Namibia?

He had to get to the bottom of all this. Tomorrow, he'd take his chances and go directly to Cullum's office. If he got kicked out, so be it.

He had a date with Judith early in the evening, and moved toward the bathroom to take a shower. As was his habit when passing through New York, he gave his ex-wife a call and they had dinner together. This time, she'd suggested eating at her place.

Three hours later, he rang the bell at the apartment on the corner of Park Avenue and 71st St. he'd left without regret seven years ago.

His heart jumped unexpectedly when she opened the door and greeted him with a big smile. At thirty-five she was still a knock-out with a gorgeous body and full breasts, long, thick hair, and a face like Ava Gardner—big eyes and a sensuous, wide mouth.

"How are you, Steve?" She gave him a quick kiss on the lips. "I hope it wasn't any problem, you coming here."

"No. Why should it be?" he answered, smiling.

"You never know. Some people don't like to return to the scene of their crimes."

"Crimes? What crimes?"

"I was just kidding. I fixed a little supper. I felt like cooking tonight. Don't worry, no t.v. dinners."

Remembering, Denton smiled again, then went to sit on the big sofa in the living room. There were good memories as well as bad of the two years he'd been married to Judith.

He looked around and saw that the apartment had really changed very little in five years. Judith had kept the W & J Sloane furniture and pictures they'd bought together—even the wood ducks from Long Island. She'd never had much interest in decorating and pretty much stuck with the stand-bys for busy, unoriginal people of good taste. "Basic Gucci" as a decorator friend of Denton's once said with a condescending smile.

Judith held out a glass of J & B and sat down next to him.

"Steve, I want to tell you again how sorry I am about what happened in Paris. I know this must be a terrible period for you and it was nice that you called me. Are you going to be in New York long?"

"I don't know. I have some business that could take a few days."

"If you need anything, don't hesitate to ask me," she said sniffling a couple times before lighting a Marlboro.

"Got a cold?"

"No, I'm fine. A little hay fever probably. So, is it Geographic business that brings you here?"

"Yes. I'm having trouble getting an appointment with this guy to get permission to use pictures of his mines in Namibia. David Cullum. Do you know him?"

"Cullum, sure I know him."

"How so?"

"I know everybody in New York, remember? Seriously, I've been in charge of VIP accounts at the bank since this summer. You know, champagne, private drawing rooms, and menus a la carte for those who have more than a million dollars in their account. Obviously we're not going to make them wait in line for a teller. All the major banks in New York do this. And Cullum is one of our customers—probably our biggest. He's absolutely drowning in money."

"You see him often?"

"Only occasionally. And I don't deal with him directly. I think the last time I saw him was three weeks ago. He hasn't been in very good shape since he lost his daughter."

"He did? What happened?"

"In a car crash. In Texas I think, or some place like that. Nobody said much about it."

"I see. That's why he looks sad. Do you know anything else about him?"

"Not much. He's extremely private, like most billionaires. They're scared silly about kidnapping. I can imagine it's tough to get an appointment with him . . . Hang on, I'm going to check on dinner."

She got up and went to the kitchen, leaving behind a strong whiff of perfume. He started to sip his Scotch when it came to him. He stopped cold. Of course, that was the answer. . .

He jumped up and went to the kitchen which reeked of garlic. Judith was warming up two dozens *escarcots à la bourguignonne.*

He winced. Garlic was the only ingredient he hated in French cooking.

"Judith, I've got an idea. You see Cullum from time to time on business, right?"

"Right. Why?" she answered without turning around.

"Well, I wondered if there wasn't some way you could arrange a meeting with him for me?"

"What?"

"You heard me right. You make an appointment with him and I come along."

"Are you crazy, Steve? It would be the end of me at the bank if I did that. Keep in mind with a big fish like Cullum . . ."

"I guess you're right. I hadn't thought of it that way. But isn't there anyway of doing it discreetly without becoming directly involved?"

"What do you mean?"

"Oh, I don't know. Like having a secretary call. Or in calling yourself under a different name and saying that a certain Mr. Smith or somebody is coming by to get some papers signed."

"That's doable, I suppose. But what's going to happen when he finds out that it's you? He'll be furious, and it'll be my head that rolls."

"Don't worry. Once he sees me, I promise, he'll have a lot else on his mind."

She crossed her arms against her front and stared at him a minute.

"Steve, there's something about this I just don't get."

"What?"

"Why go through all this grief just for permission to take pictures of a mine?"

Denton hadn't had time to think all this through. For a few seconds, he hesitated.

"Well . . . listen, that's not the only reason I want to see him. I have some personal reasons too. Because of something that happened to me in South Africa. I'd like to talk it over with him personally, face to face."

"It must be pretty important for you to go to such lengths."

"It's too long and complicated to explain. But believe me, I'm not undertaking this lightly."

"Let me think it over and I'll let you know if it's possible. In the meantime, let's eat. The *escargots* are ready."

They went in the small dining room where Judith had set the table with flowers and the best dishes—something that had rarely happened when they lived together. Denton was frankly surprised to see this, and to find Judith so energetic, so dazzling, so glib. But as dinner progressed, he began to sense something forced in her nervous energy, something strange that he couldn't quite put his finger on.

"Judith, are you still happy in New York?"

"Yes and no. It gets crazier and crazier here. And as if there weren't enough other problems, now we've got AIDs. You really get the feeling you're risking your life every time you touch a man. It's so frustrating! But you'll see, you'll have the same problem in Europe soon. Care for a nightcap?"

"A nightcap? No thanks. The whiskey and wine were enough for me."

"Oh, but I've got something even better. Something that will really do you some good."

"What's that?"

"Wait a second, you'll see. I'll be right back."

She got up to go into the bedroom. Puzzled, Denton left the table and settled into the sofa that he knew so well.

"Here it is. And I promise it's good stuff. It'll make you feel great—you'll see."

As she settled down next to him, Denton finally understood. She held a little packet of white powder and a thin glass plate.

"I don't believe this. What are you doing?"

"You see perfectly well what I'm doing. It's the best on the market. The doorkeeper delivers it to me. . ."

"My God, Judith, I didn't know you were into this."

"That's because I never told you. But tonight I thought maybe you could use some."

"No thank you! I wouldn't touch the stuff. You must be crazy. It's stupid, it's dangerous to take that."

"Come on, Steve, cocaine isn't dangerous. Everybody in New York does it. It's the only way you can keep going. What would you have people do? Sure you don't want some? Men who take it say afterwards they can make love all night."

"Night and day, no doubt!" Denton couldn't help himself from uttering a snide cliche.

"Steve, do you want to fuck me?"

He felt himself blush, like an embarrassed adolescent. He had once been used to the explicit words used by his ex-wife, the raw words of sex they had always spoken during moments of physical passion. But now he didn't know what to say, probably because he didn't know what he wanted.

But she didn't give him time to answer before she came to him, enclosing him again in the familiar scent of her heavy perfume, which always unleashed a stirring of desire. He bent toward her half-way, then suddenly he felt her mouth against his, her breasts against his chest, her tongue in his mouth with an intensity he remembered, which had always amazed him. She had told him once, after their first time together, that the tip of the tongue was one of the most sensitive of all the erogenous zones of her body. That remembered detail came over him now with a rush. In a moment they were half-undressed, impatient as two lovers who haven't been together in a long time. Denton felt the urgency of her wanting in the bold caresses and the hungry words she whispered in his ear. And he felt the desperation of his own longing, so painful it excluded any possibility of tenderness.

He grabbed her by the shoulders and pushed her down, her stomach against the sofa and entered her between her two buttocks. She still had on her high-heels and her blouse, but Denton, out of his mind with desire, pushed himself in deep. She turned her head to look at him, her mouth half-open. Then she reached up with one arm, grabbing his hair in her hand and pulling his head towards hers, and his lips to her mouth. It was an imperious, willful gesture which only made him want her more.

He lost himself in the ferocity of their coming and bit the tongue she thrust into his mouth. Then, feeling his desire rising again, he pushed her down on the couch and seized her hips to come into her even deeper. She cried out her own satisfaction with the coarsest words she knew, and he exploded, releasing himself at last into pleasure at the same time he let go of the tension and frustration that had built up in him for over two weeks.

He stayed in her a long time, not moving, his face in her neck, and tried to not crush her with his weight. Then he sensed that she wanted to get up, so he loosened his embrace and rolled to his side. She rose and went toward the bathroom. It was the last thing he remembered before falling into a deep sleep.

The next morning when he woke up, she'd already left. He was surprised not to have heard anything, because he was usually a light sleeper. She'd even covered him with a sheet on the sofa where he'd spent the night. He made his way toward the kitchen where he smelled hot coffee and poured himself a cup before noticing a piece of paper on the table. A note from Judith.

"Steve, call me at work. I'll try to get you an appointment with C."

CHAPTER 24

Luderitz, January 18

"**O**.k., that's it, that house with the wrought-iron railing." Gudrun von Bach pointed out the German doctor's hilltop villa overlooking the port to Johannes Viljoen.

"Thanks. I'll hurry over there and come back to the tourist bureau after."

"You never told me why you were so desperate to get there. Just like your friend, the American. He saw the doctor, too, you know . . ."

"I'll tell you all about it later."

Viljoen began climbing the road which led to the house, happy to be able to see the doctor at last. He'd wasted almost two weeks in Pretoria obtaining the permit to re-open his paper which had been shut down by authorities at the end of December. Then he'd had to wait four days for the doctor to return from a trip south.

He'd called for an appointment, pretending to be a doctor friend of Piet du Toit, whom the German knew vaguely. It was 10:00 in the morning. The sun was already high and Viljoen was sweating by the time he got to the house. He knocked a couple of times using a gong in the shape of a lion's head. Then he waited about twenty seconds.

A shuffling sound from inside let him know he'd been seen, and the door opened up on the German doctor who stood in the entrance hall. His servant was probably out shopping. He looked anxious, his face creased with fatigue.

"Hello Doctor. . . ."

". . . Verplank. I hope I'm not inconveniencing you. Piet du Toit urged me to pass this way to see you." Viljoen gave a big smile.

The German eyed Viljoen suspiciously. With his bushy hair, cotton pants, rumpled shirt and informal bush jacket, the journalist hardly had the demeanor of a doctor.

After a moment's hesitation, the German stepped aside to let his visitor in. They went into a living room with heavy oak furniture, where the thick drapes let in very little light and preserved the cool air, but also gave a certain morbid feeling to the room.

"Sit down, Dr. . . . Verplank. May I offer you a beer? You must be hot if you visited the town this morning."

"Yes. Thank you. In fact it is quite hot."

The doctor left the room briefly to go into the kitchen and fetch two beer mugs and some bottles of Namib. Viljoen had sat in the armchair nearest the door.

"Well, doctor, just what did you wish to know? It's not every day we have a top specialist from Johannesburg coming to consult with a poor colleague isolated in middle of nowhere."

The German spoke in a jovial tone, which helped to soften the bitterness of his face. He handed a mug to his visitor.

"Thanks. That's very kind of you, Dr. Schlammer. But I'm not a top specialist, far from it. I'm an epidemiologist and wanted your opinion on a strange epidemic which has just been observed in the northern part of the territory. Nobody's been able to pinpoint what caused it."

"Well, what are the symptoms?" Without betraying the slightest emotion, Schlammer finished pouring a second beer and placed the bottle in front of him.

"Very peculiar symptoms which aren't quite like anything we know. A sort of a bubonic plague you might say. You haven't seen anything like this in the south? Or maybe heard about such a thing, since you know the country so well."

The doctor remained calm, reflecting a moment before answering. "No, I haven't heard of anything like that," he said, lifting his mug to his mouth.

Viljoen leaned close to him. "But I thought you were a specialist in this kind of disease, Dr. Sorge." He spoke very softly.

The German's arm froze in place, his mug at his lips, as though he'd been struck by lightening. After what seemed an eternity, he turned, livid, toward Viljoen.

"What? What did you say? My name is Schlammer, Konrad Schlammer."

"Come on Sorge, you can cut out the innocent crap. I know perfectly well who you are and what you did during the war. I haven't got any time to waste, and you'll understand soon enough why I'm here. So you can tell me what happened to the Ovahissas in the Kaokeveld."

Without answering, the doctor gently placed his mug on the low table in front of him. He made a determined effort to recover himself. "I don't understand what you're talking about," he finally said. "I am Dr. Schlammer and I haven't been in the Kaokeveld for years. What's this all about? You must have mixed me up with somebody else."

"You already gave your line to Steve Denton, the American journalist who came to see you in December. This time it won't work and you're going to tell me everything." Viljoen didn't hide the threat in his voice.

"You're crazy. I have nothing to say to you and I'm going right now to look for the police." The German was yelling as he got up and went for the door.

Viljoen leapt up from his chair, grabbed him by the shoulders and pulled him back. Unable to resist, the doctor let himself be dragged back to the couch where Viljoen forced him to sit down.

He took a sip of beer, his hand trembling, before he lifted his head. "I repeat, I have nothing to say, and even if I did, I don't see how you could force me to talk. I won't tolerate this. Who are you, anyway?"

"My name is Johannes Viljoen and I publish the *Windhoek Examiner*. Believe me Sorge, I didn't come here to amuse myself. There have already been enough deaths in this affair. There's no way you can hide out in Luderitz. If you don't cooperate, within two days my paper will come out with your picture on the front page and the whole story of what you did during the war for the Nazis."

"That's impossible. You've got no right," the German countered, suddenly very nervous.

"No right to what, Sorge?" Viljoen's tone was insistent. "I thought you didn't have anything to hide?"

"You, you don't have the right to publish lies about me," stammered the doctor.

"These aren't lies, and you know it. But I do have the right to denounce fakes, and you won't be the first. Some of them have committed suicide, you know. Dirty scum who wallowed in hypocrisy. I don't know what made you do it Sorge. All I do know is that you're rotten. You might as well tell me everything today. It'll take a big load off your mind and may even help to spare a few lives."

The doctor raised his eyes briefly to look at Viljoen, then grabbed a pack of cigarettes from the coffee table and lit one with a shaky hand.

"In any case, I'm not leaving here until I've gotten what I want from you," Viljoen said. "I have a gun with a silencer with me, Sorge, and I assure you I'm prepared to use it if you don't want to talk."

Sorge snuffed out his cigarette in a pewter ashtray and put his hands over his eyes. Then his shoulders sank as the energy drained out of him, and with it, his will to resist.

"All right Viljoen, what do you want to know?"

"What happened in the Ovahissa village?"

"They forced me to do that experiment." His voice was a listless monotone. "They took the airplane I use, the one the Cullum

Company bought a few months ago, to drop the gas that I made over the village. Then for three days we hid behind a nearby hill to watch what happened. They wanted me to verify that it worked like it was supposed to . . ."

"Who are 'they?' "

"The mercenaries and the pilots hired by Marais. The ones who've been training at Naukluft. Everything went fine until the helicopter came. Afterwards, they quickly brought in trucks and bulldozers from the mine at Tsumeb. The bodies were evacuated in them and buried about fifty km. from the village. Not a very pretty sight. That's the mass grave the Lutheran missionary discovered in the north."

"Who's behind all this?"

"Marais's the one who forced me to make the gas. He knew that's what I did during the war. I don't know how. He threatened to tell everything if I didn't obey."

"He must have been informed about you by the South African secret police. But what does he need this gas for?"

"I don't know. He wanted a gas that could be dropped from a small plane. It had to be completely odorless and undetectable and capable of causing a slow, horrible death in two or three days, with an incubation period of twenty-four hours. That is, a gas that a person can breath without knowing and without feeling any effects until a day later. I had worked in Germany on the production of such a gas, which in its most sophisticated form came from Yperite, or mustard gas. I came up with the formula again pretty easily. They gave me all the materials and everything I needed and I had the laboratory in the mine to myself for several weeks. It was guarded by mercenaries."

"Was?"

"Yes. More than three weeks ago, they all left on the trawler with the gas."

"What? What trawler?"

"The *Sarah of Man*. It's a converted trawler of the Cullum

Company that was anchored in port. That journalist from the Geographic took a picture of it when he left my place."

"And where did it go?"

"I'm not exactly sure. Marais never wanted to give me detailed information about what he was doing. And the others hardly said anything."

"Come on, you must know something. They must have given some clue. Think!"

"I overheard several times some talk of an Omega Base in the Mediterranean. After a number of allusions, I came to suspect that it was somewhere in Greece, but I'm not at all sure."

"Nothing more than that?"

"No. I've told you everything I know."

Sorge looked at him anxiously. He'd aged ten years. "What are you going to do? Alert the authorities? Tell the whole thing in your paper? In any case, I'm finished now."

"I don't know yet. First I have to warn someone so they can try to stop Marais. I'm going straight away to the tourist bureau."

"And then you're going right back to Windhoek? In that case, take me with you. I'm no longer safe here. I'm under constant surveillance and my phone is tapped. If they learn I told you anything, I'm dead. I'll have 'an accident,' just like the helicopter pilot at Windhoek."

"So they killed him?"

"Yes. By sabotaging his helicopter. Marais told me about it as an example of what would happen to me if I talked."

Sorge twisted his fingers nervously, and his face grew pale. He got up suddenly to look out the window. Viljoen could not resist posing the question he'd been dying to ask.

"So tell me, doctor, why did you agree to do it? Couldn't you have said no?"

The German turned to him, his drawn face the face of a hunted man.

"It was impossible. Marais threatened to reveal everything about me, everything I'd done during the war. He even said he'd give my name to Israeli agents, who would come looking for me. And that would have prevented me from doing what I've been getting ready for all these years."

"What?"

"Going back to Germany, to finish out my life. I've gotten everything ready and thought I'd be able to do it without too much difficulty, when Marais dropped this on me. It's almost forty years since I've seen my country, my homeland, and I still have family there. There hasn't been a single day since I left Germany that I haven't dreamed of going back."

Sorge's voice had broken, like the voice of a man who's just lost all hope.

"It's strange how life repeats itself," he said in a weary tone. "The first time, too, I was also a victim of blackmail. They threatened my wife, my son, my parents if I didn't go to Luneburg. I was afraid, and like a coward, went to work in their labs instead of fleeing with my family. The worst happened anyway. My wife and son were killed during the Allied bombing raids. It was horrible. The fires turned some of the underground shelters into actual ovens, if you understand what I'm saying." He put his head in his hands, as though trying to conjure up images.

"When the war ended, it was like I had gone mad. I had witnessed such horrors in the experimentation chambers. Men who died slowly, eaten by gas, or else very fast, like they'd been touched with a torch. I still have nightmares sometimes. I lost everything. As for my parents, I couldn't bear facing their questions, to say nothing of the investigations the Americans had already begun. I was able to get on a boat leaving for South Africa. And then, after all this time, it all started up again a few months ago. The blackmail. The fear. . . . I thought after this, it would be over, that I'd finally be able to get back to Hamburg. But now I know it's finished for me. I can't stay any longer in this stinking backwater. You've got to take me with you."

Viljoen studied the man a minute, thinking it over, then got up from his chair. "O.k., I'll take you. There's space in the rented plane I came up in. But let's get going."

They started out, Viljoen carefully looking around before stepping out the door. He saw nothing suspicious, and they quickly headed down toward the port and the tourist bureau.

"Gudrun, quick, a phone," Viljoen called out as he entered the office. "Can I call New York? It's urgent."

"Yes, of course. What's the number?"

She got an international line, dialed the number he recited, and handed him the phone. After three rings, a sleepy voice picked up the receiver in Denton's mother's apartment.

"Steve? Viljoen here. I'm in Luderitz. How are you?"

"All right, even though it is 5:00 in the morning. How's the doctor?"

"I've just talked with him. Listen to this. It's really unbelievable and much worse than even you imagined. Have you got a pencil . . ."

Ten minutes later, Viljoen hung up, while Gudrun looked stunned. She couldn't believe what she'd heard.

"This is absolutely incredible . . ."

"True. I'll tell you everything in detail later. We've got to get to Windhoek fast so I can talk to the authorities there. The local police won't understand a thing and would think we're crazy— especially if we accuse Cullum people. Can you take us to the airport in your car?"

"Of course. Whenever you like . . ."

Five minutes later they squeezed in Gudrun's little Toyota and headed for the airport just outside the city. There wasn't much traffic in the late morning, just a few commercial vans, and Viljoen asked his friend to speed up. He was desperate to leave.

Sorge sat in front, next to Gudrun. Behind him, Viljoen was thinking over the enormous implications of what Sorge had confessed, and wondered how the story would be received in Windhoek.

They were only a kilometer from the airport, and he looked up from his notebook to see a convoy of three orange mining trucks lumbering up the road opposite them. He figured they must be trucks from the Naukluft mine, similar to the ones at Tsumeb which had carried the Ovahissa bodies. He straightened to get a better look.

He didn't even have time to lift his head all the way up. Without warning, the middle truck shot out of line and veered right on the highway. Gudrun von Bach hit the brakes desperately, pulling out toward the shoulder. But it was too late. The car slid under the front of the truck to the shattering sound of metal and glass ripping apart.

CHAPTER 25

New York, January 18

"**M**r. Cullum will see you in a minute, Mr. Barnes. Please have a seat."

Steve Denton, dressed in a proper gray suit, a coat over his arm and carrying a briefcase, walked to one of the leather chairs Cullum's secretary pointed out in the small waiting room. For the first time in eight years, he'd put on a tie and carefully brushed his hair back. He sat down, trying to look as serious as possible, as though he really were a bank official who'd come with important documents for a billionaire to sign. Judith had managed to get him an appointment using the name of one of the officers of First National.

Viljoen's early morning call had convinced him the situation was urgent. If the boat had left three weeks earlier, it certainly must have already arrived at the mysterious Omega base. The doctor's revelations were truly astonishing! Denton would have to call Viljoen a little later in Windhoek to see if there was anything new. In the meantime, he had to see Cullum, to feel him out. His plan was ready.

"Mr. Barnes, if you would please . . ." Kay White addressed him with a pleasant smile and showed him the door of Cullum's office.

Denton rose quickly and went in. Cullum was seated at his desk and glanced up indifferently when he came in. "Hello Mr. . . . Barnes, is it? Sit down, please. I'll be with you in just a minute." He gestured to an armchair across from him.

Denton sat down and observed him for a moment, at once intrigued and impressed. He was an imposing man, clearly used to being in charge, yet whose rigid face seemed drained of all life or emotion.

He closed the file which he was in the process of reading, and looked up. "Well, Mr. Barnes, would you like to give me the papers I'm supposed to sign? There shouldn't be any problem."

Denton opened his attache case and took out a folder that he placed on Cullum's massive mahogany desk. Cullum began looking over the papers, a slight frown forming across his brow. Then he closed the file and handed it back to Denton.

"You must have made a mistake. There's nothing in there but some newspaper articles about Namibia." Cullum spoke calmly, looking Denton right in the eye. Denton himself leaned forward.

"No sir, no mistake. It's Namibia that I wanted to speak to you about."

"But . . ."

"I made your secretary believe that I was from First National Bank. In fact, I'm Steve Denton and I work for *National Geographic*. Does that mean anything to you?"

Cullum, still calm, took back the file on Namibia.

"Mr. Denton, the name does ring a bell. You're the one who's been trying to see me for some time. But I can't understand your persistence. I replied to the Geographic that I couldn't let you visit the mine. The matter is closed, and I find this subterfuge really ridiculous. Now, if you'll excuse me. . . ."

"No, sir, contrary to what you may think, the matter is not closed. First of all, why won't you let anyone visit Naukluft? Have you got something to hide?"

"Of course not. It's a policy we've always followed, and you're not the first nor the last journalist to be turned away." Cullum's face showed no emotion apart from a trace of exasperation.

Denton touched the tie which squeezed him around the neck and wondered how anyone could stand to be strangled all day by a piece of cloth. Now it was time to show his hand.

"Have you read this folder I gave you? Open it. You'll see an article about a mass grave discovered in northern Namibia. Some villagers exterminated by a strange disease and buried mysteriously. Do you know what I'm talking about?"

"I read about it in the papers, yes. But I don't see what that has to do with me."

"Mr. Cullum, listen to me. I'm in possession of detailed information which indicates that Piet Marais ordered this massacre by dropping a lethal gas over the tribe with the help of one of your company doctors at Luderitz and mercenaries hired in South Africa."

"What? Why that's preposterous. You'll say just anything, won't you?"

"No. What I said is perfectly true. The doctor swore it. He also revealed that another operation is underway that will also use this gas."

Cullum could not prevent a slight shadow of anxiety from crossing his brow. He sat down again quickly, paying keen attention to Denton.

"This story is ridiculous and your accusations grotesque. I don't know where you got all this, but your imagination is too vivid, like all journalists. Besides, if this were true, you wouldn't be here, but with the police or the F.B.I."

Denton hesitated for a minute. Actually, he didn't have any formal proof, only what the German doctor told Viljoen. But Viljoen ought to be back in Windhoek by now and would have alerted everybody. . . .

"Don't worry. The police will soon be all over you if you're mixed up in this. I didn't make any of this up, Cullum, and I'll tell you why. I didn't make it up, because somebody really has tried to kill me several times. Nor did I just imagine that my good friend was killed in Windhoek. And I certainly didn't make up that my fiancee was assassinated in Paris. Don't you believe that's enough?"

Cullum seemed truly astonished, to the point where Denton wondered if perhaps he didn't know anything after all, if it had all been done by Marais.

Cullum addressed him in a consoling tone. "I'm truly sorry about what happened to your fiancee. But, I repeat, it has nothing to do with me. Believe me, I sympathize with your grief.

Incapable of containing himself any longer, Denton got up and leaned over Cullum's desk. "Sorry! Sorry! What's that supposed to mean? What do you know about my grief? You don't know what it means to lose someone who is everything to you, to see her massacred, to. . . ."

He couldn't finish the sentence. The rage rose in his throat and stopped him from speaking clearly. Across from him, Cullum turned ashen. His fists shut, as if he too were holding himself back from exploding. He lowered his eyes, as though hoping to find some response he wanted on his desk. Then slowly looking up, lips pinched and eyes fixed squarely on Denton, he spoke in a low, hissing voice.

"I can't allow you to speak to me that way. Nor have I any lessons to learn from you. Life is hard, and you're not the only one to suffer, you know."

Taken aback, Denton stopped speaking for a moment, then started up again. "Look Cullum, I don't know if it's you or Marais who's responsible, but it comes down to the same thing. There have already been a lot of innocent victims, and it's got to stop."

Both hands bearing weight, Denton leaned threateningly across the desk as he spoke to Cullum, who reached for a telephone, and then thought better of it.

"I could call security and have you thrown out of here, but I don't think that will be necessary. I don't care to discuss this with you anymore. I don't know what's gotten into you, but I assure you you're barking up the wrong tree. There is nothing I can do for you. You know the way out."

Cullum's expression was rigid once again. Mechanically he began arranging a few folders on his desk, as if completely disinterested in his visitor.

Denton decided it wasn't worth trying to talk to him any longer. He looked around. Everything seemed orderly in the luxurious, comfortable office. He had always liked old globes and noticed the one on Cullum's left, a big russet ball which showed a peaceful, serene world. Only a few red marks disturbed the perfect order of that world, but he didn't have time to figure out what they represented. Cullum had just gotten up without a word. Denton stepped back and stared at him.

"Cullum, I don't know exactly what you know or what Marais is planning to do, but I urge you to call it off if you still can. Otherwise, you're going to be in enormous trouble. You can count on me to stop you in any way I'm able."

He was aware of being a bit theatrical and felt awkward in his tie and well-cut suit. But he couldn't think of anything else to say to Cullum, who remained closed-mouthed and unresponsive to his challenge. Denton picked up his briefcase and headed for the door. Passing the secretary, he thought she looked at him uneasily. She started to get up as though she wanted to tell him something, or maybe just retain him. But she sat down again and let him go without a word.

Pushing the elevator button, what Judith had said about Cullum's daughter suddenly came back to him. He'd completely forgotten the story about the girl's accident. He would have to get in touch with Aberder as soon as possible, right after calling Viljoen in Windhoek.

Cullum sat in his leather armchair, stricken. He sat lost in thought for five minutes, looking at the globe beside him. Then he picked up the receiver of the nearest phone.

"Kay, please get Richardson for me at La Guardia. Ask him to get my plane ready right away. I've got to leave in two hours."

He hung up, then grabbed a second phone a little further away, and looking grave, began dialing . . .

CHAPTER 26

Washington, January 18

Leaning over the mahogany desk, the three men listened carefully to the tape that unwound in front of them.

". . . Marais, I think you're exaggerating. We'll talk about this later when Operation Boomerang is over. This murder in Paris didn't seem necessary. I hope the operation isn't compromised now."

"Don't worry. This morning we eliminated all the witnesses in Luderitz, including the doctor. I honestly didn't think he'd crack. Only Denton is left. I thought he'd give up after leaving Paris. Any possibility of shutting him up?"

"Difficult, if not impossible. This isn't South Africa. He's a risk, but a small one. Nobody would believe his story without the testimony of the doctor. And I don't think he's alerted the authorities. In any case, I don't have time to take care of it. I'm leaving New York in an hour. We're going to proceed as if nothing had happened. I'm absolutely firm about keeping the anniversary date. Call me from Omega the night before."

"But, sir, at least you should get Denton out of the way for a few days, you never know. . . ."

"That's enough, Marais. You've made enough blunders. I don't wish to discuss it further."

"Very well, sir, as you wish . . ."

Thomas Aberder stopped the tape recorder and looked at the others who were seated across from him in the comfortable office-library.

"Philip," he said to the man on his left, "I think Steve Denton is right. Up to now, I've had some doubts about what he told me, but things certainly heated up over the past twenty-four hours. Something very serious is underway, and we better find out what it is and intervene before it's too late."

Philip Carrington, Assistant Director of the C.I.A., a man with an angular face and set jaw, looked like Charlton Heston. He straightened up, adjusting the bow tie of his dinner jacket. Giving in to Aberder's request, he had agreed to have a meeting in his Spring Valley home, one of the most elegant residential areas of Washington, before attending a Republican dinner at the Mayflower Hotel. He turned toward Denton, who had rushed to Washington after a call from Aberder.

"Mr. Denton, Tom has confidence in you, and that's enough for me. However, this business implicates someone of great importance, so we better be damn sure of what we've got. The DCI comes back tonight from San Francisco, and we need to have a better file than this one to present to him. If not, I'll get my knuckles rapped. Especially for this illegal taping."

Aberder looked slightly pained. Denton settled into his leather chair, frankly worn out. What else did the man need?

He was even more on edge than just before leaving for Washington. He'd finally been able to get in touch with du Toit in Windhoek, having tried in vain to contact Viljoen. Then he'd learned the bad news. Sorge and von Bach had been killed instantly in a car accident just outside Luderitz airport. Viljoen was in a coma, and the doctors didn't know whether or not he'd pull through. Denton was sure this was another job done by Marais and his thugs.

"Mr. Carrington," he said, "I don't understand your hesitation. The tape you've just heard gives concrete proof. It was made this morning just after my meeting with Cullum. He's behind this all the way. What does it take to arrest him? Or at least to interrogate him?"

"Hold on, hold on. Not so fast. You can't just go around arresting people like that," Carrington answered. "Especially people like Cullum. Let's go back. We know that right now some sort of trawler with a helicopter and deadly gas aboard is some place in the Mediterranean, with the apparent intent to use the gas somewhere. Where? A mystery. Why? We have less of a clue about that. Now this is a bit thin to sound a general alert on, let alone going around arresting everybody."

"But don't you see that time is working against us? These guys don't fool around. They've gotten rid of everyone who might cause trouble except me. This tape isn't good enough for you? What do you need?"

Carrington adjusted his bow tie once more, and looked disapprovingly at Denton's open collar.

"Take it easy, Steve," Aberder broke in. "It doesn't do any good to get worked up. Philip, did you bring in the file on Cullum? Maybe there's something interesting inside which could shed light on this."

"Right. I looked it over before coming. It's a restricted file, as you know. There's evidentally plenty in it—Cullum's such an important man, if you see what I'm saying. I did note one or two interesting things, however."

"Like what?" Denton couldn't stay still in his chair.

"The first thing is that he wants to increase the capacity of his uranium mine in Namibia," Carrington answered. "The Naukluft mine, near the Atlantic coast, if I read that right. That's quite surprising, because the world market in uranium is in a huge slump. Of course, part of this uranium does go to the USSR, at least to be enriched."

"Hmmm, that's interesting," Denton said. "The mercenaries were supposedly hired by Cullum to protect the mines in Namibia. The one at Naukluft is very heavily guarded. I certainly found that out when I went through there recently. No way to get within 500 yards of it."

"Why? Has Cullum got something to hide?"

"I honestly don't know. His right-hand man in South Africa, Piet Marais, is an extremely shady character who seems capable of anything."

"True. But Cullum is definitely mixed up in this. You heard the tape. What if they've produced this gas to protect themselves against a SWAPO attack, or something like that?" Aberder asked.

"That's what I used to think. But why transport it to the Mediterranean with a whole band of mercenaries?"

"You're right. It's all very strange. What else have you got there, Phil?"

"The other notable thing is the death of his daughter, Melissa, under conditions that were . . . well, dramatic, shall we say."

"Yes, I know. In a car accident."

"That's the official version."

"What?"

"You heard me. Melissa Cullum was not killed in a car accident, but in circumstances that have been kept secret," Carrington went on, glancing through the folder.

"I'll be damned. I didn't know anything about it, did you Tom?"

"No," Aberder replied, wrinkling his forehead in astonishment. "What happened?"

"Very few people know, and Cullum succeeded in hiding the truth from the press. His friends think that Melissa died in a car accident in Paris. In fact, she was killed by a bomb in Paris, near the Champs Elysees. And she didn't die right away. The attack, which was made with a phosphorous bomb, killed only one person outright, but dozens were burned, some horribly."

"And she was one of the victims? That would have made headlines."

"Yes. Only nobody found out. That's because she was staying in Paris under her mother's maiden name, Elizabeth Lacarrière. Her mother's French, and she always used her mother's name when traveling, mostly to avoid the press. Her father rushed to Paris and didn't want to leave her in the hospital where she was being treated. She was hanging between life and death, completely disfigured with third-degree burns. He was determined to bring her back to the States and asked the Director to help him so that, with the aid of the French, it could be done as discreetly as possible. We put a specially equipped plane at his disposal and brought Melissa to the burn treatment center in San Antonio. It's an Army hospital, so discretion was assured."

"Then what happened?"

"She lasted two weeks. Cullum and his wife moved into the room next to their daughter and watched over her day and night. She put up a fight for a few days, and the doctors had some hopes of saving her. But then she just started to go downhill. They could do nothing. Her system just wasn't strong enough. It must have been awful for him. According to the Director, Cullum became a different man after that."

"God, what a terrible experience. But I don't see what it has to do with all this business," Aberder remarked, leaning over to pick up his glass of whisky.

"Wait. Let's think this through a bit," Denton answered, motioning with his arm for them to stop. "Let's get back to the attack. How did it happen?"

Carrington looked over the file, turning the pages in a few seconds.

"Here it is. It took place about a year ago near the Champs Elysees, on rue du Colisée. It was noon and lots of people were on the street. Nobody took credit for the attack, but it evidentally was intended for an Arab newspaper opposed to the extremist regimes of the Middle East, like Iran and Libya. It's published in Paris and its offices are across from the place where the bomb exploded."

"And what did the investigation turn up?"

"We helped out the French in return for their promise to say nothing in public about Cullum's daughter. This is what we were able to figure out: the attack was carried out by a group of terrorists led jointly by Iranians and Libyans. This revolutionary group is based in Libya near Tripoli. It is suspected to have carried out another attack in the Jewish quarter of Paris in 1982. Rachid Habas himself went back to Baalbeck, in Libya, where there is a big concentration of Iranian extremists. They're the driving force behind operations mounted by Teheran and make appeals to the most experienced terrorists when they can't launch a suicide attack like the one against the Marines in Beirut."

"And did Cullum know about this hypothesis?"

"Oh, I'm sure. The Director no doubt talked to him about it. They were very close, you know. But why? What are you getting at?"

Suddenly rigid, Denton didn't answer. He was distracted by the globe behind Carrington. All at once he could see himself again in Cullum's office, just before leaving . . . those red marks on the globe, where had they been placed? He tried to concentrate, and the image became clearer. That was it, along the Mediterranean to the south and east. In a flash, he knew he'd found the answer, something he'd confusingly grasped for the last few minutes.

"Steve, what's going on? Are you day-dreaming or something?"

Aberder leaned over toward Denton who was totally lost in thought.

"No, I'm not day-dreaming. Just the opposite. I think I just figured out what's going on. One more question. Cullum spoke of an anniversary, didn't he? What was the exact date of the Champs Elysees attack in Paris?"

"Wait, I'll check," Carrington answered, flipping quickly through Cullum's file. "Here it is. January 21st of last year."

"O.k., that's what I thought. You've got just three days to try to stop this. . . ."

CHAPTER 27

"**P**aul, I can't believe my ears. Do you mean to say that for some kind of personal vendetta, David Cullum would decide to drop deadly gas on Tripoli, Damascus, or wherever? It's absolutely incredible."

Vice President Walter Fareast spoke to C.I.A. Director Paul Moseley in an extremely skeptical voice. It was he who had hastily called the meeting of the special crisis council at the White House. Besides Fareast and Moseley, around the rectangular table of the Situation Room there were Jack Sherman, Secretary of State; Peter Worth, Director of the F.B.I.; Edward Reston, assistant to the President; James Whitney, National Security Advisor and his assistant, David Glatzman, as well as Undersecretary for Defense, Carl Thomas; and Chairman of the Joint Chiefs of Staff, Admiral Robert Gibson.

"But it's true, Walter," answered the white-haired Moseley, a craggy-faced man of sixty-five. "We have a bundle of proof and all sorts of information pointing to an imminent operation. I called this meeting so we could quickly decide what steps to take to stop this thing before it's too late."

Fareast pushed back the hair that had fallen over his forehead and adjusted his glasses, scowling at Moseley. He was in a bad mood because he'd had to interrupt his golf game at Burning Tree to rush to the White House. There was nothing he hated so much as a crisis popping up in the middle of his favorite sport, especially now when the weather was unseasonably nice for the end of January.

The job of vice president was supposed to be all relaxation—foreign funerals and gala dinner parties—but that was not taking into account a president who himself liked to take it easy. He was at his ranch in California, and having learned of the affair, had asked Fareast to take care of it and send the Crisis Council's decision for his approval.

"And how have you collected this proof? If I'm not mistaken, Cullum is an American citizen and lives in the United States." The F.B.I. Director spoke in a smooth voice to Mosely, who threw him a weary look. It was the old story of territoriality. Worth was very strict about it.

"Peter, we'll talk about it again later if you want. For now, we better stick to the main point, which is, according to what we've found out, that the operation will take place in two days and that one of Cullum's boats is in the Mediterranean right now, although we don't know the exact location. All our posts have been alerted and our satellites are trying to find it. If it's found, are we going to stop it with one of our ships from the 6th Fleet? Even in international waters? Jack, what do you think?"

"It's perfectly illegal, of course," answered Jack Sherman, the Secretary of State. Anyway, in a case like this one, we could forget about the rules. But we have to be careful. We don't want to be a laughing stock again."

Sherman, an overweight fifty, usually showed little expression on his tired face, although now it registered exasperation. In the four years he'd been on the job, fate had dealt him a bad hand, and the problems just kept mounting up.

He'd been in up to his neck with the fools in the Middle East, the hot-heads in Central America and scheming advisors in the White House who'd betrayed his confidence with their Irangate caper. And that was without even mentioning South Africa and the Namibian problem—a real bone-cruncher, which was fortunately being resolved. Compared with that, relations with Moscow were a real piece of cake. He should have remained an international lawyer raking in $400,000 a year instead of coming into the government.

"And if we do nothing at all?"

Sherman and Fareast jumped at hearing that suggestion from David Glatzman, Whitney's assistant on the National Security Council.

"What are you saying?" asked the Vice President.

"You heard me right, Walter. Why not let this thing, whatever it turns out to be, just go ahead as planned? Nobody's going to miss terrorists who assassinate our diplomats and American tourists around the world and plant bombs on our planes."

"My God, David. Think of the hundreds, the thousands of innocent people who could die a horrible death if we don't intervene."

"Well, how about the innocent victims of terrorists? Besides, it's completely by chance that we learned what's going to happen . . . If we don't do anything, it's just as if we never knew and nobody will be the wiser."

"I'm not so sure about that. As you know, there's no way to keep the slightest secret in this administration. I'm taking this opportunity to remind you of your duty to keep quiet about this affair."

"No question about that, Walter, we certainly agree there," answered Edward Reston, the personal assistant to the president and a man who liked the good life. He was often seen with influential journalists at the Palm or Duke Ziebert's. "But we've got an urgent decision to make here. Can you explain your view, David?"

Glatzman straightened up and adjusted his glasses, conscious of being the center of attention. Whitney glanced with dismay at his assistant, who looked like a forty-five-year-old, slightly disheveled version of Art Buchwald. One more guy who thought he was Henry Kissinger and wanted to play the sorcerer's apprentice! The President liked him because he told good jokes and made him laugh. They both had arrived at the same time at the NSC, and Whitney wondered if his underling wasn't plotting to replace him.

"Well, look," Glatzman was saying, "we never stop talking about reprisals and punishment against terrorists. But what we've done in the past few years doesn't add up to much. It was all well and good to bomb Tripoli and quiet down the Libyans, but so far as I know, we didn't kill a single terrorist, and even missed Kadhafi. Now here comes along a second chance. Why not take advantage of it and let somebody else do the dirty work for us? We still haven't even paid back the killing of our Marines in Beirut. And we even know where that attack came from, if I'm not mistaken. Now the French—they didn't hesitate to drop a few bombs in the Bekaa."

"That's right. In fact, where are the special teams you were supposed to put together for just this purpose, Paul?" The director of the F.B.I. spoke in a smooth, honeyed voice to his counterpart in the C.I.A., who did his best to keep from exploding.

"As you know perfectly well, Peter, and so does everyone else here, my men are ready to go. They need only an order and they're prepared to take care of Arafat or any other terrorist. Any time they're asked."

"Are you sure? When the C.I.A. tried to get rid of Castro with toxic ink or some crazy invisible gadget, the results were hardly brilliant. Are you planning to poison his hashish, or maybe send him a booby-trapped letter?"

Moseley turned red and clenched his fists, as if he were ready to punch out the F.B.I. director. "Peter, don't be ridiculous. This isn't the sixties any more, and the Agency has changed a lot."

"Gentlemen, please. Enough squabbling," the Vice President finally broke in. Peter Worth, with his close-cropped hair and angular, scornful face really got on his nerves. To say nothing of his goddam bow tie.

"What you're proposing is very interesting, David, but do you really think it's worth it?"

"Listen, in all honesty, wouldn't you like to be rid of the Ayatollahs or Kadhafi or Assad? Those scum cause disruption everywhere they can and are doing everything they can to get the atomic bomb. Just think for a minute what would happen if they succeed. Now suppose we let Cullum take care of them, and maybe even a few hundred terrorists along with them, and I say he's done us a favor. It's all well and good to flex our muscles off the Gulf or to bomb Libya, but that doesn't even touch the killers, the ones who plant the bombs in Paris or Rome."

"Right, but do we really know where Cullum is going to drop this gas? Are we talking about Libya, Lebanon, Iran, or what?"

"Actually, we really don't know, Walter," Moseley interrupted. "There are lots of things we don't know for sure. The main thing is to locate the boat."

"O.k., fine. Let's say you find it in the next few hours. Then what? Do you sink it, merely stop it, or let it go? And what if it's in a Greek port? Jim, what do you think of David's suggestion? He's your assistant, after all."

"He's my assistant all right," Whitney answered, not even trying to conceal his irritation with Glatzman. Maybe the moment had come to teach him a lesson and to bring him down a peg or two in front of the highest ranks of government.

"It's an appealing idea in its way," he continued in a soft voice, "and I'd be the first to rejoice if we got rid of Khadafi or any one of a number of terrorists. We could close our eyes on the whole thing and let it alone. But then what? We don't have any idea of the real objectives. Suppose there end up being hundreds of casualties. Think about the reaction internationally, the fury of the Arab countries—without even mentioning the American hostages who would be killed. And then, even if it isn't known who actually did this, we will get the blame, no question about it."

"That's possible," Glatzman answered, "but we're used to all this righteous indignation. The Israeli's are used to it too, but it doesn't stop them from bombing P.L.O. camps. Look what happened after Grenada or Tripoli. Everybody screamed at us publicly, but most of our allies quietly sent their congratulations. Besides, we can hope that Cullum is very well prepared and will cover his tracks without a trace. Why not lay blame at the feet of some shiite zealots, or even the Egyptians or Iraqis!"

"Why not?" interrupted Reston, the president's assistant. "Paul, if I remember right, the attack in Paris was organized by Rachid Habas's group, wasn't it?

"Yes. As you know, he splits his time between terrorist camps in Libya and Syria. I think that . . ."

Moseley suddenly stopped speaking. Now he understood why Cullum had asked so many questions after his daughter's death! At the time, he hadn't made much of Cullum's intense curiosity, which he'd put down simply to a father's grief.

"What's going on Paul?" said Worth. "Actually, you knew Cullum, didn't you? Too bad we couldn't contact him directly. That would have been the simplest solution."

Moseley threw a furious look at the head of the F.B.I. "That's true, but there's a problem. We don't know where he is. And Marais, who organized the operation in South Africa, has also vanished into thin air."

"The problem is," said Worth, nailing Moseley with an unblinking stare, "we were notified a bit late. We just missed Cullum by a hair. It seems he left U.S. territory only yesterday in his private jet. Destination unknown . . ."

"Anyway, Cullum or no Cullum, that doesn't really matter if we decide to just let him go ahead." It was Glatzman's turn to speak out, hoping to set back Whitney's offensive.

But Whitney just smiled at his assistant. He'd saved the best for last. "That's true. But I think there's a whole other aspect of this business we haven't taken into account. Do you think we can morally let this go forward without sinking to the level of terrorists ourselves? If we act like they do, we might just as well seal the lid on our own pretensions of leadership in the civilized world. Our credibility was already seriously damaged after the Iranian affair."

"No argument there, Jim," Reston broke in. "If we conduct ourselves like terrorists, the world will become a lawless jungle. It's up to us to maintain our moral integrity. I'm certain this is the President's view."

Glatzman winced. If Reston, who had the ear of the President, allied himself with Whitney, there was no chance. The President's assistant, who, it was rumored, had been involved in some pretty shady financial deals, was hardly in the best position to preach about morality, but it was best to not clash with him head-on.

Whitney looked at his assistant with a kind of sneer before turning to the Vice President. "Walter, what do you think? We've got to make some decision."

"What? Oh, yes. Of course we have to maintain our morality. So what shall we do?"

Fareast had been snapped back to reality by Whitney. He'd been thinking again of that birdie in the second hole. A flawless drive to the middle of the fairway and a four iron which, miraculously, had gone straight and made the ball roll just about three feet from the flag. A sturdy, if not brilliant shot, followed by a perfect putt, only one!

Of course, he always felt good at Burning Tree, maybe because they wouldn't let women in. There, at least, he no longer had to listen to his wife constantly asking why he wasn't in the White House instead of "that other man." He turned to look at Admiral Gibson, who hadn't uttered a word since the beginning of the meeting. The number two man at the Pentagon, Carl Thomas, hadn't opened his mouth either.

"Admiral, what do you think we should do?"

The Chairman of the Joint Chiefs, with his grave expression

and silver hair, was known to be something of a pompous ass. Since the Secretary of Defense was an incorrigible globetrotter, and was at that moment somewhere in Asia, he considered himself the official spokesman for the Pentagon. Yet Gibson tried to hold his tongue, unlike Reston and Glatzman, who couldn't keep their mouths shut. He was convinced that sooner or later this conversation would find its way into the *Post*.

"Listen, Walter, as you know, our position has always been very clear. Taking into consideration the geopolitics of the region, and all the other extraneous factors which you're well aware of, any attempt at destabilization would surely bring about countermeasures. The logistics of low-intensity conflicts, coupled with the state of readiness of the opposing forces and the structural analysis made by the staff on the situation in that zone which, if you will, is considered vital to our interests, demands what many would call a humid response. Having said that, many factors mitigate in favor of a tactical readjustment which might not exclude a kind of offensive immobility. In the final analysis, all our systems are operational, one way or another, and there is no doubt that some decision, whether active or passive, must be rapidly concluded."

Gibson straightened in his chair, satisfied with his little lecture. At least those two magpies would have trouble repeating what he said!

"Thank you for your thoughts, Admiral," said Fareast who had not understood a word of this gibberish and certainly didn't want to ask Gibson to clarify what he meant. Sitting next to the Admiral, Thomas raised his eyebrows and stared at the ceiling; he had absolutely no desire to get involved in this!

Those people at the Pentagon really get farther and farther out in left field, Fareast thought to himself. Not only have they gotten so much money in the last few years that they don't know what to do with it, they pose as great experts of the international scene. And as if that weren't enough, they couldn't even protect their own ground troops. With a minimum of protection, the Marines wouldn't have been killed in Beirut. And they really crowed about Grenada, which was hardly anything to shout about—more than 6000 troops against 700 Cuban workers. And as for Kadhafi, they had him in their grasp, and then blew it!

Not really knowing what to say, Fareast glanced over at Sherman, and the Secretary of State quickly came to his rescue.

"Right. It's my view that in any case we'd best not do as Glatzman suggests, and not only for all the reasons already expressed around this table. Personally I believe in violent reprisals against terrorists, even at the price of making some error, but this business of the gas goes beyond all limits. Limited bombs against precise targets, yes; but something like this, no! That would start a terrible chain reaction. And there are so many madmen in the Middle East, that we would be opening ourselves up to suicide missions, or reprisals in kind against our military installations, or even big cities. It's not so difficult to make lethal gas. The Iraqis already have Yperite and have used it against Iran. As for the Libyans, we know what they are trying to do with their 'chemical plant' in Ratba."

"I agree with you, and believe the majority are also on the same side," Whitney hurried to say. Looking around the table, he saw only nods of approval.

"Obviously, it was only one idea among many," Glatzman spoke up, trying to withdraw prudently when he saw it would be dangerous to press his case.

"Very well," said the Vice President. "Now we have to decide how we're going to proceed to stop all this. But first let's order something to drink and eat. We'll take a break for a few minutes."

CHAPTER 28

"**W**e'll never find it. It's like looking for a needle in a haystack."

Allan Barnsley turned around in his chair and lit a cigarette. The flame of the lighter flickered for a moment against his unshaved face and lines of fatigue around his eyes. The greenish cast of the screen in front of him made his features look particularly drawn.

"Pete, we're wasting our time. This is ridiculous. The fucking trawler could be hiding out in a big port like Brindisi or Piraeus and we'll never find it . . ."

Pete Sunderland lifted his eyes from the terminal to look at his colleague. He had a point; it was a thankless task, examining thousands of shots by spy satellites from the Mediterranean just to find one stupid trawler.

"Take it easy, old buddy. You know it's always like this. We always think it's impossible to find the damn thing, and then we find it."

Barnsley took a long drag on his cigarette. He knew that above all you needed patience to work at N.S.A. It was the main requirement for deciphering the info sent back from Big Birds and other spy satellites. He still got emotional remembering one of their last big finds—the cases on the wharfs of Odessa that contained the unassembled parts of MIG-21's destined for the Sandinistas. On the other hand, the hours were rotten. N.S.A. experts had a routine more like forced laborers than bureaucrats.

Barnsley, a forty-year-old confirmed bachelor, felt his heart-jump as he thought of Claire, the girl he had left in bed when he got the N.S.A. call at 4:00 A.M. He'd met her, a blond journalist for the *Washington Post*, through mutual friends in Georgetown the night before.

A new lot of shots had just arrived, transmitted by the tracking station near Cairo, and a computer was in the process of "treating" them to make them more readable. A KeyHole KH-II, the cream of American spy satellites, was now surveying the horn of Africa, and the photos of the western Peloponnesos that had just come in had been taken a half-hour earlier.

The KH-II depicted orbits at an angle of about 50 degrees from the equator. In an hour and a half, it would take the first shots of the islands in the Aegean. Barnsley thought that the *Sarah of Man*, which the C.I.A. had given him pictures of, might be found in the middle of those thousands of islands between the Greek and Turkish coasts. In other words, nearly impossible to find.

A green light blinked on the terminal, indicating that the first of the documents was ready. He pushed several keys and brought it up on the screen. Nine co-workers around him, well-trained for the job, did the same. Touched up by the computer, the picture taken from 120 miles above was nearly flawless and it was possible to identify objects less than two feet wide. Its precision was fabulous, even if it didn't come close to the best civilian satellites, whose "ground resolution" was never less than a few yards.

Launched only two weeks earlier from Vandenberg airbase in California by a Titan 34 D-7, the KH-12 had already begun to justify the some 100 million dollars it had cost the American taxpayers to construct, when it spotted the site of some antimissile missiles in a far corner of Soviet Azerbaidjan. A new violation of the ABM Treaty by Moscow, which had produced predictable cries of outrage in the halls of Congress and the Pentagon!

Two hours later, the patient process of looking still continued in N.S.A.'s main room.

"So captain, how's the fishing?"

Commander Ronald Smith, head of the deciphering service, came to find out the latest with a steaming cup of tea in his hand.

"So far we're striking out, Ron. It's not in the first "finger" of the Peloponnesos nor the far western side of Crete."

"Pay attention to the little coves. The boat might well have dropped anchor in some quiet little corner before going back to its base, wherever that is."

Bip . . . bip . . . the green light came on again, this time for the photos covering southwest Crete, Cape Krios and the islands Gavdhopoula and Gavdhos, about thirty miles southwest of the coast of Crete.

"I think I've found our boys!" Smith ran to the end of the row of computers to Owen Biddle's. His screen projected the image of three trawlers in the fishing port of Palakokhora on Crete.

"Look at that one, Ron," he said, pointing out one of the three trawlers. "It looks a lot like ours . . . same wheelhouse, same smoke-stack in the stern, bent at a slight angle, same derrick . . ."

"Hmmm. Yeah, it does come close."

Smith compared the image on the screen with the C.I.A. photos. After thirty seconds, he'd made up his mind. "Sorry, Owen. That's not the one. Look closely, the *Sarah* has a kind of white ball just behind the smoke-stack. It shelters the antenna for a satellite transmission system. This trawler doesn't have any."

"True. Also hard to say if there really is a helicopter beneath that tarp in the back."

The momentary excitement gave way to silence in the big dark room. Having scrutinized Gavdhopoula and Gavdhos, Barnsley was ready to leave his screen to stretch his legs, when a little islet appeared in the corner of the last computer-enhanced photos.

Before getting up, he consciensciously focused on the islet. After a few seconds it appeared enlarged on the screen in amazingly clear detail. It was oblong in shape with a cove facing south, and what appeared to be some kind of landing strip. A boat was tied up alongside a small jetty on the western edge of the bay. Barnsley again enlarged the shot, and his heart beat double. That was it. He knew it!

Excitement welled up in him, but he didn't want his neighbors to see. He moved only his eyes, looking impatiently for Ronald Smith, who was talking on the phone at the other end of the room. He waved for him to come quickly. Smith hung up immediately.

"Find our baby, Allan?"

"If it's not him, it's his twin brother," he answered, smiling broadly. "See for yourself. It all fits, even a helicopter on the rear platform. Have a look."

He got up to give his seat to Smith, who studied the image carefully for a few seconds before giving a loud whoop.

"God in Heaven! This is fantastic! We've got him . . . What island is this?"

"We'll find out in just a second."

Barnsley leaned forward to push several keys on the computer. The picture disappeared and was immediately replaced by some lines of text.

"Here's the poop," Barnsley said, reading the information as it came on the screen.

```
      Name: Paxikonos
   Country: Greece
Coordinates: 24 15 Longitude east
            34 30 Latitude north
Surface area: 1563 square miles
 Population: 5
     Owner: Kurt von Lassen (RFA/US)
```

CHAPTER 29

"**O**.k., now we know where the boat is, what do we do?"

An urgent transmission of the most recent information collected by the KH-11 satellite had just been sent to the White House by the N.S.A. The Vice President, who leaned across a blown-up map of the Mediterranean where he had just spotted Paxikonos, was finishing up a tuna sandwich. He turned to Sherman.

"What do you think, Jack? Do we warn the Greeks and tell them to intervene immediately, suggesting that we help out?"

"That would obviously be the quickest and easiest solution," answered the Secretary of State thoughtfully. "But I wonder if it would be the best. The socialist government in Athens has been a big pain for us for a long time now—really a bunch of extremist radicals who side with Moscow more and more while treating us like imperialists. Papandreou is really a strange bird. My feeling is if we warn the Greeks or ask their help, there'll be nothing but trouble."

"They are being a real pain in the ass about our military bases," Admiral Gibson spoke up, wanting to get in his two cents' worth. "Papandreou threatens to close them all the time, and it would certainly mean trouble if we lost Hellenikon or Souda Bay."

"I'm especially afraid that they'll try to embarrass us, to create some kind of big international scandal," said Sherman, whose normal poker face showed unusual animation. "They're going to say it's Washington's fault, even if we have nothing to do with this."

"That's right," Whitney added. "Look what happened after

the Russians shot down the South Korean jet. The Greeks had the nerve to uphold Moscow's claim that the plane had been on a spy mission. And we know for a fact that there are quite a few Russian-backed agents in the Greek army."

"O.k., o.k.," Fareast answered, "so what are you proposing?"

Sherman hesitated a moment, then said, "Well, we have enough Special Forces to intervene directly, don't we?"

"In Greek territorial waters?"

"Yes. That's a problem, obviously, but if we don't want to alert Athens, then it's our only recourse. We've simply have to stop those two planes we've got in the photos here from taking off, and we've got to do it without anybody finding out. I'm very firm on that, Walter, and I think you'd agree with me there. And we have to act in the greatest secrecy. Cullum and von Lassen are already well known, and an international scandal would be very damaging to the U.S. and the West, especially in that part of the world. We'll give them a good dressing down in private after halting the operation, but nothing public."

"I agree 100 per cent, Jack," Reston, the President's assistant suddenly broke in. Let me draw your attention to another point. In addition to his American citizenship, which he acquired a few years ago, David Cullum is one of our most faithful supporters. He gave an enormous financial boost to the Republican Party during the last election. We'll have to treat him with great care, if you see what I'm saying, to avoid any undesirable publicity."

"You can rest assured we agree on that," Fareast replied with a slight note of irritation. "So, gentlemen, how are we going to stop them? Paul, Admiral, what do you suggest?"

"Well," Moseley replied eagerly, "we have teams all ready for just this very kind of intervention. Just get them there, and the job is done."

"What do you mean, 'the job is done'? Has the C.I.A. already pulled another job like this?"

"No, not recently," Moseley acknowledged, chewing noisily.

"But our men have been training for mission like this for three years, and all they ask is to be given the chance to prove themselves."

"Paul, don't you think it's a bit risky to send units in there who aren't seasoned at this sort of thing?" Fareast was insistent.

"That's right," Worth broke in. "You only have to look at the mining of those ports in Nicaragua. Talk about terrific efficiency and wondrous discretion!"

The F.B.I. director just wouldn't let go. Moseley vowed to get his own back one of these days. There was no way a boastful son of a bitch like Worth was going to do him in.

"The situation in Central America has nothing to do with this," he snapped, barely concealing his anger. "And I repeat, our men are especially trained for just this sort of lightening attack. In this case, we only have to solve certain logistical questions. Admiral, you don't foresee any problems, do you?"

Gibson, always straight as a ramrod, shifted slightly and gave Moseley a look which said, yes, there was a problem. "Aaaah . . . yes, we can provide the infrastructure for transport. I think it will be easy to drop a commando unit on Crete and to mount an attack on the island in less than forty-eight hours. But . . . why are we using C.I.A. men? We also have highly trained units who could easily carry out this operation."

"Because, Admiral, I heard the Secretary of Defense say only last week for the hundredth time that the Pentagon didn't want to get mixed up in paramilitary activities."

"Uh . . . that's true. But this is a case of defending our vital interests in the Middle East, and our SEALS are ready to step in immediately."

"The SEALS!" Moseley exploded. "They completely blew the landing in Grenada, and you want to give them this job?"

"They didn't blow it at all," Gibson shot back, suddenly red. "If there was a hitch, it was because the C.I.A. gave us completely erroneous information."

"Really? So far as I knew, Defense Intelligence had everything they needed. Your boys informed me they didn't need any help."

"Gentlemen, please. Once again, let's stop arguing with each other and get on with this. We're wasting valuable time." The incessant quarrels between the State Department, the C.I.A., and F.B.I., not to mention the White House advisors who loved to jump into the fray, gave Fareast a headache. The President was happy enough to sit on the sidelines and watch without stepping in, leaving it up to him, the Vice President, to settle the disputes. God how he hated it.

"And Delta Force?" he threw out, trying to disengage Moseley and Gibson.

"Oh, Delta Force! Let's talk about that!" Moseley was really furious now. "I suppose I don't need to remind you of the disastrous escapade of the Blue Team in the Iranian desert. A marvelous example of efficiency . . ."

"Listen, Paul, we're not going to go over all that. This is really old stuff." Thomas, the Undersecretary of State, who planned to back Gibson even if he was stubborn as a mule, decided to step in. "Our Special Forces have appreciably improved since that unhappy venture in Iran. If anything, we have an embarrassment of riches, what with the Green Berets, Delta Force, Task Force 160, the Rangers and the SEALS. Given all those, maybe the SEALS are the best candidates for this particular job."

The Admiral spoke again. "In fact, if I understand correctly, the operation to take control of the island has to be done in the utmost secrecy. It will have to be launched from the sea, by submarine perhaps, and take place at night. I don't know of any unit better trained for this kind of mission than the SEALS."

"All right. We can't keep debating this forever," said Fareast. "Paul, it seems to me wisest in this case to let the military handle it."

"I'm not convinced. Again, I repeat, the SEALS were a disaster in Grenada during a similar kind of night operation. But I'm not going to ram my opinion down your throats. If this is what you want, I'll go along. There just isn't time to waste. I only hope we don't make fools of ourselves again."

"Thanks, Paul. By the way, any news of Cullum?" Fareast asked.

"No, still nothing. He could be anywhere on the American continent or in Europe."

"Right. If we find him by any chance, we have to pressure him quietly to stop this thing. In the meantime, let's call the SEALS immediately." Fareast was anxious to end the meeting. There was still time, after calling the President who would certainly approve the course they'd chosen, to get in an hour or two on the golf course before dark. He glanced quickly around the table and noticed that Glatzman was making himself small next to Whitney, and hadn't said anything the whole second half of the meeting.

"Once more," he said, looking directly at Glatzman, "I caution you about any leaks to the press. Each one of you will be personally responsible . . ."

"Walter, you just reminded me of something," Moseley interrupted, tapping his pencil against the table. I forgot to mention this, but the reporter for *National Geographic* who uncovered this whole can of worms wants desperately to take part in the whatever operation we mount . . ."

"Oh, absolutely out of the question," said Gibson. "No journalists on a mission of this kind. That's all we need. We had enough trouble keeping them out of the way in Grenada. And this particular one would be beside himself to spill everything."

"No, actually, it's just the opposite. He's threatened to talk, but only if we don't let him come along. If we say yes, he's promised to keep it a complete secret. You have to understand: his fiancee was brutally murdered in Paris, and he has a legitimate desire for revenge, if only to witness the arrest of the ones who were responsible."

"That's ridiculous. All we have to do is to arrest *him* and keep him locked up until this is over."

"And after that, then what will happen then? No, we've got to be fair. After all, he's the one who uncovered the whole plot," Moseley spoke again. "What do you think, Walter?"

Fareast hesitated again. "Well, Admiral, in this case I think Paul's right. And I suppose we could trust a Geographic type, not like the run of the mill journalists, you know. Now that we're in agreement, let's get down to business. We'll give you the green light as soon as the President has given his approval."

The Vice President got up and rapidly swallowed a glass of water, satisfied to have nipped this latest conflict in the bud. One phone call to California, and he could finally get out of this basement and back into the sun . . .

CHAPTER 30

Chesapeake Bay, January 19

"**B**ear away . . . bear away, the genoa isn't getting any wind."

Obeying his father, Christopher pulled the helm toward him, and the sailboat went leeward several degrees. The sails filled right away and the boat picked up speed, listing slightly.

Mike Pulaski smiled. Little by little his son was getting very good at the helm, and even seemed bitten by the sailing bug. A passionate sailor himself, Pulaski had long feared that Christopher was rejecting the sport, as sometimes happens in families who are intensely involved in a particular activity.

"Dad, haul in the genoa a bit. It's luffing a little."

"You're right, Chris. I wasn't paying attention."

Pulaski winked at his wife, Frances, who sat next to him in the cockpit, and leaned on the winch handle to trim the jib. The J-24 was over 20 feet long and with a small cabin and an extreme sensitivity to handling. As soon as Pulaski adjusted the jib, the boat leaned over its bilge.

They were coming to the end of Mojack Bay, one of the thousands in a complex design of coves and inlets dotting the edges of the Chesapeake Bay. Pulaski looked at his watch. It was 2:00 in the afternoon, and they still had an hour or two of sailing ahead before they would drop anchor again in the Poquoson River. The wind was only two or three knots, but the sea perfectly calm, making for an easy sail. And the weather was perfect, one of those glorious winter days with a pale blue sky and not a cloud in sight.

A gust of wind, stronger than most, blew up, making Pulaski

shiver, and he decided to put on an extra sweater. He handed the sail to his wife, slid open the panel of the deck, and disappeared in the cabin. The passage-way was tight for his big body, but he bent gracefully.

Just as he reached for his bag, he heard two sharp rings on a buzzer.

"Nuts, what's this all about?" And he leaned over to pick up a big green walkie-talkie he kept above the bunk. Pushing a button to stop the noise, he sat down and brought the mouthpiece up to his lips.

"STS-one, STS-one from Unit-leader, I hear you . . ."

A clear voice answered right away. "Unit-Leader from STS-one, please go back to LICNAB immediately. I repeat, go to LICNAB immediately for further instructions. Top priority. Repeat. Top priority. That is all."

"STS-one from Unit Leader. I read you. I am coming back to LICNAB immediately. Approximate time, one and a half hours. Over."

Pulaski turned off the walkie-talkie and stood still for a moment, rocked by the motion of the boat that sailed quietly through the choppy waters.

Top priority. That's the first time it's ever happened, he thought. This must be a hot one.

He pondered the best way to get back to LICNAB fast. LICNAB . . . and smiled just pronouncing the mysterious word. The Pentagon would never change! Such a passion for acronyms, although he had to admit that it was shorter than Little Creek Naval Amphibious Base.

"So, are we going back, Mike?" Frances poked her head in just above him. She had heard the end of the conversation and understood right away. The cruise on the Chesapeake was over.

She knew what LICNAB meant and also what her husband did. Although most of his best friends and close relatives didn't know, he was commander of Team Six of SEALS—the cream of American special forces. To his neighbors, he was simply Lieutenant-colonel Pulaski, head of a munitions depot at the huge Norfolk naval base at the mouth of the Bay. To his men and a few superior officers at the Pentagon and White House, he was head of the most formidable little detachment of commandos in the Western world, right up there with the British SAS and SBS and the French 2ième REP.

Little known to the public at large, the SEALS were combat swimmers, parachutists, specialists in martial arts and every kind of explosive, including nuclear. They all spoke several languages, and the rigor of their physical and psychological training would wipe out a Marine and make a Ranger look like a wimp.

To remain incognito, some SEALS, especially those in the sixth unit, had gotten rid of uniforms and were authorized to wear semi-long hair and beards. It was a liberty few abused. For Mike Pulaski, it was easier to take a "military" cover.

"We're going back, Frances. I'm sorry . . ."

"I understand, Mike. There'll be other days. I just hope you won't be gone too long." Frances looked at him for a moment, her blond hair pulled neatly back, the anxiety plain on her pretty, even face.

"I don't have any idea. Top priority. That's got to be important. What's going on in the world to merit our intervention? Did you hear anything unusual on the news?"

"No. And I listened at 11:00 this morning. Something may have happened since then."

She stepped aside to let him go out of the cabin. Pulaski ran a hand through his brown hair. His open, slightly irregular face betrayed his Polish origins.

"Chris, my lad, aim for the moorings. We're heading back."

"O.k., Dad," he answered after a moment's hesitation. He had learned it was better not to argue. Half an hour later, they grabbed the buoy, boarded their tender and rowed ashore. At 2:30 Pulaski jumped in his Chevrolet and turned onto Interstate 64 heading for Norfolk. A little before 3:00, he walked in the south gate of Little Creek base and went straight for the briefing building at the other end of the camp.

Several cars were already parked in the lot of the concrete blockhouse set among the pine trees. He recognized the blue Camaro of General Robert Lewis, chief of the SEALS. Pulaski had to show his special pass to get inside the bunker, then went several feet below ground to reach the conference room. Obsessed with fears that their secret deliberations might be intercepted, Pentagon brass had ordered the SEAL headquarters to be built with walls reinforced by steel, completely sealed off to any outside listening device.

As Pulaski walked in, the place was in an uproar. A dozen or so officers were in deep discussions, while some civilians were organizing slides and getting a projector ready.

"Mike, we were waiting just for you. I was afraid you were stuck out on the water without a motor or any wind." General Lewis was even taller than Pulaski, who himself measured more than six feet.

"I always keep a little out-board in the rear mooring-buoy, General, but I didn't need it because there was enough wind. What's going on?"

"A very delicate affair, Mike. I hope you didn't tell Frances you'd be home for dinner, because you're leaving tonight. If all goes well, tomorrow you'll be on Crete."

"On Crete? What's going on over there? They take some hostages? Some kind of abduction?"

"Better than that, Mike. Sit down. We don't have any time to waste."

The general turned to silence the room. Then he stepped up on a platform, picked up a wooden pointer, and gestured for the lights to be lowered while a civilian put in the first slide.

The black and white photo was of good quality, even though it had been taken at high altitude. The shape of an oblong island with several buildings and an airstrip could easily be made out.

"Gentlemen, what you see on the screen is the island of Paxikonos, which is a dozen nautical miles from the island of Gavdhos in the Mediterranean. On this picture, which was taken a few hours ago by one of our satellites, you will notice an airstrip, a few buildings, and a trawler anchored not far from a small wharf. Next slide, please."

The next slide, an enlargement of the first, was of excellent quality. It was easy to make out two small planes, one at the end of the runway, as though ready to take off.

"This island of Paxikonos belongs to an important European businessman, and we think that it's supposed to serve as a base for a strike against some villages in Libya, or Lebanon, or Syria, or some place where there are terrorist camps, although we're not exactly sure where. Reason for the strike? A friend of the owner wants to avenge the murder of his daughter, who was killed in a terrorist attack in Paris exactly one year ago."

"So far," whispered Pulaski's neighbor, "I don't see what the problem is. If these guys want to blow away Kadhafi, it's all right by me."

Pulaski smiled in the dark. Captain James O'Brien, his young assistant and friend, was well known in Team Six for his anti-Libyan obsession. He felt betrayed by the fact that Kadhafi had escaped the American bombing in April of '86, and maintained that Washington could easily get rid of him: all they had to do was to send in a few hundred SEALS.

"This raid will probably be carried out by the planes you see in the photo," General Lewis continued. "They are tri-engined Falc 50's which are supposed to drop a lethal, slow-action gas, like mustard gas. The gas was tested in Southern Africa, and I can assure you this is no joke. The product they came up with is frighteningly efficient. The operation seems very well organized and has every chance of succeeding if we don't intervene. But gentlemen, the President's orders are clear: this gas must not be dropped."

"I don't get it," Pulaski broke in. "I've been led to believe that Kadhafi is our number one enemy in that part of the world, and we've already tried to kill him. Why don't we just let these guys go about their business? It's in our own best interest."

"That's true," said O'Brien, his baby face reddening beneath his close-shaved hair. "They train us to fight against terrorists paid by the Libyans, and now they're asking us to intervene against people who want to get rid of them. So we're supposed to risk our necks to protect the terrorists. Isn't that a bit much?"

"I agree with you," Lewis answered. "It seems like a paradox. But orders are orders. All the international implications have been taken into account by the White House and the Pentagon. In any case, we don't have much time and this isn't the moment to argue."

But another question was asked.

"Have we tried to get in touch with the man behind this operation to get him to stop?"

"Of course. But we can't find him. We have good reason to believe that the strike will be attempted in the morning day after tomorrow. That's why you have to intervene immediately. Mike, you'll take off tonight with a hundred of your men in an Air Force Starlifter. One stop at Lajes, in the Azores, for fuel. You ought to arrive about 16:00 local time tomorrow at our base on Souda Bay in northwest Crete. From there, you'll be immediately helicoptered to one of our submarines which will take you to Paxikonos. Objective: land on the island, neutralize the planes and the boat anchored near the jetty. You do that as quietly as possible, because this is a clandestine operation in Greek territorial waters. And don't ask me why we haven't asked the Greeks to do this. It would take too long to explain."

"What can we expect in the way of resistance?" asked Steve Palmer, one of the lieutenants of Team Six.

"About twenty or thirty mercenaries and former members of elite South African forces. In other words, take them seriously, even if their weapons are probably inferior to ours. We can't underestimate the enemy like we did in Grenada. Any other questions? Good. The meeting is over. As you go out, you'll find papers prepared by our friends in the C.I.A. containing photos and a detailed map of the island and its terrain. By all means, get some sleep on the plane, because you're going to have a tough day. Oh yes, I forgot to tell you. The code name of this operation is Bushfire."

The briefing was over, and the men hurried out to get their things together, while Pulaski stayed with Lewis and his assistants to go over various plans of attack.

Specially trained for anti-terrorist operations, the SEALS's Team Six was on alert twenty-four hours a day, and its 350 men had to be ready to go anywhere in the world on a moment's notice. They also had an impressive array of equipment at their disposal: transport and assault helicopters, light planes and even submarines were specifically assigned to them. Two old nuclear subs, of the Ethan Allen class, one of which permanently sailed Mediterranean waters, had been converted to carry a hundred SEALS and their equipment in secrecy.

At 20:00, long after nightfall in Virginia, a convoy of big military trucks headed north on Interstate 64. A few minutes later, they were swallowed up in the tunnel under the mouth of the James River, separating Norfolk from Hampton. A little before 21:00, they began loading a huge C-141 Starlifter transport, parked with all the lights out at the end of the runway on Langley Air Base. It wasn't far from Mike Pulaski's house.

An extra passenger joined the commandos just before departure. The leader of the SEALS said hello and invited him to sit next to him. Strapping himself into the enormous plane, Pulaski thought briefly about his wife and son who wondered where he was going, and would never know. All destinations of the SEALS remained secret. A phone call from the base had simply warned them that he wouldn't be back for several days . . .

CHAPTER 31

Isle of Paxikonos, January 20

"What gorgeous weather! It could be Johannesburg."

Martin Davis was in top form. Humming, he checked the sights on the chart of the little three-engine Falcon 50. A gorgeous little machine, it was fast, trustworthy, comfortable, and easy to fly. Everything was o.k. The South African pilot with the round face had eased into his fortieth year looking slightly overfed, and was nothing if not relaxed. He had flown this plane hundreds of times in Africa and knew it like the back of his hand.

"All this doesn't look so bad now, does it John? And tomorrow the sweepstakes."

John Kadowicz only shook his head, his dry face and long, skinny body showing no expression as he continued his checklist. His main interest in this mission was simply to see a little action again, something he'd sorely missed since he'd left the South African Defense Forces and his Mirage III. He turned to his partner. "Perfect. You want to go over the list of emergency airports one last time, in case of a hitch?"

"No. I know them by heart. Anyway, those stupid buggers won't know what hit them."

"Yeah. And I'd rather be where we are, dropping our little present in the Bekaa instead of over Libya like Steubel and Ziegler. You can bet there are plenty of anti-aircraft systems around Tripoli. Especially since the Americans beat the hell out of them in '86."

"True. But it's not exactly going to be a picnic in the Bekka.

There's going to be a lot of flak there too. But there's not much they can do against a plane going 400 mph. 100 feet up."

"True," Kadowicz replied. "And I'm really impressed by the navigation systems they installed on our old crates in Tel-Aviv. Fantastic precision."

"The boys at Lavi Aviation are really crack mechanics. When I went to pick up that plane, they told me they copied the system used for American cruise missiles."

"I'll bet they got paid a pretty penny."

"I don't have any idea how much, except it didn't come for free, that's for sure."

Davis turned to glance at the metallic partition that separated the cabin from the rest of the plane. It had replaced the traditional small door, and a porthole allowed him to see what was on the other side, an area that was now just like a bomb-bay. Kadowicz turned too.

"Tell me Martin, are you sure these containers won't blow up if the traps don't open like they're supposed to."

"No, they can't explode except on impact—you saw for yourself during the trial runs. If they don't release, we'll take them back home. Come on, then, let's get a bite to eat."

The pair climbed out of the plane and walked over toward a second Falcon, parked on a little strip about fifty yards long leading to a crude hangar. Seeing Max Steubel and Fred Ziegler moving about in their cockpit, they waved for the two men to join them when they finished.

"John, didn't you used to know Max in the South African Air Force?"

"A little. He was on the Impala and I was on the Mirage. We were in two different squads and our paths crossed sometimes on Namibian airfields along the Angolan border. He's a real pro."

"And how about Ziegler?"

"He's solid. He wasn't really qualified for a Falcon, but he got it under his belt very fast. He told me yesterday that he'd made a lot of flights for the Order of Malta. I think he used to run arms to the Biafran rebels in the sixties."

Two men met them on the path going to the villa. Jack Hobson looked relaxed and confident, but Piet Marais seemed nervous. He spoke to the pilots. "Everything in order?"

"Everything's fine, sir," Kadowicz answered.

"Don't forget to get a good nap. You're leaving early tomorrow."

"Don't worry. We'll be in fine shape," Davis smiled.

Marais and the head of the mercenaries left for the little hangar.

"Right now everything's on target," Hobson spoke with a tone of satisfaction. Tomorrow at this time, we'll be ready to pack our bags and go home, without anybody ever seeing us or knowing we exist."

"I hope so," Marais said, wiping his forehead. "According to what von Lassen told me, Cullum was pretty nervous yesterday. He still doesn't want to take care of this journalist from the *National Geographic*. He thinks it's too risky. And this Denton's already disappeared from sight. I hope he didn't alert anybody. I suppose if he'd found something out, we'd be surrounded by the Greek Navy."

"The men are taking turns standing watch along the shore and they'll let me know immediately if there's the slightest hint of anything out of line. Where's Cullum?"

"In the Bahamas. In a very secluded place belonging to Chambers, one of his group. Von Lassen's staying in touch with him from his boat."

The two entered the hangar where about thirty containers the size of big wine jugs were stacked in fiberglas.

"They getting loaded on the planes tonight?"

"Yes," Hobson answered. "Everything seems to be going on

schedule. Now it's up to the pilots. It's not too early . . . everybody's starting to get impatient."

"I'm impatient myself," Marais said, taking off his glasses and wiping them on the end of his shirt. "Believe me, I won't really rest easy until we're back in South Africa."

CHAPTER 32

Crete, January 21

"**H**ey, Mike, we're here. You can probably already see the northwest coast of Crete out the porthole."

The commander of the C-141 had the swagger of Flash Gordon and the thick-as-molasses accent of a Southerner. Mike Pulaski took a look, then turned.

"Thanks, John. I'll go warn my men. How much time before we land?"

"Ten minutes at most. There isn't any traffic. Most of our planes are doing an exercise in the Aegean and are refueling in Hellinikon, our base near Athens."

"Are the Ch-53's there?"

"Yeah. The control tower confirmed that about a half-hour ago. Oh, I just about forgot something important—you and your officers are expected at a briefing as soon as you arrive."

Pulaski nodded his thanks, and elbowed the man sitting on his left.

"Hey, wake up old buddy. We're at Souda Bay. Things are about to pop."

Steve Denton opened one eye, managed a weak smile, and stretched. He'd hardly slept the whole trip. The seats on the Starlifter were awful, and he'd spent the main part of the trip from the base at Lajes to the Azores studying the file on the operation prepared by the C.I.A.

Pulaski, who'd just gone to tell the commandos they were about to arrive, came back to sit next to Denton and buckled his seat-belt.

"At least we'll be able to stretch out legs. If they follow the plan, we'll take the island by midnight. Are you up for this?"

"I don't have your training, Mike, but I'll get there eventually . . . far behind you, to be sure," Denton smiled. In the rush of departing and ever since, en route, he had stopped thinking about recent events and concentrated on what was going on now.

Pulaski faked a weak smile. He liked Denton well enough, but for a lot of reasons would have preferred that he hadn't come along. Yet the orders had come from Washington, and he hadn't much choice.

The wheels set down on the concrete airstrip. The C-141 continued for about 1200 yards, passing by the airfield's buildings before coming to halt in an isolated corner of the base. Two mini-buses awaited them, along with about a dozen Marines carrying M-16's.

Denton, Pulaski and a half-dozen other officers got up right away and hurried down the ramp before disappearing into U.S. Air Force vehicles, while armed Marines guarded them all around the Starlifter. Seconds later, Denton and the SEALS came together again in another heavily guarded little room. A very tall officer with a crew-cut and hard eyes behind smoke-tinted glasses, greeted them and invited them to sit down.

"Welcome to Crete, gentlemen. I am the captain of the George Gardner, and commandant of the base. I might as well tell you right away, we've had a little setback. The operation will be delayed about six or seven hours, maybe more."

"What! That's impossible," Pulaski cried out. "What's the delay for?"

"The nuclear sub has had a little problem with its boiler. But you may be assured that we're in the process of fixing it. I'm very sorry, Captain, but there's nothing more we can do."

"What do you mean nothing more you can do? From what I can see, once again the planning stinks! This delay risks the lives of my men. They're going to be more fatigued, and the surprise effect will probably be lessened if this takes place just before dawn, instead of in the middle of the night. And that's just for openers. . . ."

"Once again, Colonel, I am sorry. I'm just relaying instructions from the planning unit at the Pentagon. You'll have to revise your plans a bit—there won't be time to land the commandos on the other side of the island."

"Thank you very much! I promise you, I'm not letting you get away with this. You'll be hearing from me."

Pulaski, lips perced and beret in his left hand, was furious. When he got back to the States, he was going to complain to Washington and tell those incompetent jerks who threw billions of dollars out the window supposedly rebuilding the armed forces. While waiting, he would try to keep his cool. The main thing for now was to try to gain control of the island as quickly as possible.

"O.k., now what do we do?"

"We've fixed up a dormitory in a hangar where you can go with your men while they recuperate. They'll bring a light meal in about an hour."

"And the choppers? I hope those are working . . ."

"Yes, Colonel. Don't worry, we've got three Ch-53's. As soon as the sub is ready, we'll board you and your men."

"O.k., let's go. We've got to get some rest. We'll need all our strength tonight."

CHAPTER 33

January 21

On Board the Submarine Sam Houston

J im, old buddy, it's time. Good luck to you all. We'll be waiting for your signal."

Mike Pulaski, with a camouflage suit and black paint smeared on his face, shook hands with Captain James O'Brien, then watched the ten frogmen slip silently into the floating chamber of the sub. A heavy metal door closed behind them.

It was 3:30 in the morning. Steve Denton and Pulaski headed toward the control room of the Sam Houston, an ancient nuclear sub based in Naples and refitted to carry elite troops. Denton, who'd been introduced to the team as a "civilian observer" of the NSC, looked at the island through a thermal image periscope.

It was still pitch black out, but he could see as plain as day the trawler moored to the point southwest of the island, and the little observation bunker on the hill, just above the wharf. These were the two main objectives of the frogmen. So far, no sign of activity.

Somebody tapped him on the shoulder. It was Pulaski, a glass of rum in his hand. "Take this, Steve. It'll do you a world of good. There's nothing to do but wait. It ought to go pretty fast though."

On the Island of Paxikonos

"Be careful. If one of them falls, we'll all be dead."

With Piet Marais at his side, Jack Hobson looked on attentively

221

while three mercenaries filled the containers with gas beneath a spotlight.

They were soon finished. Two mercenaries completed filling the external tanks under the wings of the gunmetal gray Falcon 50's, while the four pilots watched eagerly. Marais approached them.

"Everything o.k.? Good. You know your instructions. Fly low the whole way to avoid detection. You'll take off at 4:15, as planned."

Martin Davis, pilot of the first Falcon, looked at his watch, glanced at the small runway, then sipped the mug of coffee he held before answering.

"Just about right. That would put us over our objectives just at dawn. There will be enough light to distinguish our targets, but not enough for us to be seen too clearly."

Marais, speaking slowly for emphasis, said, "Gentlemen, this evening you will have rendered a great service to humanity . . . and you'll get rich at the same time."

"Yeah, Marais, but first we've got to try to get back alive," Davis answered, slipping on his leather flak jacket. He glanced up at the sky without a trace of cloud.

"My lucky star has guided me so far. I just hope it gets me through today."

On Board the Submarine Sam Houston

The terse radio message had just finished blaring into control room plunged in a greenish half-light. "Trawler and bunker in our hands. No loss of human life to report. Enemy neutralized."

"Flawless!" Pulaski bellowed. "O'Brien is truly the best!"

He turned toward his men.

"O.k., so far it's clear sailing. Gentlemen, let's set our watches. It's exactly 3:45. The rubber dinghies should be in the water in ten minutes."

Along with Denton and three other SEAL officers, he made his way to the room where some sixty commandos were waiting with their gear.

A few minutes later, the Sam Houston's sail broke surface about a-half-nautical mile from the island. Partially hidden from shore by a sort of rocky barrier, the submarine stopped, its rudders gently agitating the water . . .

On the Southeast Tip of Paxikonos

Kurt Schwager was in a foul mood. He'd always hated the night watch, and he was furious at being stung for $300 at poker the night before by those shitheads Henneberger and Strudwick.

To top it all off, the pain in his lower back was kicking up again. He moved around to see if he could find a more comfortable position. The man dozing beside him mumbled a few words in Afrikaans before falling asleep again. The two of them had ended up in a sort of shepherd's hut facing to the east over the only little bay on the island.

Schwager's eyes automatically swept over the small beach and the sea beyond. He wondered if he couldn't catch forty winks when a dark shape behind the big rocks closing the bay to the southeast caught his eye. The sharpness of the outline puzzled him. This was definitely not part of the rock formation.

"What the devil's that thing?" He gave Rudolph Pienaar a quick kick in the side, and grabbed some binoculars.

"What's your problem? Are you crazy or what?" Pienaar yelled, furious.

"Get up you fucking Kaffir. Something's out there off-shore. It looks like a boat," Schwager said, adjusting the binoculars.

A few seconds later, he let them drop and stared at Pienaar, dumbfounded.

"A submarine. . . . but that's impossible . . . what the hell is it doing there?"

Pienaar grabbed the glasses to see for himself. On the beach behind the sub, shadowy figures were moving about, putting dinghies into the sea. He turned back to Schwager, nodding toward the walkie-talkie.

"Call quick! I believe we have visitors."

On the Runway, Island of Paxikonos

A walkie-talkie limp in his hand, Hobson looked like a man who had just had a bomb go off in his head. "A submarine? Have you been drinking again, Schwager?"

"No," said the voice in the box. "And the men landing aren't exactly tourists, either. And there's no way to make contact with the bunker or the ship."

Hobson looked over at Marais, who stood next to him turning pale and looking at his watch: 3:45.

"Stopping the operation is out of the question. We've got get the planes off and push back these invaders. Paxikonos is private property. Nobody has the right to land here secretly."

"Right. Schwager," Hobson spoke into the phone, "I'm sending you Venardi with a dozen men and the RPG. You've got to stop them from landing until the planes take off."

"O.k.," Schwager answered. "I'll load the machine guns and Pienaar can pepper them with Strella rockets. We'll give them a surprise welcome. Over and out."

On Board the Submarine Sam Houston

"Sir, I think I saw some shadows moving across the ground."

Ensign Phil McDermott was almost positive he noticed something moving near some kind of hut that he saw on the heights overlooking the cove to the east.

"Where?"

Tom Brockman, captain of the sub, lifted his binoculars toward the place pointed out by the junior officer. "I don't see anything. Those thugs are snoozing and they're going to get the surprise of their lives. Besides, our dinghies are going to land any minute and . . ."

In the same moment the two men saw the yellow flame that shot up from a corner of the shepherd's hut. They both dove instinctively behind the armored windshield around the lookout post. The rocket missed the base of the sail by a few inches and ricocheted onto the deck without exploding, letting fly a shower of sparks.

"Bastards! We've got to get out of here. Those shitheads are going to pick us off like sitting ducks if we stay here."

Brockman leaned over to the intercom to shout orders. The big boat, whose motors were turning already, moved forward immediately. He flew down the ladder on the inside of the sail and rushed to the control room. "Quick, let's dive. I hope to hell the SEALS can handle this, but we've got to get out of here."

In the Zodiacs with the SEALS

Pulaski and his men were about 300 yards from the shore when the first missile passed over their heads. The leader of the SEALS didn't wait for a second one. "Filthy bastards!" he yelled, letting go of his paddle. "Start up the engines and spread out. Head for the beach and we'll regroup there . . ."

The sea was soon covered with thick, reddish bubbles running with the current. The motors of ten boats roared at the same time that the dinghies shot forward, breaking the silence of the dawn.

The first burst of machine-gun fire whipped across the water just behind the Zodiac carrying Pulaski and Denton. They put their heads down and listened to the bullets whistle past. The second burst raked a boat in the middle of the little flotilla, literally cutting its occupants in two.

Thirty seconds later, in the incessant rat-a-tat-tat of automatic weapons, Pulaski's group landed on the little beach. Pulaski dashed behind a rock, dragging Denton along with him. "O.k., Steve, the fun and games are over. Don't budge from this spot."

"Don't worry, I'll keep out of sight," said Denton, who felt oddly calm. He had the sensation that the bullets that sprayed the sand around the rock couldn't reach him.

All of a sudden the fire directed toward them seemed to diminish, although the sounds of guns going off were as strong as ever. He risked a quick look around in the half-light to see that the shots at the hut were being fired from the trawler and the bunker above the wharf.

He turned toward Pulaski, whose mouth turned up in the hint of a smile. "O'Brien and his men. They're going to take the bastards from the rear."

On the Runway, Island of Paxikonos

Martin Davis adjusted his earphones and checked the coordinants on his chart one last time before turning to his co-pilots.

"So, my friend, you wanted action? Well you've got some now."

"Hmmm. Just so long as they don't have air cover," answered John Kadowicz.

"That would surprise me. If these were Greeks, they wouldn't have come in so quietly. Well enough talking. Are you ready? Don't forget a double bonus is waiting for us in Switzerland. Marais just promised."

"Yeah . . . after a small detour by way of Libya. And now we have to ditch the planes."

Davis shook his head and pulled three throttles to start the

Garrett engines of his Falcon 50. Brakes off, the little plane vibrated violently, then shot forward.

A short time after, the second jet took off in turn, heading southwest.

On Board the Sam Houston

"Shit! Get Washington for me immediately."

The two planes taking off caught the staff of the *Sam Houston*, now three or four miles from the coast, off guard.

Thirty seconds later, via satelitte, Captain Brockman was in contact with the situation room at the Pentagon. A certain Col. James Higgins was on the other end of the line.

"Colonel, we've got to act fast. Two planes have already taken off, one to the southwest, the other to the east. If they're what we think they are, we're in a hell of a fix."

"What are you suggesting?"

"That we try to intercept them. The *Carl Vinson* is off the coast of Lebanon with a naval group. For the other plane, maybe one of the F-15's from Souda Bay or Hellenikon."

"O.k., we'll look into it. And what's the situation on the island?"

"Still confused. The SEALS landed, but they met strong opposition. I'll call you as soon as I have some news."

"Good. I'll alert the White House."

On the Island of Paxikonos

Inch by inch the SEALS gained ground and made their way to the shepherd's hut. Crouched behind a rock, Pulaski set down his Heckler and Koch submachine-gun to pick up his walkie-talkie and call O'Brien.

"Jim, where are you? We're waiting for you to pick off these guys from behind. We're moving in, but slowly."

"Sorry, Mike, but we were held up. They sent out a little welcoming party to cut us off. I think that we took care of them all, but I can't be 100 per cent sure. I told the men to advance very carefully."

"Any losses?"

"Bannister took a bullet in the chest. He's not in good shape. How about you?"

"Us? We're talking Iwo Jima, pal. We've got two dead and five wounded, not counting the ones cut down in the water. We haven't gotten in position to use the Dragons yet, but as soon as we do, we'll cram as many as we can down their throats."

"O.k., we'll be there as soon as we can. Over and out."

Pulaski picked up his gun and crept forward another twelve yards. Looking up, he barely made out the head of one of the mercenaries fifty yards away. He stopped moving and aimed his Heckler. Ten seconds later, William Henneberger had half his head torn away by a 5.56 bullet. He never would get the chance to blow the wad he'd won off Schwager the night before.

Aboard the Tomcat F-14 Yankee One

"Cleared for takeoff."

The *Carl Vinson*, an 80,000 ton collossus, had just gently turned into the wind. Pushed forward by the catapults of the aircraft-carrier, the two Tomcat R-14's took off in a jet-spray of white exhaust.

"Yahoo! At least for today we won't be seasick!"

Lt. Jay Litwack was feeling fine as he played with the wings, bringing them in with geometrical precision. Then he turned to Lester Stone, his navigator. "Les, check the radio connection with Charles and Dave. We're climbing to 30,000 as planned. Heading for 270."

Stone picked the best frequency and called Charles Moorhead

and Dave Truly in the second F-14. "Yankee Two, this is Yankee One. Wake up, me lads, we've taken off . . ."

"Yankee Two to Yankee One. Thanks for telling us. We'll just have our coffee and donuts, then we'll be right along to join you," the nasal voice of Dave Truly rasped into the receiver.

Liwack adjusted his cap before entering into the conversation. "Dave, just a reminder that the first one to spot the Falcon gets to shoot, o.k.?"

"You're on. Still I'd be damn curious to find out who's in that sucker."

"Orders are orders. Shoot it down and get the hell back. Of course we have to find it first. I'm calling AWACS to see if they have anything. Over and out."

Litwack settled into his ejection seat and saw on his altimeter that they had almost reached their cruising altitude. He gently pushed the forward lever and savoured how effortlessly the Tomcat reacted, climbing so smoothly up its trajectory.

Situation Room, the White House

"Gentlemen, time's passing. The planes left twenty-five minutes ago. These are jets. They're making headway while we talk." National Security Advisor James Whitney nervously tapped the wood table of the Situation Room. It was almost 10:30 at night and the Pentagon had just transmitted the latest information on the Mediterranean operation.

C.I.A. Director Paul Moseley exploded. "I told you. The SEALS are incompetents. And of course a big cheer for our air cover! Another bedtime story brought to you courtesy of the Pentagon."

"Take it easy, Paul," answered Admiral Robert Gibson, Chairman of the Joint Chiefs. "You wouldn't want us to send a whole squadron over the island, would you? And we'll surely succeed in intercepting the plane heading for Lebanon or Syria. The problem is the other plane. It must be very close to the Libyan coast, if that's where it's going. Too late to try anything with our planes."

"Bravo!" Mosely replied, furiously crushing the butt of his cigar in an ashtray.

"Paul, when are you going to quit smoking those awful cigars?" the Vice President broke in, overcome by the smoke that filled the little room.

"'Awful cigars'? These are Cuban Partagas. Drobnikov sent them to me. Direct from Havana via Moscow."

"Wonderful! I hope they aren't wired. But back to business. What do we do now? Warn Tripoli?"

"Why not?" answered Whitney. "Except that might take forever. And since we bombed them, they don't have much confidence . . ."

"What if we notified the Soviets? They have several fighter squadrons in Libya. They could do the job."

Whitney raised his eyebrows and looked at David Glatzman, his assistant, who had just made this suggestion.

"Truly, David, you do have strange ideas. Enlist Moscow in the fight against terrorism? . . ."

". . . against counter-terrorism, you meant to say," Moseley broke in. "I think he's got a good idea this time. What do you think, Walter? This is the time for cooperation with the Kremlin, isn't it?"

"That's right," Fareast replied, pushing back the unruly hair from his forehead. "I don't expect that Moscow particularly wants the Mediterranean to go up in flames at the moment. And how would we warn the Evil Empire? On the hotline?"

"Too complicated," Whitney said. "Why not just call Drobnikov and explain the problem to him. If he's in town he could be here in ten minutes."

"He's in town. I saw him at an opening at the Corcoran. I'll go call him right away." Moseley got up from his chair.

"Tell him to get here immediately. I'll meet him and tell him the situation. With him this could move fast." Fareast said, looking relieved. "Say, mind if I have one of your cigars. . . ."

Aboard the F-14 "Tomcat" Yankee One

"I've got it, Jay."

"Are you sure? We can't afford a mistake. And we can't exactly do a fly-by without getting picked up on their radio."

"Don't worry. That plane's exactly where the AWACS spotted it, flying low over the water."

"Good. Tell the others and the *Vinson*."

Jay Litvack let up a little on the two Pratt and Whitney engines and set in motion the hydraulic jacks to gently bring the wings back toward the front. The plane's speed stabilized at Mach 1.2. He turned on the target radar and prepared to fire the Phoenix missiles. Only light pressure from his fingers was enough to push the deadly rockets to nearly Mach 3, as they zoomed toward the target guided by infrared auto-pilot.

"Jay, we should see them now. They're in front of us, at one o'clock. We'll be on top of them in thirty seconds."

Aboard the Falcon 50 en Route to Lebanon

"Good. Everything should be quiet until we get there. Nothing on the horizon. Call Marais to let him know everything's going well."

Martin Davis relaxed in his chair and grabbed a chocolate bar. Their quick departure from the island had made him hungry. At more than 300 mph, the small tri-engined plane headed straight toward its target.

"I just can't believe we're out of the woods yet," John Kadowicz replied. "There aren't any planes waiting for us. Who tried to take over the island, anyway?"

"No idea," muttered Davis, his mouth stuffed with chocolate. "The main thing is we're on the right course. You able to get ahold of Marais?"

"Wait a sec."

Kadowicz turned two or three knobs on the radio before signaling the pilot.

"I've got the island. Hello, Marais? Falcon One here, all's going. . . ."

He never finished the sentence. The first missile hit the Falcon, transforming it instantly into a huge ball of fire. The second went harmlessly into space

The White House

Vladimir Drobnikov had just been led into the small office of the Vice President in the basement of the White House, not far from the Situation Room.

In shirt sleeves, with a cigar hanging from his lips, Fareast looked tired and upset. Still, he greeted Drobnikov warmly.

"Ah, my good friend, how are you? Your cigars are quite good, you know?"

"My cigars?"

"Yes. I'll explain later. But please, sit down. I'd like to speak to you about a very serious matter which requires urgent action on your part."

Puzzled, Drobnikov settled into his comfortable leather chair. Five minutes later, amazed, he understood.

"Mr. Vice President, what you're telling me is unbelievable."

"I understand your astonishment, because I also had trouble believing this story. But I assure you, the situation is extremely serious. Our two countries can cooperate to prevent disaster."

Drobnikov reflected a few seconds while examining Fareast.

The Vice President was naive, not cunning. He decided to trust him.

"All right. I'll call Moscow immediately to tell them to alert our pilots in Libya . . . if there are any."

"I hope there will be." Fareast answered with a big grin. "Here are the particulars of the plane and its likely course," he added, handing a piece of paper to Drobnikov and pushing him toward the phone.

It was the Ambassador's turn to smile as he got up.

"No thank you. I prefer to use my own telephone."

On the Island of Paxikonos

The Dragon, carefully adjusted, went off with a large "whoof." Two seconds later, the shepherd's shelter was pulverized.

Schwager and Venardi were thrown to the ground by the explosion. They got up slowly, trying to assess the damage some fifty yards below.

"God damn . . . we barely escaped."

"Yeah. Thank God they've stopped. They're throwing everything under the sun at us." He put down his burning Kalachinikov and shook the dust from his walkie-talkie. A cracked voice came through the speaker, barely audible through the noise of gunfire.

"Hobson here. Is that you, Schwager? What's going on over there? Are they attacking with cannon?"

"Almost. We can't hold out here, we're almost surrounded. We'll fold up and come back to the villa, all right?"

"Are there many of you left?"

"No. Most of the blokes are killed or wounded."

"O.k. I'll tell Marais. He's glued to the radio. He lost contact with one of the planes, but the main thing is they got off the island. Our contract is fulfilled. I'm going to try to convince him that it's best to surrender."

"Understood . . . shit . . ."

A mortar shell exploded right next to them; Schwager threw himself on the ground again.

Getting up, he felt something against his leg and glanced down. It was a forearm, neatly severed. Blood still ran from the gaping joint. He stood up further and could see, about three yards away, the badly shredded body of Venardi. He reached out his hand, as if there were still time to pull his comrade-in-arms back to life. Then the expression of surprise on his face gave way to a sickened grin. He got up and fled toward the villa.

Ghurdabiyah Airbase, Libya

"Comrade-Colonel, a cable from Moscow. Top priority."

Colonel Leonide Sverdlovsk looked sleepily at Captain Vladimir Barin, who had just burst into his bedroom holding a cable. He rubbed a hand across his face swollen by sleep and a formidable hangover. God, what night it had been! But what was there to do in this fucking base in the middle of the fucking desert except enjoy a little vodka?

"What's this all about?" He grabbed the satellite-transmitted message. As he read through the message, his body slowly stiffened.

"You're sure this isn't a joke?"

"No."

"*Blyatz* . . . Well, better get cracking. Call General Tarchenko in Tripoli immediately."

Sverdlovsk rose clumsily, pulled on pants and a shirt, then rushed into the waiting room where four MIG-25 pilots were ready. Already alerted by Barin, they had put on their anti-G jump suits and their flight boots.

"Comrades, this time it's serious and not an exercise. You take off in five minutes. Objective: intercept and destroy a tri-motor

Falcon 50 heading for Tripoli to drop bombs, or God knows what. The plane hasn't been detected yet. We only know it took off from an island off Crete about an hour ago, and must be flying very low."

"An American?" asked one of the pilots.

"I can't tell you anything more. Concentrate on looking for it along the approaches to the Gulf of Sidra and the coast across from Tripoli. You'll receive further instructions in flight."

On the Island of Paxikonos

A piece of white cloth had just appeared out of one of the villa's windows.

"Hmmm . . . they've finally finished making up their minds. Let's go, but be careful," Pulaski said. "Steve, stay a little behind. You never know with guys like this."

The SEALS had sent a half-dozen rockets into the villa before the white flag had appeared. About twenty men approached one wing of the ramshackle, U-shaped building, white in the first light of the day. Pulaski signaled to O'Brien, who jumped into a gaping hole made by one of the missiles. The others followed. They quickly passed through a small ground level room buried in plaster to turn into a darkened corridor. Checking out every room, one by one, they worked their way toward the center. Suddenly, a door at the end of the hall opened, and a tall, blond man appeared, his hands in the air. He paused for a moment before crying out, "Don't shoot, don't shoot . . . we surrender."

"Move out slowly, keep your hands in the air," O'Brien called back, who, out of surprise, had failed to shoot.

Then things moved fast. A man appeared suddenly behind the mercenary, and let loose a short round of fire from a Kalachnikov, before disappearing. O'Brien, leaning out to see what was happening, took a bullet in the right eye. His head half-blown-off by the impact, he sank slowly on his side.

The others fell to the ground. Pulaski got up first to dash to the body of his second. A quick look and he jumped up straight, crazy with rage.

"Those dirty bastards," he bellowed, tearing down the hall. "They're going to pay for this."

Ghurdabiyah Airbase, Libya

Col. Leonid Sverdlovsk was growing more nervous by the minute. He'd ordered four more MIG's to take off, plus others which had left from the base at Okfa-ben-Na'fi near Tripoli. But so far none of them had been able to spot the Falcon. There was no visual contact, and none by radar.

"Shit. I just knew this would be shitty," he said to himself, heading to the radar operators in the control tower. His hangover had given way to a different kind of discomfort. Just three months from returning home—they'd promised him the air district of Crimea—and now his whole carrier was in jeopardy.

"Anything?"

"Still nothing, Comrade-Colonel. I have all our planes on the screen, but nothing else."

"And that little speck on the left?"

"That's an Air Algeria Boeing. We just verified it. The problem is if the Falcon comes in at a very low altitude, it will escape our radar. Only other planes will be able to spot it . . . Oh, I think I've got an echo . . ."

"Where?" Sverdlovsk roared.

"There, in the lower right corner . . . It's disappeared now . . . no, there it is again. It's going pretty fast . . . Damn, it's gone again."

Sverdlovsk also noticed the little yellow spot. "That's it. I'm positive. Position?"

"About fifty km. from Tripoli, along the coast near the ruins of Leptis Magna."

"Tell our planes immediately."

Aboard a MIG 25

Lieutenant Pavel Gramov didn't understand a thing. He and his wing forward Roman Kopayev had borne down toward the position Ghurdabiyah had pointed them, but the two planes hadn't found anything. The Falcon had magically disappeared, as if it had never been there. They had gone back along the coast following the Tripoli-Al Khums axis, and had drawn a blank.

"What shall we do, Pavel? Look off the coast or in the interior?"

"Maybe we ought to go for the interior. But I'll be surprised if we find much."

"With the sweeping radar we've got below, we might as well give it a shot. We can tell the others to look off-shore. Wait a second, what's that?"

Like a bat out of hell a fighter plane zoomed in front of them, making them change course by veering sharply to the right. Gramov opened his eyes wide trying to identify the intruder.

"That's a Libyan plane. What the hell is it doing here?"

"I don't know any more than you do," Kopayev answered. "What kind of plane was it?"

"A Mirage FI I think. They're pretty good, those French planes, but in the mitts of the Libyans, they're a disaster. They barely know how to make the things take off. I'm going to call them in English."

"Mig 25 here calling Mirage. What are you doing here? Repeat, what are you doing here?"

"Mirage 25 from Mirage. Lt. Ahmed Triki. By order of the Great Leader of the Revolution, we're joining you in the search for the imperialist aggressor, enemy number one. May Allah be with us in the sky."

Gramov cut communications and turned to Kopayev. "Did you hear? I didn't know we had told the Libyans. Let's really pull out over the interior. Maybe we'll lose him . . ."

He swung his plane toward the left wing. The huge, interceptor steadily headed south, making for 210 . . .

Aboard the Falcon 50 over Libya

His gaze fixed on the sandy soil which rushed by in the breaking dawn, Max Steubel tried to keep the Falcon flying as low as possible.

"There's one job well done. Do you see where we are now?"

"Yes," replied Fred Ziegler, his co-pilot, "about seventy km. southeast of Tripoli. Pretty soon we'll have to change course and go north again. Do we have enough fuel?"

"With the extra tanks, plenty. Do you think we ought to notify Marais?"

"Not before we've completed the mission. It's too dangerous now. We'll establish contact when we're over the sea again. If Marais's still there, that is . . . I wonder what's happened on Paxikonos."

"Hmm. We'll know soon enough when we reach our Swiss contact. Did you mark this fucking camp on the map?"

"Yeah. But what's that one in particular?"

"It's an idea of Marais'. There's a bunker in the camp, and apparently that's where the other fool stays when he comes to Tripoli. No way he's going to sleep in a tent. The Americans missed when they bombed Tripoli in 1986, but now he's cautious. He has dozens of East German and North Korean body-guards."

"Yeah. But they're not going to be able to do a bloody thing about the little present we're giving them. Go ahead and turn. I'm want to get rid of the rest of these packages as fast as we can."

Aboard Some Mig 25's

Pushed to more than Mach 2, the two Mig 25's tore up the sky, followed closely by the Mirage. Gramov contacted Kopayev.

"Is he still with us?"

"Yes, and there's no way to ditch him. He's going as fast as we are and he seems to know how to fly."

"Stupid bastard! . . . And the fucking Falcon that we've not been able to find. Let's head for the oasis at Mizdah."

"Wait a second. I've got something on my screen."

"You sure?"

"I've got it, Pavel! I've got it! It's at 2:00 . . . look in front of us and heading straight for Tripoli."

"Got it too! It must have made a big detour to come up again by the south. All right, let's go! We have to make sure it's really him before telling the base."

The planes tore in the direction of the little plane, two hawks chasing their prey. The Mirage, which had been following them, flew next to them for a minute, then dashed suddenly in front of the two Migs, as the pilot's voice squawked in their earphones.

"Friends of the Revolution, thank you for your help. I will now bring down the imperialist aggressor. Allah is with us."

The two Russians couldn't believe their ears.

"Whew, this one is completely crazy. If he brings down the Falcon, we can kiss our bonus good-bye," Gramov cried.

He brought himself up even with the Mirage.

"Comrade Triki, we have orders to finish the mission. Please clear aside and let us continue."

"Negative, comrades. The Leader has charged me with this sacred duty." The Libyan pilot responded by pushing his Mirage even further ahead.

The two Migs took out after him. All three swooped down on the Falcon which kept on its course low to the ground. The first houses on the outskirts of Tripoli appeared on the horizon.

Suddenly, when the Falcon was still more than three km. away, the Mirage opened fire with 30mm. cannons. The two Russian pilots watched the shells fall to the sand below.

"But what an idiot he is," Gramov yelled. "He knew damn well he was too far away. He's going to blow everything in the air. O.k., let's take care of this with a missile."

"Hold it! The Mirage is too close."

"No, we've got to let it go. God, what a pain in the ass these Libyans are."

Aboard the Falcon 50

"Hey . . . somebody's taking some potshots at us," Steubel roared, as watched tracer shells pass the front of his tri-motor. The plane lurched.

"Good God . . . you're right," Zeigler answered, turning around to see what was going on behind them. "Oh, shit!, we've got company!"

"What is it?" asked Steubel, his hands clasped on the joystick.

"There are two, no, three, fighters on our tail. They're going to pick us off like a sitting duck.

"Don't panic," Steubel answered. "Maybe we have a chance by going down lower."

"Don't be crazy. We're already flying as low as we possibly can. We'll break our necks."

"Any other suggestions? We've got an excellent navigation system. It's doable. Anyway, there isn't any choice. Hang on, we're diving."

Steubel pushed the joy-stick gently but firmly forward.

Aboard the Mig 25's

". . . 3 . . . 2 . . . 1, Fire"

The Atoll missile shot from Pavel Gramov's Mig, straight down at the Falcon. But after traveling a few yards, it suddenly changed direction and headed toward the Mirage, attracted like a magnet by the white-hot jet pipes of its motor.

"Shit!" Kopayev had just enough time to scream.

Within a few fractions of a second, the Libyan Mirage exploded under the horrified eyes of the two Russians.

"I told you the Mirage was too close. Now we're going to be exiled to Siberia!"

"Oh listen, tough shit for him. We can say he hit a dune. For now the thing is to not miss the Falcon."

Aboard the Falcon 50

"What was that?" Steubel asked.

"An explosion. I have the feeling they're shooting up there."

"How many are there now?"

"Two."

"Show me where they are."

"Look. One on each side. They're coming back behind us to shoot from above. We're approaching Tripoli. Maybe they'll hesitate."

Steubel jumped a small dune and glanced out to the left.

"Where is it? Oh yes, I . . ."

That was his last word. The Falcon, flying at more than 300 mph, had just smashed full-speed into a metallic structure rising up suddenly from nowhere. It disintegrated into a shower of sparks.

Aboard the Mig 25's

"Roman, did you see that? What happened?"

"I think he smashed right into a television relay station. He probably wasn't concentrating for one second. At that altitude, there are no second chances."

"Yeah. Well, at least that's taken care of. Call Ghurdabiyah. Now we can go back to the base."

"Right. But we've got to come up with an explanation for the Mirage. Sverdlovsk is going to be furious."

"The important thing is that the Falcon is down. We can just say the other business was an accident in the line of duty. Everybody knows the Libyans don't know how to fly. And don't worry about Sverdlovsk. After two bottles of Vodka, he'll have forgotten the whole thing by tonight . . ."

On the Island of Paxikonos

"Schwager, you're an absolute bloody idiot. I already had enough trouble trying to convince Marais that we had to give up without you fucking everything up. We didn't need this."

Hobson, hands on his hips, stood in the center of the grand drawing room of the old villa. Sprawled in a leather armchair and covered with blood and dust. Schwager absorbed the furious gaze of his superior without flinching.

"Sorry, but I couldn't help myself. I had to kill off one of those filthy shits to pay back for Venardi. Nielsen just got in the way. Too bad for him."

Five other mercenaries, who had escaped from the fighting, gathered in the drawing room where the doors were wide open.

After a brief disturbance outside, Pulaski with four SEALS behind him, appeared at the door, machine-gun in hand.

"Nobody move! All of you, flat on the floor with your hands on your heads. Quick!"

"Easy old man," Schwager replied without budging. "You can see we're not armed and that we're giving up."

Pulaski paled and moved slowly toward him, lips drawn. Without a word, he hit Schwager across the face with the butt of weapon. His nose seemed to burst at the impact. Stunned, Schwager moved as if he meant to get up and fight back, when

Pulaski hit him in the face a second time, cracking his jawbone. Dazed, Schwager fell back in the chair.

"The next time you talk like that, I'll put a bullet down your goddam throat," Pulaski hissed the words between clenched teeth, mad with rage over the death of O'Brien.

"I promise, you're going to pay for what you've done. Go ahead and load them up," he barked to his own men.

Denton had just come in the room.

"Have you got all of them?" he asked Pulaski.

Pulaski turned to Hobson who looked the most intelligent of the six prisoners. "Are there any others?"

"Yes, but not armed. Two servants in the cellar, and Marais, who's in the office next door."

"Who?"

"Piet Marais."

Pulaski turned to Denton with a questioning look.

"Piet Marais. Cullum's right-hand man, who organized the whole show," he said, looking at the office. "I didn't know he would be here."

"Hot damn! Let's go ask him some questions," Pulaski answered. "That asshole can pay too. You coming with me Steve?"

"Wait, Mike. I'd like to ask you something," Denton said, taking Pulaski by the arm and pulling him aside.

"What?"

"Give me five minutes alone with Marais."

Pulaski stopped and watched Denton's expression for a long moment. Then, without a word, he took his knife from its cover and his pistol from its holster. He handed them to Denton and turned his head . . .

Outside the study, Denton slowly opened the door. Marais sat on a chair facing the window, leaning over what appeared to be a ham radio. He put down the earphones and turned around, as if he sensed a presence behind him. After a moment's surprise, he narrowed his eyes and tried to compose his face lined with fatigue.

"What are you doing here?"

"Marais, you're hardly in a position to be asking questions," Denton said, coming toward him with the pistol in his hand. "You know damn well why I'm here."

"What do you want? To kill me? Don't you think it's enough that the whole thing failed?"

"Marais, I don't want to kill you. Simply to know . . ."

". . . know what?" Marais interrupted, standing up. "Poor fool . . . nobody would be dead if you'd just left us alone. But you didn't understand and caused the failure of an operation that was essential for the survival of the Western world. But you still don't understand, you shabby little journalist, that we're going to be overrun with Communists, terrorists, blacks, Arabs and inferior mixes of all sorts." Marais punctuated his outburst with threatening gestures.

"I warned you to mind your own business and to stop sticking your nose in our affairs. Now you'ved ruined everything, and if all these people died, it's your fault. Let me speak to the commando leader." Marais started to come toward him.

Denton was suddenly overcome by the irresistible desire to turn his face to pulp, to hit his weasle eyes and thin, scornful lips. When he was no more than a foot away, Denton lifted his pistol and smashed it down with all his might on Marais' head.

Marais took a step to the side and grabbed Denton's arm to stop the blow. Surprised, Denton pushed Marais, who stumbled backwards, pulling Denton with him as he fell.

The two men rolled on the ground, knocking over chairs. Denton twisted on top of Marais, who hit savagely. While holding onto the arm holding the gun, Marais freed his other hand and began to work over Denton's face, trying for the eyes. Denton instinctively reached for the knife he had stuck in his belt.

As Marais' fingers scratched his left ear and his cheek, Denton first thrust the knife in his side. Marais trembled and contracted, as if in a fit, his hand still grabbing Denton's face. Denton lifted the knife and stabbed again, then a third time, then a fourth. Slowly, he felt Marais' hand lose its grip . . .

CHAPTER 34

Palm Beach, January 21

Leaning against the terrace railing, David Cullum watched the coming and going of the waves, the blind surging of the ocean against ivory sand. The sun had almost disappeared behind the roof of the house, and its last rays caressed the branches of giant palms, standing like sentinels to guard a world that was crumbling around him.

When von Lassen had contacted him at Chambers' to tell him that the two planes had probably been intercepted and the island overrun by invaders, he felt his heart stop. All these months of preparation to have it end like that, ruined in just these few hours . . .

Wearing a white robe to cover his swim trunks and Mexican leather sandals, he slowly got up and walked toward the stairs to the lawn. Going down one step at a time like a robot, he gazed at the horizon before walking toward the beach.

One more time he saw her coming toward the shore, a sea goddess lean and firm from swimming, skin the color of copper from the sun and salt water, her blond hair blowing in the breeze. Like him, she had always preferred the relative coolness of the Atlantic to the warmer waters of the Caribbean. She could spend hours in the ocean or on the beach without ever getting tired.

He looked around at the world he had maintained and protected, but it no longer mattered to him. He had no desire to get up every day to go about his business, when it no longer made any difference. For him, the future had been Melissa, what she was going to become, what she was going to do.

After her death, an absolute desire for vengeance had sustained him, had engaged all his energy. Now it had failed. Two losses on top of each other were too much. There was only bitterness left, bitterness and the vague feeling that perhaps he ought not to have followed this course . . . At first, in his rage, after the burial, he hadn't had any doubts. But now, after a year, he wasn't so sure . . .

After getting the message from von Lassen, he hesitated a few hours, then decided to return to Palm Beach. He had expected he might be arrested, or at least intercepted, by the F.B.I. at the airport, but everything had gone smoothly. Arriving at the villa, he'd found several messages from Moseley asking him to call urgently.

Irritated, Elizabeth had questioned him. "David, where have you been? You just suddenly take off without even saying a word. It's really too much. What is going on? And why does Paul Mosely keep calling all the time?"

He hadn't bothered to answer. What was the point in arguing now? He had arrived at that moment in his life when it was useless to try to explain anything, to justify himself.

The operation had failed because of the journalist, he knew that. But what could he expect? That man, too, had wanted vengeance; it was only normal. In fact, everything had gone awry because of that imbecile Marais. Because of him, there had been all the senseless violence . . . and then the unthinkable had happened. Now there was nothing more to be done. Nothing.

He had already felt the sensation of helplessness at the hospital in San Antonio facing Melissa's slow agony. She had fought, fought with all her strength in the little room with gray walls, which flowers had done nothing to cheer up. But slowly, inexorably, death had carried her away . . .

Encircled by the gauze which covered her ravaged face, her eyes had implored him, begged him to do something to save her, to reverse the irreversible. Night and day he had stayed with her, on the brink of exhaustion. But he had been only able to cry with rage at each successive failure of the treatments tried by the doctors. Two long weeks, then an eternity of sorrow from which he'd never recovered.

The sun had disappeared behind the house, and evening approached rapidly, calming the ebb and flow of the waves. Stepping onto the sand, he took off his robe and unhooked his sandals. Then he stepped forward and felt all at once the cool, refreshing water against his legs. When he was in up to his waist, he began to swim out to sea. He felt good in the pure, clean waves, and swam with a natural, regular stroke straight toward the horizon shadowed by dusk, straight toward the inviting darkness of night . . .

CHAPTER 35

Souda Bay, Crete, January 22

Despite his fatigue, Steve Denton hadn't slept all night. He just kept tossing on his cot.

The knife . . . he couldn't stop thinking about it. He could still feel it plunging into Marais' side, still feel the quiver that came with every stab. He didn't know where the desire—the rage—that drove him to attack Marais so furiously came from. At the time, he'd felt an intense satisfaction, the gratification of revenge that wiped away three weeks of despair. But very quickly he'd been overcome by a feeling of emptiness that continued to grow with each passing hour.

He got up and glanced out the window. The sun wasn't up yet, but the first pale light of dawn broke over the bay. He washed quickly and headed for the officer's mess where he'd eaten dinner before collapsing in bed. Entering the mess, he saw Pulaski seated with the base commander, the captain of the frigate, George Gardner.

"How you doing, Steve?" Pulaski asked, seeing him come in. "Want to have a bite with us? Sleep well?"

"No, not a wink." Denton answered and greeted the Navy officer, who in turn sized him up as a fish out of water.

"I understand that. You must have been feeling a lot of things that make it tough to sleep. Me too. I got up real early this morning. Well, anyway, the deed is done. That's the main thing. We got a lot of communications from Washington during the night, especially about Cullum."

"Yeah? What?"

"It seems he committed suicide."

"What?"

"His wife notified the Palm Beach police last night. She saw him swim way out in late afternoon. After an hour, she began to worry. They found a robe and sandals on the beach, and that's all. The coast guard's conducting a search. According to his wife, he appeared very depressed. She doesn't believe he drowned by accident. It seems he was a very good swimmer."

"Yes. He probably did commit suicide after hearing his plan failed. What a disaster!"

"That's for sure," Pulaski replied in a somber voice. "Thank God you uncovered the whole can of worms, or it would have been an even greater disaster. And I can't imagine what would have happened afterward. Matter of fact, the Vice President has sent you his personal congratulations. He wants to see you when you get back to Washington."

"There's also a cable for you from the C.I.A.," the base commander added, waving a piece of paper in front of Denton.

He broke into a smile reading the brief message: "Bravo. For your info. Viljoen's better. Out of coma and sure to pull through. See you. Tom A."

Finally some good news, Denton said to himself, swallowing his hot black coffee. It was the first in a very long time. He made a vow to return to Namibia as soon as possible to see Viljoen . . . if he could get a visa.

"And everything else is taken care of?"

"I think so," Pulaski answered, turning toward the base commander.

"We think we've got everything cleaned up, at least as best we can under the circumstances. We've made contact with von Lassen who was cruising on his yacht in the Aegean. He's going to try to repair some of the damage discreetly. There were two servants on the island who won't say anything. As for him, we've advised him to go get lost for a while in Australia or Alaska."

"That's all?"

"Yup. Those are the orders from Washington. It's in the 'National Interest'. Don't ask me."

"It's really unbelievable. What about the mercenaries?"

Gardner shook his head to show his displeasure, before looking at Pulaski, whose mouth was drawn tight. He didn't try to hide the irritation in his voice.

"They've been sent back to South Africa. Their boat left the island last night with the head honcho and the survivors on it, still guarded by my men. A launch is supposed to join them this morning on the high seas to settle in a new team who'll go in convoy with the trawler all the way to Abijan. From there, the South Africans take over. The bodies of the dead have been placed in the cold storage room and will be dumped overboard as soon as it's possible—including Marais."

"God! I . . ."

"Say no more, Steve. I know what you're thinking," Pulaski cut him off in a voice laced with impatience. "In two hours, I'm taking the plane to Norfolk. The first thing I've got to do when I get there is to pay a visit to a house I know very well, and tell Jim's wife that her husband is dead. And then I have to make several other calls just like that one. You can guess what I think. But we're soldiers, and we've got no choice but to let the sons of bitches go, if those are our orders."

"The 'National Interest' again," said the frigate captain. "Washington wants absolute silence about this whole business. We've already told the South African government, and they're also eager to avoid any scandal. They're going to concoct some story saying that Marais drowned during a Mediterranean cruise, and that his body wasn't recovered."

"And the Greeks?"

"They don't know a thing. At least not for the moment. It's

quite possible that some fisherman saw or heard everything and that there'll be an investigation. There was plenty of gunfire on the island. We'll play innocent, of course."

"In the end, how many men did you lose?"

"Ten dead and twelve wounded. They were really tough opponents—highly trained," Pulaski answered. "You know, at the beginning their operation was supposed to be quite different. Hobson told us last night. He finally talked after we promised immunity. At first, their plan, which they called 'Boomerang,' was to send in two teams to clean out the terrorists. One to Lebanon and one to Libya. But the logistics were very complicated, especially for Libya where they'd have had to come in close to the coast to land the men. In the end they preferred the idea of gas."

"So do we know exactly what they were planning to do?"

"Not really, because Marais destroyed all the documents on the operation, like I told you yesterday afternoon. We think that the main objectives were a camp of Iranian militants near Baalbeck, a terrorist training camp in Libya near the coast, and a military complex south of Tripoli. We'll have to verify all this with von Lassen, but I don't know if he'll be able to tell us for sure. According to Hobson, Marais took over with a heavy hand and went far beyond his instructions. He was the one who ordered gas dropped on that village in Namibia, although it wasn't planned that way at the beginning."

"Dirty bastard! He's got to be responsible for Caroline's death too."

"Exactly. Through the mercenary Hobson contacted in Paris. In fact, it looks like Marais was acting on his own. For Cullum, it was pure and simple revenge to kill the terrorists who had killed his daughter. But Marais, according to Hobson, elevated all this to an ideological plane—the defense of Western civilization against terrorism and Communism. Hobson also had the impression that there were other people mixed up in the affair. One more thing to check out with von Lassen. . . . But in the end, all that matters is we brought down those two fucking planes."

"Did you get confirmation on the second one?"

"Yes, although it was a bit confused. The Russians said they'd taken care of it and would ask a return favor sometime. But the Libyans said the same. They sent us a strange message through the Belgian embassy which represents American interests in Tripoli. Washington sent it on to us . . . Hold on a sec, here's a copy."

Denton quickly read over the paper Pulaski had handed him. "The imperialist agent has been destroyed by the soldiers of the Revolution. Libya is not afraid of paper tigers and will not be intimidated by propaganda and the unholy threats of the Number One Enemy. It is he who will be destroyed by the wind of death and the righteous anger of Allah."

"Bizarre, isn't it?" Pulaski spoke as if in a dream, far from the present conversation. "But the Libyans will say any damn thing."

"Yeah, it's curious," Gardner replied. "But if I may be frank, we also say and do any damn thing when it comes to Libya. That started a little while after Kadhafi seized power in 1969. Not only did we give him keys to the base at Wheelus, but we even aborted a counter-coup mounted by partisans of King Idriss and a bunch of English mercenaries. I remember the story very well, because I was already in the Mediterranean at that time. Now we want to get rid of him, but there are still lots of Americans in Libya, and we've just saved his bacon. It's pretty disgusting."

"That's right and the French are doing the same thing. They fight against him in Chad, then try to woo him at the same time. Ridiculous! Some years ago, the French Secret Service had cooked up some very serious plot to topple Kadhafi, but it was squelched at the last minute by the government. Somebody in one of the French intervention units told me about it."

"Yeah . . . in any case, it wouldn't have changed anything,"

Gardner said, making a wry face. "It's not just the Libyans, and we all know it. All you have to do is look at the cutthroat slaughter in Lebanon to see that this is going to last a very long time."

"But this gas, that was still a crazy idea . . ."

"Not so much as you might think. Even here on the base we have plans to defend ourselves against chemical warfare. I'll bet you it won't be long before terrorists master the technique, if they haven't already, and threaten to use it on Washington, New York or Paris. We haven't begun to put this fire out. And I'll leave you with those comforting words, gentlemen."

The Naval officer got up, gave a stiff salute, and left the room.

"I wonder if we've really done right to put out this little brush fire," Pulaski turned to Denton. "After all, they could have done this job for us without anybody even knowing . . ."

"Maybe, but for what purpose? In any case, I'm so very sorry about O'Brien and the others you lost."

"That's part of the job . . . I suppose you end up getting used to it, even if it does make you question things. Well, I'm going to oversee our preparations to leave. You coming with us?"

"Yes. I have to pass through Washington."

"And then?"

"I swear, I don't know what I'm going to do. I have the feeling my life is in pieces. I don't even know where I want to live— except not in Paris, at least for the moment."

"I can understand that. But you'll get over it, you'll see. You're welcome at my place, if you'd like to spend a few days."

"Thanks. The worst part is not understanding why all this happened to me. I wonder if it isn't some punishment from heaven. All I wanted was to get away from reality, to find a peaceful way to live, then I found myself in the middle of all this violence. I left my wife and the woman I loved . . . is gone . . ."

"It's ridiculous to talk this way. It's just fate and nothing more— no use looking for other reasons . . . Look, I could ask you why Jim bought it yesterday and not me. But there isn't any reason, any justification."

"True. But in my case, I received a warning and didn't listen. I knew that I shouldn't keep on going in Namibia, that I should have returned to Paris, but didn't do it. No, it's not just fate here. I wonder what pushes us to act in certain ways, to do what is really against our best interests. Our destinies catch up with us in the end."

"Really, Steve. Cullum's daughter was killed by accident. You can't say that there was any reason, any explanation . . ."

"It's possible. But then why seek vengeance from fate. That doesn't make sense. Nothing makes sense any more . . . but I'm boring you with my two-bit philosophy. It's just that I was thinking all night."

Denton rose and glanced out the window of the mess. He felt exhausted, the aftermath of a sleepless night. The first rays of the sun shimmered on the choppy waves of the bay. It would probably be a gorgeous day. Caroline . . . they had been so happy on their recent cruise to Greece. In just a few weeks his life had shifted from blissful satisfaction to total confusion. He had to get ahold of himself again, but he didn't know how. It was absurd. It had all meant nothing, absolutely nothing . . .

CHAPTER 36

Tarhuna Camp, Libya, January 22

The heat . . . Rachid Habas should have been used to it, but the temperature in the camp seemed nearly unbearable. How hot was it? 105, 110? And so early in the morning! The *Ghibli*, the burning wind from the desert, had come up last evening and its hot breath had blown incessantly toward the sea. It was an unusual occurrence for this time of year . . . He had slept badly and had trouble breathing during the night, only to wake up feeling like he was suffocating.

He rose with difficulty and walked to the door of his little, prefabricated house. Truly, he was too old to continue supervising these training sessions. This was definitely the last time! Two more days, and he'd be back in Tripoli.

Outside, the first rays of the sun touched the Mediterranean, lighting the ruins of Leptis Magna in the distance. There was hardly a ripple in the sea as it lay still beneath the wind that carried sand from the beach. Why was he having so much trouble breathing?

Swallowing with difficulty, he touched his hand to his throat. Suddenly he noticed a swelling beneath his fingers, something like a large boil. Concerned, he ran his fingers over his face and found two others, one on his forehead and one on his left cheek. He hurried to the makeshift bathroom inside the tiny house. In the mirror there were three ugly blisters just where he had felt the boils. But what could they be? He rushed to awaken his assistant, Yasser Hachim, who slept restlessly, face down, in the second bedroom.

He tapped him on the shoulder, and Hachim turned over, groaning. Rachid Habas looked at his face and jumped back, horrified. There was a cyst oozing infection on his forehead. Without saying a word, he tore outside and began running to the infirmary on the other side of camp. But feeling a burning in his chest, as though his insides were on fire, he stopped short. He tried to catch his breath again, but didn't succeed. Then he felt a hand on his shoulder and turned around. Yasser Hachim stared at him, a look of terror crossing his astonished face.

"But what is it? You're covered with great boils."

"I don't know what it is. You are too. You've got them everywhere. Wait, what did we eat yesterday?"

"Nothing special. Lamb, cucumbers, artichokes, a few dates, just like usual."

"Let's go see the others."

Breathing heavily, they made their way toward a row of tents lined up against a dune, when Rachid Habas stopped suddenly and cried out in pain. Barefoot, he'd just stepped on a piece of broken plastic. It had come off one of those containers dropped the day before by the plane flying in from the sea. Leaflets, at least the ones that hadn't been picked up yet, swirled around in the hot desert wind.

Reaching the tents, they went from one to the next, waking up the men who slowly staggered out, many half-naked. Surprise quickly gave way to panic: almost every one of them was covered with spots and was having trouble breathing.

As a group they headed for the infirmary where they were used to going for the odd wound or cut incurred during training. A violent burst of wind came up, blowing a leaflet into Rachid Habas' unshaven face. Unnerved, he grabbed it, ready to tear it up, then changed his mind and read once again the Arabic words written in bold red ink:

"Remember January 21. The anger of God is upon you. The

wind of death has just swept over you. Repent before it is too late."

They had all wondered what this meant when they'd read it for the first time. The day before had been January 21 on the Christian calendar, but it wasn't a special day of any kind. And what did it mean, "the wind of death"? The plane had disappeared after leaving behind those "sonic bombs," the containers which exploded and spilled out these leaflets—just like the ones used by certain groups in Beirut or Tehran. An officer from the garrison at Al Khums had come to collect some of the tracts and take them back to Tripoli. Afterward, nothing had happened. Probably it had just been a trick of those fool Egyptians who were trying their hand at propaganda.

This time, however, he felt there was something more—something terrible—in the message. Especially in the second part:

. . . Remember the words of the Koran:

We have unleashed against them an impetuous wind

to last throughout their ill-fated days

that they may taste the punishment of shame in this

world . . . a wind that contains a mournful punishment

and that will destroy all

at the bidding of its Lord . . .

It became more and more difficult to walk, so Rachid Habas knelt in the sand, facing the sea. Where had he been January 21 last year? Beirut? Paris? Rome? Rereading the message, he suddenly felt that it wasn't worth the effort to struggle, that something irreversible had happened to him. He looked at the others circled about him, and saw only the fear and emptiness of their incredulous eyes.

Exhausted, he threw down the leaflet still clutched in his hand. A gust of wind carried it away, twirling it a few seconds in the air before slowly blowing back toward him, sticking the paper up against his chest. Helpless, he closed his eyes, feeling the pain in his lungs, the evil which was slowly, inexorably, eating away his body . . .

The End
Gilbert Grellet and Hervé Guilbaud, Washington, D.C.,